ALWAYS ELI

FOREVER LOVE BOOK ONE

CHARLIE NOVAK

Jodi,

Thanks for being the
best assistant ever!
#RARE22 Edinburgh

Love
Charlie xx

This one is book ten, and this one is for me.
Look how far you've come.
Look how much you've grown.
Now keep going.

CHAPTER ONE

Eli

"WHAT THE ACTUAL FUCK? You've got to be kidding me!" I stared at the two digits at the top of my banking app that represented the minuscule amount of money I apparently had to survive on until the end of the month. Below that, in the most wonderfully fuck-you manner ever invented, was the very large negative number that told me my credit card was maxed out.

Well, that was just bollocks.

So much for that backup plan.

I tapped on my current account, scrolling through the outgoing transactions to check I hadn't actually been robbed. I had, but only by myself. And my drag career. God, why was everything so fucking expensive? It wasn't as if I regularly bought thousand-pound lace front wigs for crying out loud. The last one I'd bought had been twenty quid off eBay, and I'd spent an entire weekend trying to make it look less like some shit a cat had dragged back-wards through a hedge. Half my drag costumes came from charity shops and careful internet shopping, and I relied on two pairs of shoes—one pair which I regularly spray-painted so I could have different colours—to get by.

The make-up was the expensive thing, but that was because I'd discovered my skin was sensitive as fuck, and attempting to use whatever cheap plasterboard foundation I could find in Primark or Superdrug inevitably resulted in horrible breakouts, and I was too old and fuckless to be dealing with a spot the size of Piers Morgan's ego on my chin. My skin seemed to think it deserved to be treated like a queen without giving a fuck that our budget was no higher than that of a bargain basement trash goblin.

Whoever said being a drag queen was glamorous was a filthy fucking liar.

I sighed, muttering darkly under my breath as I squinted at my phone, trying to figure out how I could magic up money for food for the next two weeks that wasn't the cheap-as-fuck Pot Noodle equivalent from Aldi.

"Everything okay, babe?" The warm arms of my best friend and roommate, Orlando, encircled my neck as he leant over the back of the sofa and pressed a soft kiss to my cheek. "You look awfully cross."

"Just contemplating the misery of my existence," I said, tilting my phone so he could see the screen. "Why the fuck did I think I could make drag work full-time? What magical confidence did past Eli have that made him believe we could survive off Pot Noodles and thin air?"

"Wow, you really are broke." I felt Orlando wince. His

arms disappeared from around my neck, taking my phone with them, and two seconds later he climbed onto our sofa beside me, resting his head in my lap like a large, pretty kitten. I brushed his soft, blond hair out of his face as he scrolled through my phone, his lips settling into a pout. Orlando really was the prettiest man I'd ever met with a magical genetic code that seemed to keep him looking eternally youthful. He wasn't quite twenty-eight, but he didn't look a day over eighteen. A fact he used to keep men wrapped around his bratty little finger. I lived in eternal awe.

"Did you really need to buy doughnuts last week? Or whatever you bought through the Nintendo store." he asked, looking up at me through long lashes, disapproval written across his face.

"Excuse me for wanting some small pleasures in life," I said, poking him in the stomach. Orlando grinned. "I need to have some fun."

"How's that working out for you?"

"Horribly." I laughed, but it was more a hollow chuckle of despair.

"So, what are you going to do?" Orlando handed me my phone, and I dropped it onto the cushion beside me like it was a venomous beast about to strike. I sighed and ran my fingers through my wild hair as I mentally surveyed the options before me.

I wasn't going to lie: there weren't many of them.

"I guess I'll have to get a job. A proper one." I'd done it before—the whole working a full-time job and doing drag in the evenings and on weekends thing. The money had been nice. The stress and exhaustion less so. But at least the people at Monster energy drinks would make a nice profit from my suffering. "Maybe I'll see if I can get something at a coffee shop," I said, turning ideas over in my mind. I needed something that would leave my evenings free, which ruled out bars and restaurants because they always wanted you to work Friday or Saturday nights, which was prime drag time. Fast food would do if it came to a push, but it would depend on the shift pattern I was offered. "Or retail. Fuck, I'll have to go back to being nice to stupid people." I gave a dramatic shudder, and Orlando giggled.

"You could get a temp job," he said. "There's always things like admin contracts going. And they won't be very long either. I'd imagine the longest you'd find would be covering someone's maternity leave."

"That's not a bad shout." An office admin job would be fixed hours and steady money. And if it was only a temporary contract, it would mean I wasn't stuck forever. The work would be easy as well—most likely just answering emails and dealing with endless reams of paperwork. It would mean I'd have to suck up to people and probably wear a suit or at least a shirt and trousers. But the trade-off might be worth it if I didn't have to man the tills at Primark and deal with assholes trying to return clothes they'd clearly worn on a night out or the underwear they'd had sex in.

The memory of that encounter was seared into my memory from my university days, and no amount of brain bleach would ever let me forget it.

"See? I'm more than just a pretty face."

"You sure are, baby." Orlando smiled up at me, and I grinned, gently booping him on the nose with one finger. He really was adorable. We'd tried dating once, but it hadn't worked because neither of us could be what the other needed. In Orlando's case, that was someone who wasn't going to let him brat about all over the place but would still spoil him rotten. In my case, that was someone who didn't mind that I had a tendency to be a dramatic bitch and needed a little control. Orlando was the best friend and roommate I'd ever had though, and I still loved him—just as more of a friend than the love of my life. We still fooled around occasionally when we were bored or stressed, and the sex was always fun. We just weren't ever going to make anything like a relationship work long-term.

"You know," Orlando said, a mischievous glint dancing in his baby-blue eyes. "If you want to get an office job, you probably ought to do something about your hair."

"What about my hair?"

Orlando gave me a pointed look. "It's a mess. Nobody will hire you looking like that."

"Harsh. It's not that bad." I tugged self-consciously at the nearest strand that was resting over my shoulder.

"It looks like an eighties hair metal mullet fucked a noughties MySpace emo profile picture," Orlando said, sitting up and climbing into my lap, twisting a strand in his fingers and brushing the rest out of my face. I rested my hands on his thighs, grinning at the rainbow-coloured joggers he was wearing.

He might have a point about my hair, loathe as I was to admit it. A couple of years ago I'd shaved one side to see what would happen. Then I'd shaved the other, leaving a wide, fluffy strip all the way down the middle. Then I'd let it grow. It was now well past my shoulders but still hideously uneven in what I vaguely pretended were deliberate layers. And, given the fact it was naturally thick and wavy, it did have a tendency to stick out, especially after I washed it. If I went out in the wind, it looked like I'd stuck half a can of hairspray in it. It was also getting harder to put under a wig. I usually ended up having to pin it flat with a thousand fucking bobby pins, and by the end of the night my head was sweaty and itching. But as stubbornness made up a good thirty percent of my personality, I hadn't given in and shaved it all off on principle.

I was starting to think principle or not, it was going to have to go.

"I can do it," Orlando continued, giving me a full-on puppy pout. "It wouldn't take me long, and I promise to make you look sexy."

"This was your plan all along, wasn't it?"

"What? Make you go broke so you'd have to get a job and finally let me get my hands on your hair?" He grinned. "You saw right through me." His voice was dripping with sarcasm, but his eyes were sparkling. "Can I do it now?"

"Now?"

"Yes! Before you change your mind. Plus, I'm going out this evening, and I'll be tired tomorrow."

"Fine," I said before I talked myself out of it. I'd probably regret it in the morning, but that would be tomorrow, and it would be too late by then. Orlando had been dropping hints about this for months, and if I refused, he'd only bring it up again and again until I relented. Might as well get it over with. "But only if you make me look sexy."

Orlando clapped his hands, kissed me, and then hopped off my lap to go and find his scissors. Given that Orlando was a trained hair stylist, I wasn't worried. This wasn't going to be a hack job like that time I'd decided I could make myself look like the lead singer of Black Veil Brides when I was fifteen. I thought I'd looked cool. Photo evidence proved that was a lie.

"Can you go wash it?" Orlando asked, sticking his head around his bedroom door. "It'll be easier to style if it's wet."

I sighed begrudgingly and hauled myself off the sofa, picking up my phone to take one last photo of my hair in all its glorious infamy. I still wasn't sure how I'd gone from bemoaning my lack of funds to being forced into a haircut in the short span of half an hour, but I was just going to roll with it. It wasn't like I had a choice. My options right now were to make money or starve, and I quite liked food. The myth of the starving artist was all well and good until it was staring you right in the face, and although I knew neither Orlando nor my family would let me struggle, I didn't like the idea of taking advantage of them.

I'd gotten myself into this, and I could get myself out.

And if I couldn't? Well, then I'd light the beacons and call for aid.

I walked into the bathroom and shrugged off my clothes, hoping our temperamental shower wasn't about to dump icy water all over me. I turned it on and put my hand under the spray, waiting until it vaguely resembled warm before I stepped in. If I had my way, I'd have the water so hot my skin turned pink on contact, but warm-ish was about as good as it got until the letting agency *finally* decided to answer our complaints and fix the fucking shower. Apparently they'd decided as long as it still worked and was chucking out water that it wouldn't kill us. We were not their biggest problem.

In the background, I heard Orlando firing up some clippers and singing along to whatever was on his Spotify. Just how fucking short was he planning to go?

I grabbed the cheap bottle of shampoo off the side and began to scrub my scalp. At least if it was shorter it wouldn't be such a pain in the fucking ass to wash. Or dry. I'd miss my hair metal fluff though. It was a wonderful talking point, and it annoyed my oldest brother, Richard, to no end. Which may or may not have been another reason I'd been so determined to keep it.

If Dick liked something, you could guarantee it would be boring. That man was as exciting as the colour beige.

Eventually, I couldn't waste any more time in the shower, and it was time to say goodbye to my hair. May it rest in peace. I stepped out and towelled off, wrapping the rough, dark material around my head before scooping my clothes off the floor and wandering into Orlando's room. I was still naked, but it didn't really matter. It wasn't like Orlando hadn't seen it before.

He grinned when he saw me and winked. "Very nice. But I'm going to play later so not today."

"Damn, there goes my planned distraction." I laughed, pulling on my boxers and tank top. They clung to my damp skin. "Still enjoying your men?" I asked as Orlando directed me to head back to the kitchen, which I supposed would be the more practical venue for the massacre about to commence. I tried to think where the dustpan and brush might be for later. I didn't fancy scooping hair off the floor with my fingers or picking it out of the brushes of our shitty hoover.

"Yes! They're so much fun!" He giggled and gave a happy wiggle as he directed me to a chair and plugged the clippers in by the kettle. Orlando was currently sort of seeing a married couple, one of whom was a Dom and the other a switch. Having a bratty little whatsit like Orlando to play with was fun for all parties involved. I was almost a little jealous because he got spoilt rotten and always came back utterly fucked out. Not that I wanted spoiling, not unless someone just wanted to give me money and buy me wigs and maybe a large takeaway, but the fucked-out part would be nice.

No money. No sex. And now forced to get an actual job. Damn, my life sounded bloody depressing. Teenaged Eli would have been very disappointed. Then again, teen Eli thought I'd be a famous West End star by now.

Teen Eli also hadn't known about drag or the wild and beautiful discovery that awaited him.

Orlando grabbed a brush and gave me a wicked smile. "Are you ready?"

"Full speed ahead."

CHAPTER TWO

Eli

THE EXTERNAL FRONTAGE for the offices for Green & Wodehouse, estate agents to the rich and wanting, could only be described as Fancy. Capital *F* and everything. Located in the Bailgate area of Lincoln, not far from the Cathedral, they'd taken up residence in a converted Georgian building with deep navy window frames and signage decorated with gold lettering. There were a variety of properties displayed in the window, going for such eye-popping prices that even if I sold both my kidneys, my liver, and all the blood in my body, I'd never be able to afford more than the front door.

It was also the place that had hired me to be their new administration assistant, a decision that still utterly baffled me. Perhaps it was because Orlando had packed me off to the interview in a crisp suit, freshly ironed shirt, and sporting a new haircut that was styled to within an inch of its life. He'd even made me remove my nose ring under pain of torment, a threat I'd readily succumbed too.

Perhaps I really was as charming as I'd thought and the interviewers had been blown away by my natural vivacity, wit, and charisma.

Or perhaps they had limited options and had been forced to reach deep into the rubbish bin of life and had thus been rewarded with me—a being that looked vaguely human but was largely a raccoon in disguise.

Either way, there I was, once again sporting a brand-new, ironed shirt Orlando had forced me to buy, along with some dark grey suit trousers and a sensible blue jumper. I was even wearing a tie. I'd sent my mum a picture to prove I could scrub up nicely when required. She'd sent back heart emojis while her wife, and my beloved stepmum, Mimbles, had asked when I'd been abducted by aliens. I'd just laughed and told her I'd finally succumbed to the wrath of capitalism.

I reached up and nervously touched my hair again. Four weeks and I still wasn't used to the new length. Although that might be because Orlando had cut it again last night to "tidy it up" and get me ready for my first day. You'd have thought I was starting fucking primary school, not an office job. Orlando had done a nice job though; I'd give him that. He'd shaved the sides shorter but left it much longer on top, then he'd run some wax through the waves and pulled them together so it looked like I had a natural pompadour. It was cute. And it fit under my wigs so much better.

Adjusting my bag—which contained the lunch Orlando had insisted on packing for me—on my shoulder, I headed for the front door. It was just before half past nine, which was when I'd been instructed to show up for my induction.

I took a deep breath, pasted on a smile, and pushed open the navy door. An electric buzz and the sound of ringing telephones greeted me. There were some rather nice-looking armchairs off to my right clustered around a glass coffee table. And in front of me sat a large desk with a "Green & Wodehouse" sign attached to the front of it. Behind it sat a round, older woman with elegantly styled grey hair, bright purple glasses, and red lipstick, who was wearing a pretty polka-dot blouse. If my memory served, she'd been there when I'd come for my interview, but I hadn't spoken to her because I'd been whisked off upstairs before I could open my mouth.

"Good morning," she said as soon as she saw me. "May I help you?"

"Good morning. My name is Eli Baker. I'm the new admin assistant. It's my first day." I gave her my best beaming smile and reached out across the desk to shake her hand. I always made it a point to be nice to receptionists, counter staff, or anyone else I met first because they were the gatekeepers and the ones who always got treated like shit. It was the same rule I applied to everyone in retail and food service and the cleaning staff in hotels.

It could largely be summed up as *only be a dick to people with power. And only then if they strike first.*

"I'm Pamela, not Pam, and I'm the receptionist and other admin assistant." She shook my hand and grinned at me, and I saw a spark in her eyes. We were going to be friends. I could tell. "You're here covering Jaz's maternity leave, aren't you?"

"I believe so. You'll only have to put up with me for a maximum of a year, and then I'll be out of your hair."

Pamela laughed. It was a warm, friendly sound, and I felt myself relax. "I think we're going to get on famously," she said. "Wait here a minute, and I'll let Holly know you've arrived." She picked up the phone and pointed at the armchairs. "Take a seat. I don't know when she'll be down."

My bum had barely touched the seat when another woman appeared from a door to the left, which seemed to lead to a set of stairs. She had lots of dark curly hair and a wide smile but clever, calculating eyes that seemed to study every inch of me. It had been the same look she'd given me during the interview. She was wearing a business suit and a rather spectacular pair of heels, and I was now quite glad Orlando had forced me to acquire more work wear, even if it had come from Primark and the lowest budget tier of ASOS.

"Hello," she said, shaking my hand and squeezing. "It's nice to see you again, Eli. Would you like to follow me?"

It was phrased as a question, but it wasn't as if I really had a choice in the matter. Not if I wanted a job. And given that I'd spent the last four weeks eking out whatever money I'd had left and living on the kindness of Orlando and some leftovers I'd acquired from my mothers, I didn't.

"Of course."

And so began my first day at Green & Wodehouse.

Holly was one of the directors of the business, which she

co-owned with her husband, Andrew. She oversaw the office staff, finances, and marketing, making her my boss. I got the impression that as long as I did my job, I'd be absolutely fine, and we'd get on as well as could be expected. If I fucked up, then it would be a monumentally different experience. She directed me to my desk, which happened to be behind Pamela's, and talked me through some of my responsibilities before she gave me a tour.

Given that the building was fairly narrow, the offices were located over several floors. On the top floor was an office shared by Holly and Andrew, who was a chartered surveyor and did some of the valuations. He gave me a half-smile and a curt nod before returning to whatever he'd been staring at on his computer. On the middle floor were three offices in what I assumed had once been three bedrooms. The largest was shared by the three members of the sales team—Alistair, Rebecca, and Michael—who looked at me with a range of expressions from welcoming to disdain. I made a note for later in case I was ever required to make anyone coffee. Treat me like shit and I would make you drink sludge.

Another office held a young man named Hayden, who did all the marketing and design for this office and the various other branches they had across the East Midlands. He looked up at me from his enormous iMac and gave me a small wave. There was another desk in there, which belonged to the accountant, but she was apparently out sick.

The third door was closed.

"We have an in-house finance and mortgage adviser,"

Holly said, gesturing to the little gold plaque on the door. It had a name on it, but I wasn't close enough to read it. "He's technically an independent professional, but we recommend him to all our clients. If the door is closed it means he's in a meeting or on the phone, but I'm sure he'll come down and introduce himself later."

Holly didn't mention his name, and I'd totally forgotten to ask before Holly launched into an explanation of their in-house charity fundraising programme. I added it to the mental list of things I needed to remember as she led me back downstairs. Pamela smiled at me from the front desk as Holly pointed out the downstairs meeting room used for client appointments, a bathroom, and a small kitchenette with a fridge, microwave, kettle, water cooler, and a rather nice coffee maker.

"You're welcome to bring your own mug, but please make sure the design is tasteful. No rude slogans or explicit designs." I nodded, hiding my smile as best I could. Given that half the mugs Orlando and I had were printed with slogans that included some variation of the word *fuck* or were covered in dicks, I thought I'd probably need to pick up a plain one from Tesco. Or maybe I'd see if I could get a pride one off Amazon. "We also have cups and glasses available for client drinks, which you'll need to make if requested," Holly continued. "Do you have any questions?"

"None so far." From what she'd explained, it seemed like a dead hamster would be able to do this job. My one issue would be keeping the snark in check if someone decided to take umbrage with me. And given the expression I'd seen on the face of at least one member of the sales team, it was definitely going to be *when* and not if.

"Good. I'll leave you to get logged in and set up. Pamela will talk you through the phones and your email and get you started." Holly gave me another smile, then retreated upstairs, her heels thudding on the carpet.

I grinned at Pamela, who'd rolled her chair back and was smiling at me again.

"Fancy a cup of tea?" she asked.

"Pamela, dear, I think you read my mind."

By the middle of the afternoon, I was convinced a dead hamster would indeed be able to replace me with very little inconvenience.

My job seemed to largely consist of directing phone calls from clients at various stages to the appropriate person, making viewing appointments, answering emails, sending out property details, and dealing with a phenomenal amount of paperwork, despite the fact that everything could easily be digital. The printer and I had already had words, and I'd promised it I was not above giving it a swift kick if it refused to do as I asked and kept scrawling up random chunks of paper.

Pamela had turned out to be a rather wonderful woman, who'd been working here for nearly ten years, seemed to know everything that went on, and had an opinion about everyone.

"Michael has no people skills but seems to be able to sell everything under the sun, Rebecca is very sweet but doesn't mess around, and Alistair has as much charm as a slug in your shoe unless you have several million pounds in your bank account," Pamela said over our afternoon cup of tea. She'd produced a tin patterned with Christmas teddy bears and filled with biscuits from under her desk and let me help myself to the last chocolate one. I made a mental note to grab some more tomorrow morning to refill the tin. It seemed like she and Jasmine, the girl who'd gone on leave, had been close, and tea had been one of their little rituals. I was more than happy to partake, given that I was naturally a people person. Or as my brother Lewis said, "an obnoxiously chatty asshole". He was probably my favourite brother, tied in equal place with Jules, my only sister, for favourite sibling.

My family was large and chaotic, but I loved them all. With the exception of Richard.

"Got it," I said, dunking the last of a chocolate hobnob into my mug. "Michael is asocial, Rebecca is the one I'll like, and Alistair is a dick."

Pamela laughed, shaking her head at me. "Exactly. And don't ever let Alistair talk down to you. Jaz was terrible for that." She looked at me shrewdly. "Then again, I don't think you'll have that problem."

"No," I said, smiling sweetly. "I don't think I will."

"Good."

The phone rang, and we went back to work. I spent the next few hours becoming *familiar* with the current portfolio of properties on offer, which basically meant perusing the website and becoming more and more convinced money very rarely equalled taste, particularly when it came to decor. If this was what rich people wanted their houses to look like, then I could have made a fortune shoving lemons into a glass jar, sticking it on an overpriced table, and calling it good.

There was another clattering on the stairs. I glanced up from my computer to see who was going to grace us with their presence. So far, I'd hardly spoken to anyone else, even when a couple of them had popped down at lunchtime to either use the microwave or disappear out to see what was on offer elsewhere. Clearly being *just* the administrator made me unworthy of bothering.

I froze, a sudden chill sliding down my sternum like I'd drunk too much of a cold drink at once.

The man entering the office was altogether too familiar, though so far today we hadn't been introduced. He had golden hair and sparkling grey-blue eyes that shined like the sea under a stormy sky and a body that had been perfectly sculpted to carry off the designer suit he was currently wearing.

He saw me and strode over, sticking out his hand with a charming smile on his soft, rosy lips. There was no hint of recognition in his expression, which stung because I'd known him in some capacity for nearly twenty years. Granted, he wasn't *my* friend. He was Richard's.

"Hi," he said, grasping my hand tightly. "I'm Tristan Rose. I'm the financial adviser here."

A warm rush spread across my skin like I'd suddenly dunked it in hot water, and I had to resist the urge to cling to him for just a second longer. It startled me.

"Hello, Tristan."

CHAPTER THREE

Tristan

"Hello, Tristan."

The man's voice was oddly familiar and so was his playful smile. I stared at him, trying to fit the pieces together in my mind. It took me longer than it should have, and the realisation of who he was stunned me. Mostly because the last time I'd seen him he'd been wearing a tank top that said, "Training to beat Goku" and sporting both a nose ring and what could be politely described as a mullet.

Now he looked... handsome. At least, more conventionally so than before.

"Eli?"

"There we go," he said, his dark eyes dancing with an expression I couldn't place. Mischief perhaps? Or maybe it was scorn? After all, I'd known him since he was ten and I was fourteen. He was my best friend's brother. The second of his four younger brothers to be precise. "I wondered how long it would take you to recognise me."

I swallowed, regaining some of my composure. "Well, I've not seen you in a suit before," I said pointedly, trying to get myself back on even footing. "And you've cut your hair."

"Yes." He touched it with one hand in a gesture that was almost self-conscious as if he were still getting used to it. "The demands of capitalism require me to look the part." His lip twitched into a smile. I wasn't quite sure how to respond. That was the thing with Eli, he always threw me. Whenever I spent any time with him, I could never get a read on him. All I had to go on was the feeling in my gut and the picture Richard had painted, which was never flattering. Eli was the last person I'd expected to find working at Green & Wodehouse, but demanding an explanation for what he was doing there was only going to make me look like an arse.

"It suits you," I said somewhat lamely. Eli's smile widened. "So, are you covering for Jasmine then?"

"Yes, I'll be here for the next year or so while she's on maternity." His answer was surprisingly civil, and it threw me even further because I'd expected sharp sarcasm.

"Great. Well, you won't need to do much for me, just send through the occasional phone call. I have my own line, but clients tend to forget and just call the office. And you might have to pop some contracts in the post, things like that."

"Of course," Eli said. "Whatever you need, Mr. Rose."

I got the feeling he was mocking me, but I wasn't sure

why. There was a tight feeling in my chest combined with a sinking lead weight in my stomach. I cleared my throat and glanced up at the clock on the wall. I had a client call in five minutes, which gave me an excuse to escape.

"Thank you. I've got a call to get to, but it was nice to see you again, Eli." I turned tail and walked to the stairs, hoping it didn't look like I was running away.

I was still confused by the whole thing at the end of the week when I met Richard and his girlfriend, Ruby, for dinner.

I'd spent the week largely avoiding Eli and talking to Pamela when I needed something. I got the feeling he'd noticed, but he hadn't said anything. Luckily, I'd had a lot of client meetings and stacks of mortgage applications to process, so I'd been too busy to dwell on my new co-worker. Still, it did seem strange to me that Eli would take up an office job given what I knew about him. I knew he was a drag queen and that he'd been doing it full-time for a while because Richard had spent a lot of time ranting about it. Richard spent a lot of time ranting about Eli in general if I was being honest.

Out of all his siblings, Eli was the one who frustrated Richard the most and had for years. Richard was my best friend, so I was happy to let him vent to me, and sometimes I did think he had a point. Creative work was great, but I wasn't sure it was a particularly stable career, and Eli wasn't too far off thirty and still living a student lifestyle as far as I was aware. Not that I thought everyone needed to settle down and get married, but didn't everyone have to grow up at some point?

Although my sister Alexis would probably disagree with me on that. She was a similarly free spirit. Albeit one who owned a very successful interior design business.

"Hey," I said, sliding myself into a wooden chair opposite Richard and Ruby. "Traffic was a nightmare."

"No worries. We only just got here." Richard smiled at me. "I ordered you a drink, and they've got a slow-roast pork belly and lamb hotpot on as the specials."

"Oh good, I really liked the pork belly last time they did it. I hoped they'd do it again." I glanced down at the menu in front of me, even though I already knew what I was having. I rotated between three or four dishes unless they had a special that really grabbed me. It sounded boring but we'd been coming here for so long that I'd already tried everything I wanted to and had picked my favourites.

Richard and I had been meeting at the same pub for dinner on a Friday night every two or three weeks for the past four years, and it was a part of my routine that I cherished.

We'd been friends since we were fourteen and we'd found ourselves in the same set for science. We'd ended up being paired together, and after an initially awkward start, we'd clicked, and that had been that. We'd kept in touch through university when I'd gone to Oxford and him to Reading, and then afterwards when I'd moved to London to go into finance and him back to Lincolnshire to become a Chemistry teacher.

Richard had been there for me through all my awkward

teenage years, my freakouts at university, and my low years in London. He was the one who'd given me the courage to leave banking when I found myself drowning under the pressure, and he was the first person I'd ever come out to. In return, I'd been there for him through the days when his family drove him crazy, listened to him stress about work and debate whether he really wanted to keep teaching, and supported him through every single one of his misguided dating adventures. If I hadn't known I was gay by the age of fifteen, Richard's escapades with women would have put me off for life.

Luckily, he seemed to have found someone sensible in Ruby.

It had been nearly a year since they'd started dating, and she hadn't tried to get him to join a pyramid scheme, convinced him to get their names tattooed on each other after only two weeks, thrown all his possessions out a bedroom window, started a bar fight in his name, or tried to throw him a surprise wedding. And Richard hadn't tried to propose after three dates, to convince her that jumping out of an aeroplane was the best way to conquer her fear of heights, or spent all his money booking a dream holiday to the Maldives only for him to discover she was still married.

I was praying their relationship stuck if only for my own sanity. Richard was my best friend, but even my patience had limits.

"So, how've you been?" I asked after a young waitress had dropped off our drinks and taken our orders.

"Did you know Eli got a job?" Richard said. I stared, not sure whether to answer the question or not. Did Richard know we were working together? Had Eli said something? I wouldn't have put it past him if he wanted to wind his brother up.

"Er—"

"He won't tell us where, but mum insists it's an actual job for once, which is something, but the fact he won't tell us means it's probably something really shifty. I bet he's making porn with that roommate of his."

"Rich," Ruby said, nudging his arm. Her tone was gentle, but I noted her raised eyebrow. "Remember what we said."

"Sorry. I'm just frustrated." Richard sighed. If he was bringing it up this early in the evening, then it had clearly been bothering him. I wondered if I should say something, but it wasn't my news to share. If Eli hadn't told his family, he probably had a perfectly good reason for not doing so.

"I just wish he'd apply himself," Richard said, taking a large sip from his glass of red wine. Ruby was drinking Coke, so I guessed she was driving. "He's so smart. He got a fucking first from Leeds Law School for Christ's sake. I just don't get why he isn't doing something with it. I know mum says she just wants us to be happy, but I know all our parents wish he'd do something productive with his life, and Dad's really worried about him. He'd never say it to Eli's face, but I know he doesn't want to watch Eli waste his life and be destitute by forty. I know I wouldn't want that for my kids." Richard sighed again, shaking his head. "I mean, if Eli wants to insist on making a twat of himself on stage, then that's fine, but he can do that part-time. It's not like he's ever going to achieve anything with it. Why can't he just do it as a hobby like a normal person?"

I took a sip of my own small glass of wine to give myself a minute to think. I knew Eli had a law degree, but I'd never realised he had a first. It seemed even stranger to me now that he'd want to spend his days writing emails and answering phone calls for other people. Leeds was a top law school, and while a law career wasn't for everyone, there were plenty of things he could have done with it instead. Part of me wanted to agree with Richard like I'd done so often in the past, but something stopped me. A tiny pull in my chest that said *No* like an invisible hand guiding me away from that path.

"Maybe this is him trying to figure things out?" It was more placation than actual answer, but it would do. "Maybe the reason he hasn't told you is because he wants to work out what he's doing before he tells you."

"See?" Ruby said. "That's what I've been telling you." She grinned and poked Richard in the side. "I wish you'd listen to me. I do actually know what I'm talking about. Maybe Eli doesn't want you jumping down his throat before he's worked out what he's doing. You just have to let him get on with it and realise he's an adult, and as much as you wish he'd do things differently, you can't stop him from making poor choices."

I smiled. I really did like Ruby.

"Why are you so smart?" Richard asked, giving her a soft look. "What did I do to deserve you?"

She laughed and leant over to kiss him. "Don't let Eli get

under your skin, babe. I bet he doesn't give you as much thought as you give him."

"That's definitely true," Richard said.

The waitress reappeared carrying our food and the conversation broke off to follow other topics. I was glad of the subject change. Something about this situation was bothering me, but I couldn't put my finger on what it was. At least it was the weekend now, and I could spend two days not thinking about Eli.

That was the plan anyway.

CHAPTER FOUR

Eli

"He's such a smug bastard! He avoided me all week because he clearly thinks dealing with me is beneath him, and I bet he's gone straight to Richard to tell him all about it. I deliberately didn't tell my family what I was doing because I didn't want to deal with shit from Dick, and yet here I am, lost at sea without a paddle. Sunk by Tristan fucking Rose. I'm going to freeze to death in the icy waters of the Atlantic without a door to climb onto. And if there was one, Dick would just shove me off and tell me to fucking swim!"

I threw my beauty blender down onto the small desk that served as my make-up station and watched it bounce across the surface. I grabbed a brush and my contour palette, preparing to shape my face beyond all recognition. Orlando watched me from his seat on my bed, grinning as he hugged some adorable but ridiculous avocado plushie to his chest. A gift from his men.

"Are you done?"

"Not sure," I said, sweeping dark make-up across my temple and down my cheekbones, nose, and jaw. "Maybe? But then again…" I sighed. "How long do you think it will be before the family chat goes nuts with the news that I have indeed gotten myself a *sensible* job." I shuddered. "They'll think I'm becoming an actual adult."

"You are nearly thirty."

"So are you."

"Nope. I'm going to be twenty-one forever," Orlando said with a grin.

"You'll stop looking twinky one day, bitch. You might even get wrinkles."

"Like you?"

"Mine are distinguished," I said as I started to blend the fuck out of my face.

"Says you."

"Feeling sassy today, aren't we? Are you coming to see my show or are you off to get spanked?" I looked at Orlando in the mirror and watched his grin widen, his cheeks flushing a delightful peach colour.

"Both. I told Daddy and Sir they have to come see your show at some point because you're amazing. So they said we could go tonight and then I can go back to their house." He sighed happily. "They bought me new toys."

"Of the electric, silicone, or plushie variety?"

"I hope it's all three."

"Well, you know where I am if you need anything," I

said, shaping my nose. Luckily, my drag persona wasn't of the pageant queen variety, so I never intended to look particularly feminine or pretty. Bitch Fit was more hair metal, emo queen trash goblin. She was my inner self brought to life.

I turned to Orlando, looking him in the eye and repeating the same three phrases I said every single time he went out. "Have fun. Be safe. Call if you need me—for anything."

"I will. Promise."

"Good boy."

I looked back at myself in the mirror and nodded. Close enough. I reached for some setting powder.

"Hey, can I ask you something?" Orlando asked. I glanced at him in the mirror, trying not to frown. He usually just came straight out and said things.

"Of course, baby. Everything okay?"

"Have you ever considered doing drag competitions?"

"Like *Drag Stars*?" I asked, raising one eyebrow. The television show was a cult phenomenon, but I had *opinions* about it. Largely around the prescriptive narrative it seemed to require of drag and its lack of inclusion of both drag kings and trans performers. I'd been asked whether I'd consider auditioning for the UK version at least twice a month for the past two years, and it was starting to get on my tits. I'd instituted a rule at The Court where anyone foolish enough to ask me that question when I was on stage had to get up and lip-sync. Depending on whether I liked it or not, I'd either give them a free drink or I'd roast them mercilessly. Don't fuck with me, honey.

"No. Duh, I know you hate that show." Orlando rolled his eyes and gave me a pitying look. Brat. "I meant like local stuff."

"Such as?"

"*It's a Drag!* It's the one they're holding in Nottingham this year. The charity one. This year they're raising money for a trans children's charity and an LGBTQ suicide hotline." I turned in my chair and found Orlando looking at me with wide, earnest eyes in the same way Labrador puppies did. "It's their third year, and they really want to make a splash, and I thought since it's not so prescriptive, you'd be interested. Their past two winners are great: Snow Woke and Rick N. Roll."

"Rick N. Roll is wonderful," I said, nodding my head. Rick was a drag king and had done a couple of guest slots at The Court in the spring. "He's got amazing stage presence. I didn't realise he'd won."

Orlando nodded. "He did! Remember? I told you I went to watch. It was your dad's birthday, though, so you couldn't come with me."

The wheels in my brain turned slowly. We'd all gone out for a huge family dinner, and I'd deliberately sat at the other end of the table from Richard so I could enjoy the meal. I'd spent the whole time talking to Lewis and Finn about *Final Fantasy* games and horror movies. It had been a good evening. "I remember. You got drunk and came home with two loaves of bread. You ate half of one and then spooned the other."

"I was hungry."

I chuckled. Now that I'd thought about it, I remembered

Orlando mentioning it to me last year as well. I'd brushed him off then, although I couldn't remember the reason. "When's the final?" I asked. "If it's the same date as last year then it'll be a no. Mum would kill me if I missed Dad's birthday, and I don't know if they'd come and watch."

My family was big, queer, loud, and largely supportive, but I doubted Richard would come to anything like that and then mum would get sad. Plus, Dick would kick up a huge stink if it was on the same date and no doubt accuse me of trying to take over Dad's birthday for my own nefarious purposes. In his mind, I was a work-shy narcissist who'd never amount to anything, and this would be proof of that. And as much as I hated Dick, I didn't want to cause a rift in my family.

"It's on the eleventh of December. It's a Saturday." He grinned. "It's two weeks later than last year, so you won't have to miss your dad's birthday. And you'd be so good. They're crying out for talented entrants, and I know people would love you. Just think about it, please. For me."

He batted his eyelashes ridiculously, his lips forming a doll-like pout.

"Fine. I'll think about it."

"Yes!" Orlando hopped off the bed and threw his arms around my shoulders and squeezed before dancing out of the room.

"That doesn't mean it's a yes," I called after him. He wasn't listening though.

I sighed and reached for an eyeshadow palette.

· · ·

The Court was full of laughter and cheering faces as I stood backstage, humming quietly to myself as I watched some of the other performers. Not only was The Court Lincoln's one and only gay bar and nightclub, but it was also their premiere drag venue.

We did a mixture of full variety drag shows, comedy nights, guest slots, and smaller shows with just a couple local performers.

That night was one of our variety weekends, and the show was in full flow.

I loved these nights mostly because I got to go out and do whatever the fuck I wanted within some very loose limits. Usually it was comedy and lip-syncing with some parody songs and maybe a dance skit here or there. I knew the audience well because I'd been coming to The Court since I was a very naive eighteen-year-old baby queer, and even when I'd gone away for university, I'd come back at least once a month.

The Court's owner was one Miss Violet Bucket— pronounced *Bouquet*, after Patricia Routledge's legendary character from *Keeping Up Appearances*—or Phil if you ever met him outside his sequins and enormous Marie Antoinette-style wigs. Violet was the one who'd first suggested I get up on stage and give drag a try. I'd done a lot of drama at school and was a natural show-off, but drag had been a whole new world for me. Theatre was fun, but drag called to my soul. I'd still been terrified of actually getting up and doing it, but after several months of practising in front of a mirror and spending countless hours playing with make-up, I'd been brave enough to give it a try.

The first time I'd set foot on The Court's little stage, I'd known I was home. The feel of the lights on my skin, the music, the first laugh I'd coaxed from a slightly drunken audience, the applause as I'd finished and tottered off the boards in the new heels I could barely walk in—it had all been intoxicating. A boost of confidence I'd never experienced before. As soon as I'd come offstage, I wanted to do it again.

That was nine years ago, and I hadn't looked back.

"Hello, darling." Violet appeared beside me, her sequined dress glittering in the low backstage lighting. Her hair was a towering mass of lavender, flowers, and hairspray that seemed to have a life of its own. If I put a match to it, it would probably go up faster than a chip pan.

"Honey, what is that wig?" I asked, giving her a wicked smile. "You look like you've stolen a buttercream wedding cake from the eighties and stuck it on your head."

"Oh, thank you, darling! That's exactly what I was going for." Violet smiled and patted her wig fondly. "I see you've gone for the raccoon look again, dear. Perhaps if we bought you a little rubbish bin as a dressing room, you'd feel more comfortable."

I laughed. "So kind of you Miss Bucket," I said, deliberately using the traditional 'bucket' pronunciation, watching to see if it made her wince, "to think of this small, humble trash goblin."

"My dear, I don't think you could do humble if you

tried." I laughed. "So, how's things?" Violet continued. "I see you survived your first week in an office."

"I did. And I didn't stab anyone with a pencil either, although I'll admit it was close." I'd spent several hours lamenting my monetary worries to both Phil and Violet, both of whom had been largely sympathetic. There wasn't really a way for Phil to offer me more work at The Court, but he'd promised to keep his ear out for more gigs and try to direct as many people my way as possible.

"That bad?"

"No, not really. Just quite tedious. But it will pay my bills until TikTok makes me wildly famous."

Violet laughed. "My darling, if anyone can make money by making a spectacle of themselves, it's you."

"Why thank you. I try." There was a round of raucous applause as the dancers on stage came to the end of their performance.

"Do you need me to get you anything for later?" Violet asked. "I'll get the bar to send you up some water, and I popped a few snacks in the basket for you."

"You're a star. Just send me some Fanta now and then, and I'll be fine." After the show ended, The Court would convert into a nightclub, and I would be DJing until the early hours of the morning. It was Friday night, though, which meant I could play a wonderful mix of trashy cheese, gay shit, bouncy pop, and whatever new club music I could stand to listen to for more than thirty seconds. Then tomorrow it would be sleep, rinse, and repeat.

The dancers trouped offstage, looking exhausted but

wildly happy. Violet greeted them all like some mother hen before shooing them away to get a drink.

"Good luck, my dear," she said, handing me a microphone. "Have fun."

"I always do." I took a final deep breath to calm the last of my nerves and felt excitement sweep deep in my stomach. Then I adjusted the bottom of my skirt, wiggled my hips, grinned, and strutted out onto the stage. The audience cheered.

It was just like coming home.

CHAPTER FIVE

Tristan

ON MONDAY MORNING, I'd been determined to be a better man and stop avoiding Eli, but that lasted as far as walking in the door and being cornered by Holly, who wanted to talk about client services. It was the last thing I wanted to do at eight thirty on a Monday morning, but I'd dutifully obliged. I'd only managed a quick glance at Eli before I headed upstairs. He'd been in the kitchen with Pamela making coffee, a wry smile on his face that made something catch in my stomach.

By the time I'd escaped Holly and her plans, I'd found myself knee-deep in emails, phone calls, spreadsheets, and client meetings, which I spent the rest of the morning wading through.

I put the phone down after a particularly irksome client, who seemed to think just because he was buying a house worth a rather large amount of money, he should get preferential treatment from everyone he encountered. And while the mortgage provider he was applying for said up to twenty-eight working days for the paperwork to come through, he seemed to expect it to be hand delivered to him the next day. I rolled my eyes and rubbed my temples, very glad I had an office to myself so I could mutter darkly under my breath.

Looking at the clock on my desktop, I realised it was nearly lunchtime. I hadn't remembered to pack anything, so I'd be doing my normal mosey up and down Bailgate to see what I could find. And if I felt very, very lazy, I'd get on Deliveroo and order something to the office.

I wondered what Eli was doing for lunch today.

Did he bring food with him? Last week, I thought I'd seen him eating what looked like a Pot Noodle at his desk, so I assumed he did.

I was up and out of my chair before I'd really thought through what I was doing. I shoved my wallet into my jacket pocket along with my phone and clattered down the stairs to reception. Eli was on the phone and jotting a note down in a little spiral notebook with a purple pen. His head was tilted to one side, his mouth pursed in mild annoyance. He was wearing a rather dashing shirt, waistcoat, and tie combination in a jaunty but tasteful blue-and-purple pattern. I'd never managed to make a waistcoat work for me, but on Eli it looked perfect—the right combination of eccentric and fashionable.

A smile pulled at the corner of my mouth while I watched him.

He hung up and scribbled something else on the jotter,

sighing in exasperation. Then he noticed me, and a tiny frown appeared between his dark eyebrows.

"Can I help you, Mr. Rose?" he asked. "If you're looking for Pamela, she's just in the kitchen finishing her lunch. She'll be back in a minute."

"No, it's fine. I'm not looking for Pamela." Why were words suddenly hard? Why was it that whenever I was around this man, I felt like I couldn't even recite the alphabet without getting everything in the wrong order? "I was looking for you."

"Oh? And what can I do to assist you?"

"Well, for a start you could stop being so sarcastic whenever I ask you something," I said. I'd meant it as a gentle rib, but now I wasn't sure whether I'd gone too far. There was a moment's pause, then Eli threw his head back and laughed. The sound echoed around the room like a brook bubbling happily over stones on a summer's day.

"Oooh, you've got a shiny spine today. I like it." He grinned, and I swallowed. "What else can I do you for? Or did you just come to reprimand me?"

"I just wanted to apologise. For avoiding you last week. I guess it kind of threw me, seeing you here, and I was a bit of a dick about it. I just wanted to say I'm sorry." I watched him carefully as I spoke, taking in the way his dark eyes flickered and his mouth twitched. One thing I'd always been good at was watching the way people reacted. I could tell a lot about a person from the way their expression shifted and body moved when I spoke. I think it was because I'd been a quiet, awkward child, much to my father's chagrin, and I'd spent a lot of time watching people rather than joining them. That was before my father had forced sport upon me to "build my character".

Eli had always been hard to read though.

"I accept your apology," he said graciously. I felt like a peasant being forgiven by a king. "And I suppose I should apologise for speaking ill of you to my roommate because I can imagine I wasn't who you expected to take this job." He considered me for a second. "What did my brother say when you told him?"

"Richard? I didn't tell him anything." After Ruby had changed the subject on Friday night, Eli hadn't come up again, and I'd made sure to keep it that way. "He knows you've got a new job—your mum told him—but he doesn't know what it is. And I didn't tell him because it's none of my business," I said, somewhat put out by the insinuation that I'd tattle. Then again, I was Richard's best friend, and I supposed Eli's suspicion was justified.

Eli was staring at me slightly open-mouthed. If I didn't know any better, I'd say I'd stunned him into silence. Then a smile slid onto his lips—the sort of smile a cat gives a mouse it's considering eating for lunch. My insides twisted, and I suddenly felt very warm, despite the fact the office was quite cool.

"You are a surprising person, Tristan Rose," Eli said. "Thank you."

"You're welcome." I smiled. "He's frustrated he doesn't know though. He, er…" I tried to think of a tactful way to say what Richard had said on Friday. "He thinks you might be doing something shifty."

"Does he now?" Eli's wicked smile widened, and I saw

something forming behind his eyes. Probably some scheme to drive Richard insane. I wondered if I should have just kept my mouth shut.

"Would you like to get lunch?" I asked, blurting the question out into a moment of silence. I'd wanted to change the subject, and I'd wanted to offer Eli lunch by way of an apology, but that wasn't quite the way I'd intended to do either thing. "I was going to get some food, and I wondered if you'd like to come too? My treat."

"He'd love to," said Pamela, suddenly appearing behind Eli. "Go on. Get your stuff. It's a nice day, and the fresh air will do you good. And lord knows you could do with something more for lunch than a Pot Noodle." She raised an eyebrow at him.

"I like Pot Noodles," Eli said with a huff as Pamela chivvied him out of his chair. "By the way, that purple note is for Alistair. Mrs. Elliot rang about the house in Caythorpe. She has some questions about the plumbing and the carpets. I told her he'd be happy to answer all her questions as soon as he returned to the office." He grinned sweetly, and Pamela laughed.

"You're going to get me shot."

"Oh no, Alistair won't shoot the messenger. And if he wants to know where I am, you can tell him I'm in a very important meeting with our good friend Mr. Rose here." Eli patted me on the shoulder and grinned at me as he pulled a battered, denim jacket covered in patches on over his office attire. "I'll be back in an hour."

He was already halfway out the front door by the time

I'd registered what was happening. I almost had to jog to catch up.

"So, where are we going for lunch?" Eli asked, grinning slyly at me as we walked towards the cathedral. "Am I allowed to make requests?"

"Sure. What do you fancy?"

"Have you been to the Minster Deli before? I've had the occasional sandwich from there, and I'm craving some of their meat."

I laughed. "I have. We can definitely get you some meat."

Eli grinned. "You see, this throws me because if I'd said that to Dick, he'd have lectured me about making sex jokes."

"I'm not your brother though," I countered as we passed a group of old ladies pottering along the pavement.

"True, true, but you are his best friend, so I expected you to have a similarly dull sense of humour."

"Are you saying you expected me to be boring?"

"Yes," he said. "Does that bother you?"

I wasn't sure. I hadn't expected him to be so honest about it or come right out and say it. "I don't know. But you might be right. I'm not particularly exciting."

We passed the post office, rounded a corner, and I saw the familiar green frontage of the deli. It wasn't a particularly big place, and on some days, there was often a queue out the door. But it was already past one on a Monday, so if there had been one, it had cleared. I just hoped there were still sandwiches available.

"Oh, come now. You can't be that boring," Eli said. "What do you do for fun? Do you have any hobbies? You still have the dogs, right?"

"Yes, I do. I didn't know you knew about them."

"Mum told me I think. They're Labradors?"

"Yes, Indy and Solo. They're three and four now." I resisted the urge to pull out my phone and show him pictures. Not everyone wanted to see countless photos of random dogs, and while I thought they were the cutest things on four legs, that didn't mean everyone else did. I was surprised Eli even knew about them, and I was almost more surprised he'd remembered and cared to ask.

"Did you name your dogs after Han Solo and Indiana Jones?" Eli asked, giving me a wry smile as we stopped outside the door.

"Maybe..."

"Interesting." He hummed and pushed the door open, and I was left to follow him wondering whether that was a good *interesting* or not.

The deli had a little seating area on the first floor, so we ordered some sandwiches, drinks, and a giant piece of millionaire's shortbread to split between us before heading upstairs. There was a table available in a corner by the window, and Eli sat down opposite me, placing the tray of food down between us.

"So," I said, unwrapping the printed greaseproof paper around my focaccia filled with spinach, thick slices of brie, and cranberry sauce. "What made you get this job?" I winced, realising it sounded like I was asking the opening question at a job interview, not a lunch date. Not that this was a date. Just a lunch.

Only a lunch.

Eli chuckled, unwrapping his own sandwich, which was loaded with salami, cheese, salad, and sun-dried tomatoes. "Honestly? I needed the money, and this seemed easy. Plus, it's only a year-long contract, so all I have to do is suffer through twelve months and then I'll be free." His honesty surprised me, and it must have shown on my face. "Did you want me to pretend I've always wanted to be an administrator?"

"No," I said. "I guess I'm just... surprised."

"Oh?" Eli looked at me, and I couldn't help noticing how long his eyelashes were. "Were you and Dick hoping I'd finally gotten my act together and gotten serious? Grown up a bit? Started settling down?" He rolled his eyes.

"It's none of my business what you do."

"No, but you're my brother's best friend, and you know all his dirty little secrets. I'm sure he's vented to you about me as much as I've vented to Orlando and my other brothers about him."

I had no idea who Orlando was, but the rest was a fair assumption. I took a bite of my sandwich to avoid answering.

"See?" Eli continued, sitting back in his chair and folding his arms.

"I didn't tell him though." And for some reason I resented the accusation that I would. I thought Eli had accepted my apology, but clearly he was still suspicious of me. "And I could have. It might have helped. Richard thinks you're doing porn with your roommate, and I don't see how working at Green & Wodehouse is much worse."

"Does he really? How fun." Eli's mouth flickered into another of his smiles. "Also, if I ever hear you degrade sex work or sex workers in front of me again, Mr. Rose, then whatever this is will be over before you can speak because I will personally throw you into the sun."

"I'm sorry," I said, feeling my face heat. "That was low of me."

"Good, I'm glad you know that." Eli fixed me with an interested look. "You know, I can't figure you out. You're my brother's best friend, which ought to make you a huge twat just by association."

"It feels like there's a *but* there." I'd practically forgotten about my lunch at that point. I was too intrigued by the man sitting across from me. He was everything and nothing like the person I expected him to be.

"But I think you might just surprise me," Eli said. He picked up his sandwich again. "So, you were telling me about your dogs. Do you have pictures? Because if so, I want to see them right now."

The rest of the hour passed quickly with Eli cooing over photos of Indy and Solo before the conversation turned to office gossip. Eli wasn't impressed with Alistair, but then again, I didn't know anyone who was. How that man managed to sell anything was a miracle modern science hadn't yet unravelled. Everyone I knew thought he was an enormous knob.

Lunch was fun though, in a surprising way, and I found myself regretting the passage of time.

By the time Eli and I got back to the office, the strange weight I'd had on my chest had been replaced by an entirely different one. One I wasn't even sure had a name.

All I knew was that it was connected to Eli.

CHAPTER SIX

Eli

I STARED up at my pockmarked bedroom ceiling and sighed. It was late on Sunday morning, and usually I'd still have been asleep, but I'd woken up after an intense dream and now my brain had decided we were up.

The dream was still fuzzy, no more than shapes, colours, and lingering sensations on my skin, but there was a stubborn feeling of heat blossoming across my torso, and my dick was more than a little interested in whatever fantasy my brain had been indulging in. I just couldn't remember what it was.

It was probably just a random sex dream.

I'd been going through the most hideous dry spell, which wasn't helped by Orlando coming home every weekend with red marks all over his ass and then curling up with me to tell me all the delicious things his men had done to him all night long. I was happy for him because he deserved to be loved and cherished, but at the same time, I was a jealous hag because fucking dammit, I needed to get laid. Where was my willing, slutty bottom who'd let me play with their ass for hours on end?

The image of Tristan in his navy suit trousers, which perfectly hugged his little, round ass, strolled lazily into my mind.

I debated swatting the thought away like a fly. After all, this could not lead to anywhere but trouble. It was not a yellow-bricked road to a magical city but more a red road to pain. Tristan was my brother's best friend, and if Richard thought my intentions were impure, he'd probably punch me.

Then again, when had Dick's disapproval ever stopped me from doing something? It usually made me want to do things more, and like a giant red button labelled Do Not Touch, it was far too tempting to ignore.

My hand wandered down my chest, lazily grazing my nipples on the way. One day, I was going to get them pierced because I thought I'd love the extra sensation. I just wasn't great with needles—something I'd figured out when I passed out on the day I got my nose pierced.

In my mind, I watched Tristan bending over in his suit trousers like he'd done on Thursday when he'd been trying to reload the printer. I'd only been watching him because I thought he'd need rescuing. Not for any other reason at all. His ass had looked lovely though. Very squeezable.

My brain helpfully conjured up a desk, and fantasy Tristan bent over it, looking over his shoulder at me with flushed cheeks and swollen lips where he'd pulled them between his teeth. His perfect, golden hair was mussed, and there was a desperate look of need in his eyes that made my cock throb. God, I just wanted to pull his trousers over his ass so his hole was exposed, open my fly, pull out my aching dick, and fuck him so hard that all he could do was cling to the desk and moan for me before he shot his load all over the polished surface.

I wrapped my hand around my cock, letting the fantasy play out in my mind as I stroked myself. My head was buried between the pillows, eyes falling shut as I thought about fucking Tristan in his office, the door shut and locked so we couldn't be disturbed. Shoving his tie into his mouth to keep him quiet so nobody realised. Fucking him rough and hard until I came deep inside him, whispering in his ear that he was mine, then leaving him to go back to work full of my cum.

Fuck. That would be hot.

Maybe get a little plug for him to wear.

Then he'd have to sit through the rest of his day with it in, and every time he shifted in his seat, he'd be reminded he was mine.

"Shit," I said loudly, spitting on my palm before jacking myself faster and harder. I was stupidly close already. My breath came in pants as my brain began to supply images of Tristan on his knees, sucking me off in his office because he was so desperate for my cock. "Fuck!"

I came with a grunt, painting my fist and stomach with my release. I lay there for a moment, letting my post-orgasm high sink into my bones. Whether it had been an advisable fantasy or not, it had been fun. And it wasn't as if

Tristan was ever going to know I was indulging in thoughts of him taking my cock.

Later that afternoon, after I'd dragged my tired ass through the shower and done a few chores, I'd hopped into my tiny, old car and headed south to see my family for Sunday dinner.

My family situation was often described as unusual, but I preferred to describe it as messy, queer, and slightly chaotic.

My parents lived next door to each other with their respective partners, having separated in the world's politest divorce when I was about three. Then, when I was four, my mum and her lifelong best friend, lovingly known as Mimbles, realised they were in love with each other after Mimbles's husband died from cancer. After that declaration, the two of them had wasted no more time and created an enormous, blended family with their six children. My dad had met his partner, Paul, when I was eight, and they'd been together ever since, living right next door because dad never wanted to miss out on being a parent.

The funniest thing was that dad and Paul hadn't told us they were dating for years, even though we'd all figured it out. Apparently, they'd been worried about telling us, but none of us had batted an eye. Then again, there was only one straight person in my entire family—Richard.

My siblings and I were all fairly close in age, and we'd grown up in the middle of the Lincolnshire countryside living a semi-feral existence. As there were six of us, it made for a good split for teams, and we'd never ever done it as one family versus the other. Mostly because Richard and I refused to be on the same team. But I'd never viewed Oscar, Jules, and Finn as anything other than my siblings. Blood relations or not, they were my family, and I loved them more than anything else in the world.

Even now, as adults, we were still ridiculously close and nosy about each other's lives. I knew it would drive some people crazy, but I loved it. Most of the time.

Recently, our youngest brother, Lewis, had acquired a boyfriend in the form of the charming television and theatre actor, Jason Lu. I'd met him a couple times, and I very much approved. Not only was Jason ridiculously handsome, but he seemed very grounded and down to earth, and he took excellent care of my baby brother. Poor Lewis had never had much luck with men—bless him—but Jason was wildly different than everyone else he'd dated before. They'd bought a house in Lincoln in the spring, and I'd spent many happy hours lounging on their sofa watching Jules and Lewis move furniture while Jason was in Canada wrapping up filming for his show.

I'd declined to help with the moving because Jules was ten times stronger than me from hefting car tires around, thus it was much easier to let her butch ass do it. Plus, it was Lewis's house, and I didn't want him telling me I'd done it wrong. Much easier to just sit and direct like a queen.

By the time I pulled up to mum and Mimbles's house, there were already several cars in the driveway. I must have been one of the last to arrive.

"Hello, hello," I said as I wandered into the large kitchen where everyone tended to congregate. There weren't as many people there as I expected. "Did you miss me?"

"No," Jules said with a wry grin. She was leaning against the counter, drinking a bottle of beer, her dark-blonde hair scraped back off her face in a messy topknot. Her t-shirt had an oil stain in the corner, and I wondered if she'd been looking at someone's car. Separating Jules from an engine was largely a pointless endeavour. One day, I was going to clean her up and stick her in a suit. She'd do very nicely on lesbian thirst trap and attack dog TikTok.

"I didn't miss you either, bitch," I said, taking the bottle she handed me and pressing a kiss to her cheek. She laughed.

"Hello, darling." My mum engulfed me in a soft, floral-scented hug, her pastel-pink hair brushing my face. She cupped my face, her numerous bracelets jangling as she scrutinised me. "You look very tired. Are they making you work long hours at this new job? You need to make sure you're eating enough."

"It's fine. I shall endure," I said. "Just feed me and tell me I'm pretty, and I'll be fine."

"You're very pretty." Mum kissed my cheek before wandering back towards the oven at the other end of the kitchen. "Orlando did a lovely job with your hair. He's so talented. You should have let him cut it ages ago."

"Absolutely not. I can't let him get a bigger ego than he already has. There's only room for one ego in our flat."

"And it's already yours?" Jules asked with a grin.

"Precisely." I looked around the kitchen. Apart from Jules and mum, there was only Finn, who sat at the table reading something on his phone. Finn was the quiet, soft one, the family cinnamon bun as it were. He was so enthralled by whatever he was reading, he hadn't noticed me coming in. Or if he had, he'd chosen to ignore me, which I found improbable.

"Hello," I said, throwing my arms around his shoulders. "Reading anything fun?"

"Just a novel I'm recording this week," Finn answered, twisting his head and giving me a small smile. "It's a romantic suspense."

"A good one? Is there a murder?"

"Yes, there's a murder. Do you want to know who did it?"

"Absolutely not! It'll ruin my enjoyment when I listen to it." I grinned. I bought and listened to every single audio-book Finn narrated, whether I liked the story or not. It was the best way I knew to support him, and Finn was a fabulous narrator. "Are there smutty bits? Will I need to fast forward?"

Finn's skin tinted slightly. "Only a couple, but they're not very long."

"My darling baby brother, I love you very much, but I do not need to hear you making dramatic breathing noises while reading dirty words. It's very confusing." Jules laughed from behind me, and Finn's face flamed. He mumbled something quietly, and I kissed him dramatically. "No, I'm not going to stop listening to them. You're an excellent narrator, and I like books with murders. Are you going to be doing any more in that mystery series? The one with the rich, layabout detective who's an absolute chaotic bisexual dumbass?"

"I think so," he said, his smile returning. "We're just sorting dates now."

"Excellent. I love those."

"How's your new job?" Finn asked, twisting in my arms so I had to release him. I pulled out the bench he sat on and slid in beside him. It was the one question everyone seemed to want the answer to, but Finn was the only one I'd tell. There was something about Finn that made me want to be honest. Lying to him was like trying to lie to a golden retriever puppy. I just couldn't do it.

"It's fine, very boring, but they are giving me money, and all I have to do is answer the phone, write emails, and try not to throw shade at Alistair in sales." I sipped my drink. It was a fruit cider flavoured with pineapple and raspberry, and I'd happily have drunk it in one long swig, but since it would be my only drink of the night, I was going to savour it. Somebody needed to invent home tele-portation so I could get drunk and then zap back to Lincoln in an instant. It would be so much easier. "Luckily, the other person on my floor is a gorgeous human called Pamela who insists on twice-daily tea and biscuit breaks, wears the most fabulous glasses, and I'm sure has a lipstick collection that would put mine to shame."

"That doesn't sound so bad," Finn said. "I guess it could be worse."

"I think I just feel sorry for the poor suckers that have to work with you," said Jules, wandering over from the counter and sitting down next to me so I was sandwiched between her and Finn. "How long before they find out you're a complete bitch?"

"How rude! I've already been there two weeks, and everyone thinks I'm charming."

Finn chuckled softly. "I give it a month then."

"Smart," said Jules. "I'll go two."

"I don't like either of you anymore." I grinned. "Where's Lewis? He'll take my side."

"He's in London with Jason for the weekend," Mum said, breezing past us to get something from the fridge. "And Oscar is in New York. He's writing a piece about city breaks."

"Why doesn't he ever take us on these breaks with him," I grumbled. "I'd like a weekend in New York." Oscar was a travel journalist and was always jetting off to beautiful parts of the world. Earlier in the year, he'd reviewed an exclusive resort in Bora Bora, and I'd drooled over the pictures he'd sent us. Then I'd Googled how much it would cost to stay there and cried. The only way I'd ever get there was picking up a rich sugar daddy—or mummy, I wasn't picky—or by selling all my organs.

"Oh, he's sending Mimbles and I to Rome for a week for our anniversary next year," Mum added. "Isn't that sweet of him?"

"So he's not only swanning off to places himself, but he's making us look like bad children," I muttered. Jules laughed.

"I think he just feels guilty he's not here a lot," she said quietly. "This is a way to make it up to them."

Jules had a point. Most of us hadn't gone very far. Even if we'd moved away for university, we'd all come back again. Lewis had been the last. Except for Oscar. I didn't think he'd ever stick to one place. Mimbles always said there was too much wind in his soul, that he'd never settle until he found a reason to stay.

It seemed like she was trying to be poetic, but honestly, it just made me think of Oscar as a stray cat.

The back door swung open, and I heard a collection of voices. Twisting on the bench I watched Mimbles, Dad, Paul, Richard, and his girlfriend, Ruby, appear.

"Hello, Eli," Mimbles said, giving me a smile as she washed her hands in the sink. She was wearing an old pair of gardening jeans and a jumper she'd had since the nineties, her grey hair in short curls with her glasses nestled in the top of them. She was almost the complete opposite of my mum, but that was probably what had kept them together for so long. "Love the hair."

"Doesn't it look nice?" Mum said. "I said he should have let Orlando do it years ago."

"You know, at this rate, I'm just going to grow it back out again," I said, folding my arms stubbornly. Finn snorted, and Mimbles laughed.

"How's work? Not too tedious?" Mimbles asked, drying her hands. I sighed internally. I should have expected all these questions given that it was the first time I'd seen them in person since I'd started the temp position, but it was irritating already.

"It's fine. Not particularly exciting." I saw Richard watching me, and my conversation with Tristan from the beginning of the week began replaying in my mind. I felt myself start to smile. "But then again, they're paying me, so I'll do whatever they want me to. No matter how *hard* it might be."

Richard's face twitched in irritation and smug satisfaction filled my chest. Mimbles gave me a shrewd look but obviously decided against pushing the issue.

"And what is it you're actually doing?" Richard asked, standing at the head of the table and looking down at me. "Mum said it's a proper job. What does that mean?"

"Rich," Ruby said softly, like a gentle warning, from behind him.

"Like I said, I'm doing whatever they want."

"And who's they?"

"Wouldn't you like to know?" I sipped my drink. I knew I was being a petulant child. In fact, I was delighting in it. But there was something about my brother's imperious demands that got under my skin. If nobody else had told him, I certainly wasn't going to. Not yet anyway. Besides, the moment I told him, I knew I'd get a lecture about how it either wasn't a good enough job or how pleased he was to see me growing up and taking life seriously.

I couldn't think of anything worse.

"Jesus Christ, Eli," Richard snapped. "Why are you being so childish about this?"

"Why do you instantly think I'm doing something shifty? Or at least that *you* view as shifty. It's none of your damn business what I do for work."

"Yes, it is."

"And why is that?" I asked, anger rising in my chest. I'd

told myself I wasn't going to get irritated, but it wasn't working. One look at his smug face and I was ready to explode. "Why do you, Dick for brains, have to know every single detail of my life? Is it because you want to know exactly how much of a disappointment I am to you? You're not even my parent for fuck's sake. What does this have to do with you?"

"You are a disappointment." He was yelling now, and everyone was staring at us. "Why don't you just grow up and behave like a normal person? You have a bloody law degree. Why don't you fucking use it?"

"Because," I said coldly, rising to my feet, "if being normal means being like you, I can't think of anything worse." I pushed the bench back, sliding out past Finn. "You're a judgemental asshole, and if all you're going to do is criticise my choices and jump to conclusions, then I'm done here."

I pulled my keys from my back pocket and pushed past him, heading for the front door and leaving everyone in stunned silence behind me. Anger and frustration pulled at my chest, and I hated the fact that my eyes were prickling with tears. Nobody ever made me feel ashamed of myself except for him. I'd known what he was going to say, but it still stung to hear those words: *a disappointment.*

The worst part was that nobody else had said anything, which meant they were either too stunned to speak, or they agreed. I could probably put money on who was in each camp, but somehow that made everything worse.

I didn't understand why Richard couldn't just leave me

alone. He'd been the same for years—acting like the worst combination of parent and teacher.

Enough was enough though. I wasn't going to sit there and be interrogated by him.

Not anymore.

CHAPTER SEVEN

Tristan

"ELI? ARE YOU OKAY?"

"Hmmm? Did you say something?" Eli looked up at me from behind the reception desk where he was covering for Pamela on Tuesday afternoon. He had a faraway look in his eyes I hadn't seen before, and there was almost a flash of pain before he blinked and looked up at me.

"I just asked if you were okay," I said. Richard had spent Sunday evening blowing up my phone with long rants about how Eli had childishly walked out of their family dinner because he'd refused to tell Richard about his job. Part of me wondered why Eli hadn't just told him since Green & Wodehouse wasn't exactly MI5, but a smaller part of me understood that if he told Richard, his brother would simply hold it over his head as an example that Eli could apply himself.

I felt caught in the middle, unable to move. It would be

easy enough for me to tell Richard what was going on and pacify him, but if I did that I'd prove to Eli what he'd thought about me all along. And something inside me didn't want that. It wanted to be different.

My feelings about Eli were like a tangled mess of wool, and I didn't know where or how to start unpicking them. I didn't even know how they'd become so tangled in the first place. One minute, he was just Richard's brother, and the next, he was my handsome co-worker who threw me for a loop with every wry smile he shot my way. It shouldn't have been complicated, but somehow it was.

"Never better." Eli smiled at me from his chair, but it didn't reach his eyes. "Did you need something?"

"No, I just… I wanted to check on you." I said the last part very quietly, like it was a secret I didn't want to admit. Eli's eyes narrowed.

"Dick tattled on me to you, didn't he?"

"It was more ranting," I said. "He was, er, upset you walked out on Sunday."

"Well, then he should learn to mind his own fucking business," Eli muttered. Then he sighed. He looked weary like the normal sparkling glow that surrounded him had dimmed slightly. I knew he and Richard fought a lot, but this seemed different. Perhaps this was the culmination of lots of different things, and the job was just the tipping point. I wanted to ask, but it didn't seem like anything to do with me.

I just wished it was.

"Do you want to get a drink?" The question fell out of my mouth before I even had time to register it. It hung in the stunned silence between us for a moment. That was the second time that had happened, and I wondered if it would always happen around Eli.

If so, it was going to be a painful year.

"You know what," Eli said, "I think I would. Come down about half five? It might be a little early, but fuck it. It's Tuesday, and I'm stressed."

"Sounds like a plan." I patted the top of the reception desk, trying to look more confident than I felt. "I've actually got a couple of client appointments this afternoon, so I'll be in the meeting room if anyone needs me."

"Is that a hint for me to make you coffee?" Eli asked with a sly grin. "If you ask nicely, I promise it won't be sludge."

I laughed. "I wasn't going to, but I'm intrigued now. So, yes, please will you make me and my clients any drinks, including coffee, as required? And in return, I'll buy you at least two drinks of your choosing later."

Eli's grin widened. "Why, Mr. Rose, I do believe we have a deal."

Several hours later, I found myself sitting next to Eli in a small cocktail bar at the bottom of Steep Hill. It had been Eli's choice, and I'd been happy to see him smile again. It hadn't really been my plan for Tuesday evening, but I'd already messaged my sister to ask her to let the dogs out and feed them. I knew by the time I got home I'd have been bombarded with photos of them curled up on her lap.

Right now, I was supposed to be studying the drink

menu in front of me, but instead, I couldn't tear my eyes away from the man beside me. From this angle, I was struck by the swell of his lips and the strong line of his jaw. I had the urge to run my fingers along it and cup his chin to bring his face close to mine.

I'd never wanted to kiss someone as much as I wanted to kiss Eli in that moment.

The certainty of that feeling almost frightened me.

"Do you know what you want?" he asked, tilting his head towards me.

"Er, I'm not sure." I hadn't even looked at the menu. "Any suggestions?"

"Depends on what you like to drink?"

"Most things really," I said. "I don't like coconut though. It gives me numb tongue. And I'm allergic to shellfish. Although I don't think that will be a problem here."

"I've not heard of oysters in cocktails, but you never know." He grinned. He'd undone his tie and unbuttoned the top few buttons of his shirt, giving me a tantalising vee of tanned skin to stare at. "Can I pick for you?"

"Sure. But if I don't like it, I'm stealing yours."

"Done. You'll like it though. Men like everything I give them." He winked at me and slid out of the booth, leaving me staring at him as he crossed the wooden floor towards the bar. My own collar suddenly felt very tight like I was struggling to breathe. I reached up and pulled at my tie, sliding it loose and tucking it into my bag before opening a couple of the buttons on my shirt. It didn't help as much as I wanted it to.

Eli returned a couple of minutes later and placed a drink

down in front of me. It was in a large hurricane glass and seemed to be varying shades of sunset colours with a curly straw poking out of the top.

"I went classic flavours," he said, settling down next to me. His own drink was pink with foam on the top and seemed to have come with an ice lolly, which was balanced across the top of the margarita glass. "That is a Cake by the Ocean—vodka, peach liqueur, passion fruit syrup, and orange and cranberry juice."

"Thanks." I took a sip, and the sweet flavours burst on my tongue. I could barely taste the alcohol, which was probably dangerous. It seemed like the sort of thing I could drink very quickly without realising. "What did you get?"

"This is called a You Spin Me Round, which I mostly picked because it came with the helter skelter lolly. I think it has raspberries in it. And possibly rum. Or vodka. Might be both." Eli picked up the wooden stick of the colourful, twisted ice lolly and lifted it to his mouth, flicking his tongue across the top of it suggestively. I stared, then took another large sip of my drink. I could definitely get drunk on these, and maybe that would be a good idea.

"What do you think?" Eli asked innocently, running his tongue up one of the grooves of the lolly before wrapping his lips around the top of it and sucking.

"Er, it's... er... it's great. Thanks."

Eli grinned around the lolly, sliding it out of his mouth with a pop. "You're welcome." I wanted to think of something to say or at least something to ask him, but then Eli slid the lolly back into his mouth, and all I could do was stare as three-quarters of the frozen treat disappeared between his lips.

If I'd ever had a brain, I didn't now.

There was a long moment of silence between us. I knew I should say something, anything, but I couldn't tear my eyes away from the swell of Eli's mouth or the way his lips glistened around the lolly. It should be illegal for him to eat an ice lolly in public.

Finally, Eli pulled off the lolly and licked his lips. His tongue was tinted red.

"So," I said, desperately searching for something to talk about before I did something very stupid like ask Eli to take me home so I could suck his cock. "What do you do for fun? Is it just drag, or do you have hobbies outside of that? I don't really know much about drag if I'm being honest. My sister Alexis keeps trying to get me to watch *Drag Stars*, but I've never gotten around to it. I'm probably not a very good gay."

I took another large sip of my drink. There wasn't much left now. Maybe I needed another? Eli laughed, biting off the end of the lolly, which he'd sucked to a point.

"I didn't realise there was a points system for queer-ness," he said. "Plenty of queer people don't watch *Drag Stars*, including myself."

"You don't? But don't—"

"Don't I have to because I'm a drag queen?" He sipped his drink, holding the lolly in his other hand. "Let me ask you this, do you watch property or financial programmes?"

"No, of course not."

"Exactly. I have some problems with some of the casting

for that show, and although it's done good things for making more people aware of the existence of drag, it's also made it very prescriptive. Many people think the only acceptable drag is what they've seen on *Drag Stars* without realising it has its own rich history as an art form. Drag is art, and therefore it is subjective. You cannot put drag into a box and neatly label it for a straight audience. That is the antithesis of the art form." He looked at me over the rim of his glass. "I apologise. I obviously get quite touchy about the subject, and I didn't mean to lecture you."

"It's fine," I said. It really wasn't something I knew much about. "It's funny. I'm gay, but I've never really engaged a lot with queer culture. Or maybe it's not funny at all. I just… I've had a few gay friends, but they're all similar to me."

"Rich, white, masculine, and straight passing?"

"Pretty much." There was no denying it. I knew I'd lived a fairly easy, privileged life. It sounded awful to admit that. Nobody really batted an eye if I went somewhere with a boyfriend because I looked and acted exactly like the rest of my family's friends. The only difference was the person who stood next to me was male.

"Plus, your best friend is the most boring straight man alive," Eli said, popping the lolly back into his mouth and sucking on it.

"If Richard is boring, then I definitely am. I mean, my hobbies are walking the dogs, giving tours at the castle in the summer, and painting historical miniatures. I don't even do any battles with them. I just like painting them." I felt my face flush. "I'm not exactly exciting."

Eli reached out his hand, his fingers interlacing with mine on the top of the table. "Who says those things aren't exciting? Dick is not exciting just by merit of being him. But you, Tristan… I think there are hidden depths to you."

"Thanks." I squeezed his hand, feeling a rush of warmth run up my arm. I wasn't sure if he was just saying it to be kind or because he meant it, but I wanted to believe it was the second, even though this was Eli, and I still had no idea how to read him.

"Okay," he said. "We need more drinks and then we are going to play twenty questions because I don't know nearly enough about you, and I'm intrigued." He grinned. "I've always thought of you as Dick-lite, but I'm beginning to suspect I've been very wrong. So, more alcohol and more questions. And then maybe pizza."

"Pizza?"

"Or we can get Chinese if you want. You said coconut gives you numb tongue, so I'm assuming Thai food is out." He slid gracefully out of his seat and headed back to the bar, hardly giving me time to process before he returned with two identical drinks in martini glasses.

"They're called Daddy Issues," he said with a grin. "I couldn't resist. I'll have to bring Orlando here for one."

"Orlando is your housemate?"

"Yes, and my best friend and occasional fuck buddy. Although that's stopped now because he's got two gorgeous boyfriends who dote on him. Honestly, I can't even get one person into bed, and now he's got two men wrapped around his finger." He sighed dramatically. "That was your first question, by the way. You get nine more."

I pushed down the odd pang of jealousy that had swelled in my chest when he'd talked about Orlando and looked at Eli. "Okay, your turn then."

"Are you single?"

"Yes," I said, unable to stop myself from smiling. "Very."

"Interesting." Eli drew out the word slowly, then raised one eyebrow and sipped his drink. "Next question."

I thought for a second. I'd always been terrible at these sorts of games. "Who's your celebrity crush?"

"Do I only get one?" Eli asked, looking at me seriously as he took a sip. "Or can I have two?"

"Er, you can have two." I hoped he didn't ask me the same question because I wasn't sure I had an answer.

"Good. I choose Sebastian Stan and Kat Dennings. Kat because she's hot and funny, and Sebastian because he's got that kinda cute broodiness to him. Also, I ship Steve Rodgers and Bucky way too hard, and I want to know if he's good in bed." There was a brief pause, and Eli grinned like he thought he'd stunned me.

"Good choices," I said, sipping my drink. It was another one I could drink easily without noticing. "I ship them too, but I always felt bad for Peggy, even if girls never did anything for me. So I'd rather they were just a little throuple together, saving the world and looking gorgeous while doing it."

"God, we'd all be fucked." Eli sighed wistfully. "I'd do whatever they said in a heartbeat, and I hate being told what to do. They could tie me up and paint me green for all I cared."

I laughed. "So your weaknesses are morally grey super-heroes with eyeliner, muscly cinnamon buns, and women who could kill you?"

"Pretty much, and I'd die a happy man."

I snorted and Eli grinned, a playful light dancing around in his eyes.

"Your turn then," I said, wondering where on earth we'd go next as I took another long drink.

"What's your favourite musical?" Eli asked, suddenly serious.

"Er, I don't have one. I've not seen many musicals." Nobody in my family liked them that much, so I never watched any. "Alexis made me watch *Mamma Mia!* with her once. The film one with Meryl Streep. Does that count?"

"I suppose it will have to." Eli looked positively scan-dalised. "But you'll have to watch more. I'll educate you."

"Big musical fan?"

"Yes." Eli's expression softened into something sweet and fond. "I used to watch them with Paul when I was growing up. He took me to see *The Phantom of the Opera* for my thirteenth birthday, and every year we go to watch one in London together. I think next year we're going to see *Everybody's Talking About Jamie* because we missed it the first time it was on. It's always been something we've done together, and those memories are special to me. Apart from Phil at The Court, Paul was one of my biggest influences to do drag. He's always encouraged me to be myself and do what makes me happy. He taught me how to sew, which is a skill all drag queens need."

"That's really cool," I said, hoping I sounded as

earnest as I felt. "I don't have anything like that with anyone in my family. My dad just wants me to be sporty so we can watch rugby and cricket together." I sighed. "He always wanted a son who wouldn't mind getting tackled."

Eli snorted. "You mean you don't like getting tackled by other men?"

"I do, but only in my bedroom, not when they're trying to break my ribs." I looked at Eli for a moment, then the two of us burst out laughing. I had no idea how strong our drinks were, but the effects seemed to have hit me suddenly. "You know," I said, giggling into my cocktail, "I never talk about my sex life with anyone. Then again, that's kind of boring too. I really am very boring. Why are you even sitting here with me?"

"Because, darling Tristan," Eli said, "I think you're quite fun."

"That's a lie."

"It's not."

"Prove it." I drained the last of my Daddy Issues and wondered if I could get another one.

"Okay, I will. What are you doing on Sunday afternoon?"

"Not much..." The question threw me. I didn't think I was doing much. Nothing important sprang to mind. "Why?"

"Good, then we're going to do something together." Eli sounded so certain, and I was momentarily surprised. I didn't think he'd meant it.

"What?"

"Not sure yet," he said with a grin. "But I'll think of something fun. Just the two of us."

I wanted to ask him if it was a date, but even in my tipsy state, I couldn't find the courage to ask. All I could say was, "Okay."

"Good. Now, do you want another drink? I think we've still got some questions to ask and answer."

CHAPTER EIGHT

Eli

"WHAT ARE YOU DOING THIS AFTERNOON?" Orlando asked, looking up from where he was lying on my bed, stretched out in a giant t-shirt and tiny underwear. He was sulking because his men had had a family party to go to this weekend, so he hadn't been able to see them. He'd spent two days moping around the apartment and sighing forlornly, and I was starting to suspect his relationship was much more than a fling. I, meanwhile, was digging through my wardrobe trying to decide what to wear for my outing, although at that point more of my clothes were on the floor than anywhere else.

"I'm taking Tristan to the Sunset Cinema at the castle. They're doing a *Mamma Mia!* singalong, and I thought it would be fun," I said. The Sunset Cinema was a touring, outdoor cinema that went around to various large castles and country estates in the UK showing a selection of films and musicals. It came to Lincoln Castle for three nights every September, and I'd been several times before with my siblings or Orlando.

"Is this a date?" Orlando gave me a sly smile.

"No. This is just us doing something as friends."

"Liar," Orlando said, throwing one of my pillows at me. "You like him."

"Absolutely not!" That was definitely a lie. I knew I felt *something* for Tristan, but I wasn't sure if it was anything more than lust. "He's just very sweet and lonely and needs to spend time in better company."

"So you're gracing him with your presence?"

"Precisely."

"And you absolutely, one hundred percent, don't want to bring him back here, bend him over your bed, and eat his ass like it's made of candy?" Orlando's smile had widened, his innocent eyes twinkling.

"I have the right to remain silent," I said, ignoring him and sticking my head into the back of the wardrobe in case I'd missed something.

"That's a yes, then."

"No comment." I grabbed a t-shirt off the floor and held it up. It was just a plain black one, but it still wasn't right. I dropped it on the floor again.

"So you didn't deep-throat a lolly in front of him on Tuesday?"

I groaned. Tristan and I had ended up having several more drinks while asking each other increasingly ridiculous questions before we'd ended up getting pizza and later poured ourselves into separate taxis. Then I'd come home and drunkenly told Orlando everything, which in hindsight had been my first mistake. "I was just teasing him! I wanted to see what would happen. I didn't mean to stun him into silence."

"It sounds like Tristan needs better sex," Orlando said matter-of-factly. "If you sucking one ice lolly suggestively is enough to shock him, then he can't have had good blow jobs in the past. Or many of them. You'll have to rectify that."

"Will I?"

"Duh." Orlando's voice dripped with disdain as though it was completely obvious and I was purposefully over-looking the point. "Of course you will. Who else is going to blow his mind?"

"I'm not going to blow him." I grabbed a loose vest top off the floor and pulled it on. Perfect.

"But you want to?"

"Of course I want to," I snapped. "God, I just want to strip him down and see how long it takes me to make him come. But I can't do that."

"Why not?"

It was a reasonable question. Usually when I'd decided I wanted someone, I'd go for it. But with Tristan, something was holding me back. There was no question that I wanted him—I'd jerked off every night that week thinking about him—but fucking Tristan came with baggage. Not only was there the whole work thing, but there was my brother to consider too, and while Dick didn't ever have to find out about it, I felt bad putting Tristan in that position. I didn't want to force him to pick sides.

Especially because I didn't know whose side he'd choose.

I'd spoken to Jules and Finn since last weekend's disaster dinner, and both had agreed Richard had been a twat, but Finn, ever the peacekeeper, had wanted to know if it would really have been so bad if I'd told him. Mum was upset, and I'd apologised over the phone, but she hadn't understood either. I didn't really think anyone truly would, except maybe Tristan.

I was banking on a lot there, and there was a good chance I was just projecting my wishes onto him. But a small part of me was holding out hope that maybe Tristan got why I didn't want to tell Richard everything, simply by merit of knowing my brother so well.

And I didn't want to muddle that with one night of good sex.

"It's complicated," was all I said.

I was still thinking about the conversation with Orlando an hour later when I met Tristan outside the castle. He looked adorable in dark jeans and a grey fleece with a hint of a dark green t-shirt underneath. He was completely the opposite of any of the people I'd previously been involved with and completely the opposite of me. So why did my heart skip a beat when I saw him?

Since when was I attracted to country casuals?

"Hey," he said, giving me a smile and a little wave when he spotted me.

"Hey yourself. Have you been waiting long?" I asked,

trying to act more casual than I felt since my insides were currently tying themselves in knots. I wasn't sure when my intestines had decided to take up shibari, but I wished they hadn't picked now to start.

"Not at all. So, what are we going to see?"

One of my eyebrows quirked in surprise. "You didn't look it up?"

"No." Tristan sounded almost offended. "You said it was a surprise. I only realised it was the Sunset Cinema when I arrived and saw the banner." He pointed to the large sign that had been hung outside the castle.

"I would have been straight on my phone to look it up," I said with a laugh. My heart skipped again. I was really going to need to see a cardiologist at this rate. "Since you said you've only ever seen one musical, I thought we'd go and see it again. We're going to the *Mamma Mia!* singalong."

A mixture of expressions cycled across Tristan's face—horror, fear, potential excitement, shock—and then he burst out laughing. "Okay," he said. "That's a new one for me. I'm not a great singer. I'll warn you now. And I don't know the words."

"If you're seriously telling me you don't know the words to *one* ABBA song, I will have to reconsider this friendship." I grinned. "And don't worry, they print the words at the bottom of the screen, and everyone will be singing, so if you really do sound like Scuttle from *The Little Mermaid*, nobody will notice."

"Okay then." He gave me a little smile, and the expression in his eyes was one I hadn't seen from many people before. It looked like trust. "Do you want to go in?" He paused. "Did we need something to sit on?"

I gestured to the old backpack I was wearing. "You don't think I would invite you out and make you sit on the grass, do you?" I asked, bringing my hand to my mouth as if utterly scandalised by this accusation. "I brought some blankets, some drinks, and some snacks. Technically, Orlando packed the snacks because he's been fucking miserable all weekend, and it gave him something to do."

I gestured to Tristan, and we began walking towards the high, open arch that would lead us into the castle grounds. I rummaged in my jacket pocket for my phone so I could pull up the booking email with the tickets attached.

"Is everything okay? With Orlando?" Tristan asked as I presented the man at the gate with our tickets. He stamped our hands, gave a cursory glance at the inside of my backpack, and waved us inside.

"Yeah, he's fine," I said as we strolled into the grounds. A gentle hum of noise surrounded us, and the smells of a hog roast and fried food wafted through the air. "His boyfriends had to go to some family event for the weekend and couldn't take him with them. He usually sees them every week, so he's sulking." I looked over at Tristan trying to gauge his reaction, my body tense. "But I get it, even if it sucks. His boyfriends are married, and this whole thing is very new between them. I'm not even sure they're actually boyfriends because it started off as just sex, but considering how miserable Orlando is—"

"It seems like there are feelings involved."

"Exactly." I felt myself relax like I'd been waiting for

Tristan to say something negative. "But I'm not going to push it. If I do, he'll start getting involved in my dating life again, and that's the last thing I need."

Tristan laughed. "Is he nosy?"

"Worse. So much worse!" I laughed. "He needs to know everything. And he's always trying to set me up with friends of his. It comes from a good place though. He doesn't want me to be lonely."

"I know what you mean, and I know where he's coming from," Tristan said softly. "I don't think anybody really wants to be alone."

I wanted to say something, but I didn't know what. There was a wistful note in his voice that spoke of heartache and loneliness, and it made me want to reach out my hand and bring him close against me, making him promises I knew I couldn't keep.

It was almost terrifying how much I wanted to make Tristan feel loved.

We'd reached a small fork in the path, and we followed it around to the right to an open lawn. A large screen was to the left of us, stretched against the wall of one of the inner buildings, and to our right the lawn was already filled with people on blankets and foldable chairs. Some of them even had immense picnics, and I wondered whether what I'd asked Orlando to pack would be enough.

"Shall we go over there?" Tristan asked, pointing at a spot towards the back where the lawn sloped upwards onto a shallow bank. "That should give us a good view."

We picked our way across the lawn, circling around various groups of people, some of whom seemed to already be down a couple of bottles of wine, until we'd reached the spot Tristan had seen. I pulled off my backpack and unzipped it, pulling out the two old blankets I'd found and spreading them across the grass. I'd wanted more than one so we'd have plenty of space to spread out. This *wasn't* a date, so there was no need for us to sit on top of each other.

I glanced back into the backpack, frowning. I'd expected there to be maybe some crisps and some brownie bites, but there seemed to be a lot more than that. There was a Post-it note stuck to a tub of mini Scotch eggs that read:

Enjoy your date ;)
Orlando xxx

That sneaky bastard! I ripped the note off and scrunched it in my hand before Tristan could see it. Then I flopped onto the ground next to him and began to pull things out, muttering variations of "What the fuck?" to myself as I spread a literal feast across the blankets.

"I thought you said it was just snacks," Tristan said, staring at a tub of mini cheese and onion muffins that I'd just stacked on one full of dinky little Cornish pasties.

"So did I." This must have cost Orlando a fortune. I was going to have words with him later. "He said it was just a few little bits."

"I mean, they are little." Tristan chuckled. He picked up a tub of fat, green olives. "I love these."

"Seriously?" I grinned. "Me too. Most people I know hate them."

"They're missing out."

"Right?" I examined everything I'd pulled out of the bag, amazed at the sheer amount of food Orlando had managed to cram into the space. I thought the bag had felt a bit heavy, but I hadn't questioned it. At the bottom, I found a couple of cans of Fanta and a couple cans of pre-mixed Pimms. They were still cool, condensation dripping down the sides. I offered Tristan a choice, and he took a can of Pimms, cracking the tab open and sitting back on the blanket, stretching his legs out in front of him. The sun was setting behind the walls, turning the sky into a vibrant kaleidoscope of colours, and beyond it, I could see a dusting of stars, waiting to emerge.

The cinema company had set up lanterns in the trees and there were solar-powered lamps hammered into the grass around the edge of the lawn that were just starting to glow. It gave the whole thing a little bit of an ethereal air. In the background, the screen had started to play a few adverts—mostly for local businesses, the castle, and other venues on the Sunset Cinema tour.

We chatted quietly about nothing much in particular as we began to pick at the food, passing various packets and tubs back and forth between us. I kept telling myself it wasn't a date, that it *couldn't* be a date, but the whole situation seemed to scream date. Every time Tristan smiled at me or offered me some food or told me a ridiculous anecdote about his dogs, my insides squirmed. It reminded me of the time we'd gone on a family holiday to France and taken the ferry, my stomach swooped and dropped like it was riding the swells of the sea, except this time I didn't think I was going to vomit spectacularly all over someone's shoes.

"Oh, I think it's starting," Tristan said, glancing over at the screen that had suddenly gone black. I looked over and saw a cinema certification fading away. The image of moonlight dancing across water appeared on the screen, and music swelled through the speakers, the first few notes of "I Have a Dream" filling the air around us.

"Are you ready?" I wasn't sure if Tristan was quite prepared for what was about to happen. I'd been to a couple of singalong screenings of various musicals in the past, and they were always fucking bonkers. Given how much some of the audience had already had to drink, I didn't think this was going to be any different.

"Ready for—" He didn't get the question out before the whole venue seemed to burst into song, in perfect albeit somewhat drunken harmony with Amanda Seyfried. I watched Tristan's face as I began to sing, unable to stop myself from smiling as I did. I knew the words to this musical by heart since Mimbles had been a diehard ABBA fan since she'd first seen them on Eurovision in the seventies. I'd grown up on the lyrics. Tristan's mouth split into a grin as he looked around then up at the screen, watching the words across the bottom as they lit up.

"Just like karaoke," I said as Sophie pushed the letters to her three potential fathers into the post box and the film cut to the three men preparing for the trip.

"I've never done karaoke before," Tristan said, sipping his second can of Pimms. "I'm very boring, remember?"

"Well, there's a first time for everything." I scooted slightly closer to him so I could nudge him with my shoulder. "There's never been a more perfect time to pop your singalong cherry! And don't worry, nobody but me is going to hear you." Tristan nodded. I reached for the tub of strawberries by my foot, ripping it open and holding it out in front of him. "Want one? They're not quite cherries, but they'll do."

Tristan reached for one, and I watched him lift it to his mouth, mesmerised. His lips wrapped around the fruit, and I wondered if this was how he'd felt on Tuesday when I'd teased him with the lolly. The only difference was I'd been doing it deliberately, and I didn't think Tristan had a clue how much he was affecting me.

I heard shrieking from the film, and I knew "Honey, Honey" was coming up. I swallowed. I'd definitely be revisiting this moment later. The crowd began to sing, and once again I was swept up in the moment, my mouth moving without me even thinking about it. I looked at Tristan, who glanced at the screen and then back at me. Then he began to sing.

He was quiet, not everyone was a natural show-off like me, but the sound coming out of his mouth was the most beautiful baritone. Fucking hell, the man had a voice! I wanted to ask him if he knew how fucking amazing he sounded, but I didn't because I knew the moment I said anything he'd probably clam up. So I grinned and smiled and sang along with him, our shoulders bumping gently.

It wasn't a date. I knew that.

But even so, it was the best non-date I'd ever had.

CHAPTER NINE

Tristan

THE CRISP MORNING air of late September nipped at my skin as I stepped outside, Indy and Solo bouncing around my feet as I tried to lock the back door. It wasn't even seven in the morning, and grey clouds hung across the sky. Autumn had well and truly arrived, and I was happy to see it. The golden glow of the rising sun began to appear over the horizon, breaking through the clouds, and in the distance, I could just about make out the towers of Lincoln Cathedral.

I lived in a small village north of the city. It was easy for me to get to work and into the city centre, but I still got to immerse myself in rural life. Growing up, all I'd wanted to do was escape, but after living in London for two years, I'd wanted nothing more than to go back to the calm, quiet pace of the Lincolnshire countryside. When I'd moved back, it had felt like coming home.

I led the dogs around the back of the house and out into

the lane, heading towards the nearby fields which we could walk around. They'd had wheat in all summer, but that had now been replaced by deep furrows where the land had been turned over. I let Indy and Solo off their leads as soon as we reached the fields, and they shot off ahead of me, hoping to find some of the local rabbit population to annoy. I dug my hands into my pockets and tramped along the grass path, lost in my thoughts.

Last night had been amazing. A *Mamma Mia!* singalong wouldn't have ever been on my list of things to do, but I'd had more fun than I'd expected. Eli had encouraged me to step out of my very small comfort zone, and I'd ended up singing my heart out, not caring if I got the lyrics wrong. We'd even gotten up and danced at the end when virtually the entire audience had been on their feet. My dancing was even worse than my singing, but Eli hadn't cared, hadn't criticised, and hadn't pushed me to do more. He'd just laughed while throwing his best seventies-style dance moves, radiating sheer joy while he did so.

It hadn't been a date, at least I didn't think it had. But it had been the most fun I'd had with a man in a long time.

Richard had always said Eli was careless and reckless, and I'd always agreed, having no more than a few brief interactions on which to base my assumptions, but now I couldn't see any of that. All I could see was a man who lived every moment to the fullest, threw caution to the wind, and embraced life. He seemed to care deeply about those he loved, and he radiated fun and passion, but I sensed there was more to him than that. There was a lingering note of pain and responsibility underlying the joy.

I got the feeling Eli liked to pretend he didn't care what people thought when underneath he cared a great deal.

"He's nothing like I thought," I muttered to myself. I looked up and realised I'd walked nearly all the way around two fields without realising. I whistled and waited for Indy and Solo to make a reappearance from under the nearest hedge, shaking leaves and dew from their chocolate coats. They pottered up to me, and I reached down to rub their heads before clipping on their leads.

"Good boys," I said. "Time for breakfast?"

Solo, who always seemed to understand any words related to food, huffed happily.

When I got to the house, I noticed the kitchen light was on. The back door was unlocked, and when I pushed it open I heard the soft strains of Billie Eilish echoing out of the speakers. I shook my head and smiled to myself because I knew exactly who was inside.

"Morning, Alexis," I said as I threw the doors open and let the dogs in, toeing my boots off on the mat. "Don't you have food at your house?"

My sister, who stood near the oven cracking eggs into a pasta bowl, laughed as she turned to face me. Her caramel-coloured hair hung in loose waves around her shoulders, the long sleeves of her floral-patterned dress pushed back over her elbows. Alexis oozed a casual bohemian air, taking life at her own charming pace and making the world bend to her will. She never seemed to be in a rush about anything. I'd never managed to exude her level of charm no matter how hard I'd tried. Alexis was truly unique like that.

She lived in the cottage next door to me because we'd

bought them as a pair with the money I had from London and a huge chunk of inheritance from our paternal grand-parents. We'd turned the garden into a communal one, and despite the fact we had separate houses, we spent as much time with each other as apart whenever she was around. She was the only member of my family I'd ever been close to since our parents weren't particularly interested in us, and we'd built a tiny shared life together. Just her and me and the dogs.

"Not really," she said. "I only got back from London last night, and I haven't been shopping. I thought we could have breakfast together. I'm making French toast."

"With cinnamon?"

"Of course. And ice cream."

"There's ice cream?" I asked, frowning as I headed through the kitchen to the tiny utility room tacked onto the side where I stored the dogs' food. Indy and Solo were already waiting, looking at me forlornly as if they'd expire at any minute. You'd think they didn't get two meals a day and whatever treats Alexis or my dog walker, Bob, slipped them.

"There is now." Alexis smiled and began beating the eggs, sprinkling in cinnamon as she did so. "You can't have French toast without ice cream."

"For breakfast?"

"It's Monday. And life must always be full of joy," she said. "How was your weekend?"

"It was fine." I mixed the dogs' food and put their bowls on the floor, chuckling to myself at the way Indy's paws did tiny tippy-taps on the tiles in excitement.

"Did you do anything fun?"

Alexis was always telling me I needed more excitement in my life. More joie de vivre. Usually I didn't have anything to tell her. "Yes, I did," I said, wandering back into the kitchen and realising Alexis already had a pot of tea stewing under the knitted cosy she'd made when she was fifteen. It had a wonky rainbow pattern and a bright yellow pom-pom on top. "I went to a *Mamma Mia!* singalong with a friend at Lincoln Castle." Alexis spun on the spot and stared at me, her mouth hanging slightly open. I chuckled because I'd never seen her so shocked. "If the wind changes, your face will stay like that."

"I'm sorry, I'm just trying to process the words you and *Mamma Mia!* singalong."

"Am I that boring?"

"Yes," she said with a smile. "But also no. It's just not something I'd expect from you. Or Richard if I'm honest. It doesn't seem like his sort of thing."

"I didn't go with Richard," I said as I finished making two cups of tea. I slid one onto the counter next to Alexis, trying to avoid her gaze.

"Who did you go with then?"

"Just a friend." I wrapped my fingers around my mug and sipped my tea. "His name's Eli. He just started at the office. He's doing Jaz's maternity cover."

I wondered if Alexis would remember Richard had a brother called Eli, but if she did, she didn't say anything. Instead, she began buttering slices of bread and dipping them into the eggs. My stomach rumbled. "And he's just a friend?"

"Yes." I didn't tack *for now* onto the end, even though I suddenly wanted it to be true. The realisation stunned me, clobbering me around the head and leaving me reeling. I suddenly needed a moment of space. "Are you okay if I go and grab a quick shower while this cooks?" I asked. "I need to get changed for work."

"Sure. You okay?"

"Just realised what the time was." I was already halfway out the kitchen and up the stairs. I managed to catch the bathroom door behind me before it slammed shut, throwing the lock in place. I reached into the shower and turned it on, letting the water hammer into the tray while I shed my dog-walking clothes. Before I climbed in, I caught a glance of myself in the mirror—blond hair askew, cheeks flushed from the cold air and the warm kitchen. I'd never considered myself particularly handsome, although Alexis and other boyfriends had told me otherwise. I'd just always thought they were being polite. But looking at myself now, perhaps there'd been some merit to their words. I'd caught Eli looking at me a few times over the last week, and I'd thought he was just watching me to make sure I didn't break his printer again. But maybe he was interested in me.

My cock twitched at the thought of Eli. I wrapped my fingers around my shaft and stroked myself to full hard-ness, watching my reflection in the mirror. I'd never been fucked in front of a mirror before, but the thought of Eli jerking me off or bending me over the sink and fucking me and making me watch had precum dripping from my slit. I bit my lip to stop a groan from escaping as I stroked myself faster, spreading precum across my skin. I thought about Eli on his knees in front of me, sucking on my cock in the same obscene way he'd demonstrated on the ice lolly at the bar. God, if he did that, I'd be done for.

There was something about the way Eli had looked at me that made me feel wanted. Desired even. His eyes had seared into my soul with a laser focus and left the images of his mouth branded there.

"Oh… oh… fuck," I said, breathing the words so they'd be lost under the sound of the shower. I knew I should be doing this in there, but I couldn't stop watching myself and the way my dick fucked into my fist, the head red and dripping. I was already close, my orgasm rushing towards the surface with ever increasing speed. I hadn't done this in a while.

Thoughts of Eli filled my mind, whispers of his voice in my ear. A shiver ran down my spine as I imagined his fingers on my skin, dirty words and commands wrapping around me in a silken vise. I'd always had a weakness for dirty talk, but I'd never really had a partner that had truly excelled at it. Somehow I got the feeling it would be Eli's forte. Just imagining him telling me what to do… what he wanted to do to me, had me gasping and panting, my hands and hips working wildly as I chased my release.

"Shit!" My cock throbbed in my hand, shooting wads of hot cum into my fist and splattering the edge of the sink. I panted, reaching for the cool porcelain to steady myself. I hadn't meant to do that, but I wasn't sure I completely regretted it.

I just wasn't sure how easy it would be to look Eli in the eye when I got to work.

. . .

I didn't end up getting to the office until after half nine. Alexis had insisted on sitting down to breakfast, and when I'd tried to argue I was going to be late, she'd pointed out that technically I ran my own separate business out of the Green & Wodehouse offices and could therefore go in whenever I pleased. I hadn't wanted to argue, so I'd just sat and eaten my French toast with ice cream and strawberries while listening to Alexis talk about the house she was designing.

Eli was chatting with Pamela when I arrived, the two of them peering at something on Pamela's screen. He looked up when the door opened, a smile sliding onto his face.

"Good morning, Mr. Rose," he said, a teasing glint in his eye. "Late night?"

"No, but my sister broke into my house this morning and insisted we have breakfast together, and by the time I left, traffic was a nightmare."

"Did you bring me any?" Eli asked, straightening up to look at me over the reception desk.

"I don't know if French toast and ice cream travels that well."

"Ice cream for breakfast?" He gave a dramatic gasp. "See, Pamela? You think you know a guy, and then it turns out he eats ice cream for breakfast on a Monday morning. How scandalous!"

I laughed. "Are you hinting that you want me to buy you ice cream?"

"Whatever gave you that idea? But since you offered,

yes please. We can go to the ice cream shop on the corner near the cathedral."

"It's nearly October."

"And? It's never too cold for ice cream. If you had some for breakfast, I can have some for lunch."

"Fine. We can go to the deli too," I said, unable to stop myself from smiling. I hadn't packed lunch anyway, and this was the perfect excuse to spend more time with Eli.

"Excellent. Orlando refused to make me lunch today, and I'm bored of Pot Noodles."

"Surely you can make your own lunch."

"Do you?" Eli asked, grinning sweetly, knowing full well the answer was no.

"Point taken." I glanced across the desk for a second and noticed Pamela watching us closely, a shrewd look in her eyes. Whatever Eli and I were doing was far too obvious. "Well, I have to go and examine the mountain of emails in my inbox," I said. "But I'll come down about one-ish. Although I'll be up and down a few times as I've got a couple of client meetings this morning and this afternoon."

"Roger that," Eli said. "I'll start the coffee now so it has time to stew for you."

I chuckled and began to head for the stairs. "If I have to drink that, so do you."

CHAPTER TEN

Eli

"Good morning. Again," Tristan said, appearing next to me as I refilled the coffee maker and slid the rainbow mug I'd brought in onto the tray. I pressed the button to dispense the coffee and looked up at him, giving him my most flirtatious smile, the one I always used to get what I wanted.

"You know, we've got to stop meeting like this. What will people think?"

"They'll think that it's only Wednesday of the longest week ever, and I seriously need some caffeine." Tristan checked the water level in the kettle and flicked it on, giving a heavy sigh and leaning against the tiny expanse of counter next to me. Over the past couple of days, ever since our *Mamma-Mia!* not date, we'd fallen into an unspoken routine of taking several drinks breaks together. I wasn't quite sure how it had happened, but this morning I'd found myself repeatedly checking the time and waiting for half ten. Pamela had even caught me clock watching.

"That bad?"

"There are days when I love my job, and then there are days like today when I remember why I left both London and banking. I hate the people involved." Tristan sighed again. "Sorry, I'm not making much sense."

"I'm going to assume you're dealing with some asshole banker, or ex-banker, who's looking to have a life in the country and play lord of the manor, and you are stuck trying to deal with his finances and or processing his mortgage application." Given the size of some of the properties we had on the market, it was the answer that made the most sense.

"You would be right."

"You could just tell him to get fucked," I suggested helpfully as my coffee finished brewing. I picked up the mug and inhaled the rich scent. Work was the only time I got decent coffee without paying through the nose for it, and I made sure to enjoy every sip. The kettle boiled for Tristan's tea, and he let out a hollow chuckle as he threw a teabag into a ceramic mug, which was patterned with a pretty blue gradient.

"I wish. But unfortunately, I have bills to pay, and dog food is expensive."

I laughed. "You can't let your children starve. They'd never forgive you."

"They'd be packing up their bags to go and live with Alexis. I'm surprised they haven't already to be honest. She spoils them rotten."

"You know the more tidbits I hear about your sister, the more I like her."

"I'm never introducing the pair of you," Tristan said, giving me a wry smile as he fished the milk out of the under-counter fridge.

"Why?"

"Because you will conspire against me, and I'll never get a word in edgeways."

"Are you saying I talk too much?" I raised an eyebrow at him.

"Yes."

"You know, I should be offended, but it's the truth, and even I know it."

Tristan laughed, the sound sending a warm rush across my skin. He began to scoop sugar into his tea. "At least you know it."

"I'm fully aware of all my flaws," I said with a grin. "Talkative, overly dramatic, and far too devilishly handsome for my own good." I knew I was pushing it, but I couldn't stop myself. Flirting with Tristan was so natural. The unspoken boundary between us was getting thinner, and any excuses I'd flimsily erected for not wanting to pursue him were melting at speed.

Tristan cast his eyes over me slowly. "I'd agree with all of that."

There was a moment of silence between us.

"Good," I said finally. "I'm glad we agree." I took another sip of my coffee, trying to calm the wild fluttering in my chest which felt like I'd just downed six double espressos. "But I think you might be even more handsome than me."

Tristan's mouth twitched, and I saw pink appear around his hairline like he'd caught the sun. "Thanks."

The phone rang on my desk, and I realised our time together was up. I sauntered out, leaving him behind to finish making his tea. "You're cute too," I said, pausing in the doorway to look back over my shoulder at him.

I didn't stay to see how pink his face went.

"Do you want a biscuit?" I asked when Tristan appeared at the bottom of the stairs on Friday afternoon for our last tea break of the week. "Usually, these are highly secret, special biscuits, but Pamela told me to offer you one."

Pamela had also had some choice words to say about our level of flirting, but I wasn't going to repeat them to Tristan. They could basically be summed up as "stop flirting and kiss the man already". At first, I had attempted to deny there was even any flirting going on, but Pamela had asked me if I thought she'd been born yesterday. I'd begrudgingly given her an overview of everything in strict confidence, leaving out some of the more salacious details like the lolly sucking. She'd given me a withering look and gone back to work, muttering something about men being daft under her breath. Frankly, she was probably right.

I still wasn't quite sure why I wasn't throwing myself at Tristan.

I mean, I was but just a lot more subtly than usual.

Normally, if things were taking this long, I'd have gotten bored by now.

The whole situation was throwing me for a loop, and I still had no idea which way was up.

"Special, secret biscuits?" Tristan asked, giving me one of his charming smiles as he strolled towards my desk. "Do I have to swear a blood oath to be allowed one?"

"Not today but only because blood is messy, and I don't fancy cleaning it up." I opened the tin of biscuits that sat on my desk and shook them at him. "Just promise me you won't tell anyone else. Especially not the assholes up in sales."

"I promise," said Tristan, crossing his heart before taking a triple chocolate cookie off the top. "Thanks."

"You're very welcome. Tea?"

"Tea."

I stood up and headed for the kitchenette. "Would you like tea, Pamela?"

"I will never say no to tea," she said. She'd spent the afternoon trying to co-ordinate the payment and delivery of some new brochures, which Hayden, our designer, had ordered. Except he hadn't told anyone he'd ordered them and then pissed off yesterday for a long weekend, leaving Pamela to pick up the pieces.

"Poor Pamela is a little stressed this afternoon," I said to Tristan, who stood in the doorway nibbling his cookie. I filled the kettle and relayed the whole brochure saga to him while he sighed and rolled his eyes.

"That sounds like Hayden. I've not worked with him much, but I get the feeling he forgets things. Or he does things he and Holly have agreed on and then doesn't tell anyone else about them."

"How helpful," I said sarcastically, pulling out some teabags and our mugs. I flitted between drinking tea and coffee depending on both my mood and the time of day. Usually it was coffee in the morning and when I needed a pick me up and tea in the afternoons and when I was stressed. There was no problem on earth that couldn't be solved with a nice cup of tea. "Not like we needed that information at all. This is why I hate people."

Tristan laughed. "You? Hate people?"

"Yes, I am very spiteful and vindictive when I feel like it. Once, when I was at primary school, one of the kids in my class stole my gel pens because they were 'for girls', and she didn't think I should have them. When I complained, I was told I needed to share because that was the polite thing to do. Plus, I was a boy, and playground rules meant I couldn't hit her. So I waited until playtime, told the teacher I felt sick so I could stay in, and took all the ink cartridges out of the gel pens in her pencil case and hid them in my sister's lunchbox."

"That is both petty and vindictive," Tristan said, looking almost impressed. "What happened?"

"Nothing." I grinned and began to pour the boiling water. "Well, I mean the girl cried and complained that I'd stolen her gel pens, but she couldn't prove it was me. And they were my pens in the first place. Nobody messes with me and gets away with it. I mean, one of Richard's ex-girl-friends is permanently enshrined in one of my drag routines because of what happened at the family dinner he brought her too."

"Ohhh, was that the pasta fight?" Tristan asked. "I heard about that. Richard was pissed. I'd tried to warn him though. MLMs are a scam, and some of the people who sell that stuff are... well... devoted to a scary level of intensity."

"That's an incredibly polite way to put it." I laughed, scooping the tea bags out of the mugs with a spoon and dumping them into the bin before I began to doctor my tea and Pamela's. "Personally, I'd have said she was batshit. We kept telling her we weren't interested in whatever fake aloe supplement shit she was trying to extol, but she wouldn't listen. And then she cornered Finn." I shook my head to myself and smiled as the memory resurfaced. "Rookie mistake there."

Oscar, the oldest of Mimbles's children and the one below Richard, was incredibly overprotective of Finn. We all were to some degree, but Oscar seemed to view his baby brother as some sort of helpless kitten. When said MLM girlfriend had cornered Finn, Oscar's warning lights went off, and the ensuing conversation ended with him dumping pasta salad all over her. Then it all went downhill from there. I think the only reason there weren't fisticuffs on the lawn was because Richard knew Oscar would hand his ass to him on a plate within ten seconds.

Tristan hummed. "I remember Richard talking it through with me afterwards. He did admit that maybe he shouldn't have brought her to meet you, and that maybe she wasn't the right girl for him."

"He admitted that? How gracious of him. Still didn't

stop him from dating more terrible women." I waved at the milk and sugar. "How do you take your tea?"

"Oh, a little milk and three sugars please. Do you want me to do it?"

"I've got it."

"You're right though. About your brother. I think after that it was the Maldives holiday woman who was still married, then the one who wanted them to get matching tattoos after two weeks."

"You know, my brother's dating adventures make my own life look very tame in comparison."

"You mean nobody's tried to throw you a surprise wedding before?" Tristan asked with a wry smile as I handed him his mug.

"Sadly not."

There was a pause for a moment. "Do you think you'd ever want to?"

"Want to what?" I asked. I got the feeling I knew what he was asking—having gotten quite good at following random conversation jumps thanks to Lewis's ability to go from Point A to Point J without any stops in between—but I wanted to be sure.

"Get married." Tristan's voice was very quiet, and he seemed to be looking into the bottom of his mug like there was something interesting stuck there.

"Perhaps. It depends really. I mean, part of me thinks marriage is a very heteronormative institution that is largely outdated, but then again, it might be nice." The cynic in me had never liked the idea of marriage, but the romantic in me liked it a great deal. I vacillated between the two depending on my general life situation. But Tristan wasn't asking for my TED Talk on my views on marriage. He was asking because he wanted to get married one day. At least that's what I assumed. Otherwise, why would he ask. I made a mental note to revisit the conversation at some point in the future. "I think if I met the right person I would. I think I'd do a lot of things I wouldn't always consider for that person."

Tristan seemed to relax slightly. I picked up my mug and shot him my cheekiest grin. "Besides, I'd quite like a day where everything revolved around me and there was a cake bigger than my head."

"It would have to be a very big cake then," he said, catching my eye.

"You cheeky bastard!" I laughed. "That's savage, Mr. Rose. I never knew you had it in you."

As I'd predicted, there were hidden depths to Tristan— deep wells full of secrets and sass that nobody had taken the time to explore. He intrigued me like a puzzle box I couldn't work out how to solve. I wanted to, though, because underneath the quiet, proper exterior was a man who never seemed to let the world see who he really was. Who'd been put in a little box and had stayed there.

I wanted to help him break free.

Even if that just involved singing ABBA songs loudly once in a while.

"So," I said, sipping my tea, "any exciting plans for this weekend?"

CHAPTER ELEVEN

Tristan

I'D TOLD Eli I didn't have any plans for the weekend beyond a Friday night dinner with Richard, but that wasn't strictly true. I did have a plan; it was just a secret one.

Even though I'd lived in Lincoln for a long time, I'd never been to The Court before. I'd gone clubbing in my youth because it was part of the university experience, and I'd done a few all-nighters in London because it was part of the culture, but I'd retired my late nights when I'd moved back. These days I spent my evenings curled up on the sofa with a warm drink, a blanket, and either a good book or some television. I hadn't been joking when I'd told Eli I was rather boring. But Eli had mentioned doing a show on Saturday night, and I'd been intrigued. One spur of the moment ticket purchase later, and there I was.

I'd debated asking Alexis to come with me, but that would lead to questions. Ones I wasn't sure I'd know how to answer just yet. Instead, I'd decided to be brave and come by myself.

One of the enormous bouncers on the door looked me over as he checked my ticket before ushering me inside. The Court was in an old building, not too far from the river-front, that appeared to have been converted several times. There was quite a crowd of people, and I found myself swept towards the main part of the downstairs, which was warmly lit with a little stage at the front with red velvet curtains hanging at either side. There was a bar in one corner and the wooden floor was littered with little tables and chairs in a layout that reminded me of the old speakeasies I'd seen in films. I grabbed myself a drink and threaded through the tables until I found an empty one near the back where hopefully it would be too dark for Eli to see me.

I hung my jacket over the back of my chair and settled myself down, sipping my glass of wine and watching the crowd. There seemed to be a mix of everyone—young, old, couples, groups of friends, and what even looked like a hen party. I assumed most of them were queer, and it felt nice for once to be among a familiar crowd, even if they didn't know me.

There was a large group towards the front on the left-hand side of the stage. One of them sported a shock of pink hair, and as he turned his head, I realised it was Eli's brother Lewis. I didn't know the people he was with, so I had to assume he was here with friends. One of them looked like a literal mountain man; another had jet black hair that seemed like it was running away and a lip ring that glinted in the light. There was a man with dark red hair and a curled moustache wearing a Hawaiian shirt and braces, and next to him was someone who I could only assume was some sort of fae masquerading as a human with sweeping platinum hair and an elaborate navy, cream, and gold coat. How he wasn't baking under the lights was beyond me.

For a second, I debated going over to introduce myself, but that would lead to awkward questions, so I remained in my seat.

I took another sip of my drink and checked my watch. As I did, the lights began to dim and some sweeping, piano music came over the speakers. The crowd cheered as a curvy queen with the most elaborate purple wig swept onto the stage, her sequined dress glittering under the lights. She had a microphone in hand and waved at the crowd like royalty might wave at peasants.

"Good evening, my loves," she said, giving us all a beaming smile. "How are we this evening?" Everyone cheered. "So you're all pissed already then? That bodes well for later." I snorted into my wine. "For those fresh faces among us I am your hostess, Violet *Bouquet*—it's a family name, some of you may remember my sister Hyacinth. I'm the pretty one in the family." There was a round of laughter. I relaxed into my seat, sipping my wine as Violet began talking to the crowd and making a few comments, gently ribbing people. It was funny and playful though, said in such a way that made you feel like you were in on the joke. She saw Lewis's table and waved to them.

"Oh, look who we have here," she said. "Mr. Lewis and

friends." She grinned and turned to the audience. "Poor Lewis is the brother of our one and only Bitch Fit, for which I am terribly sorry. I can't imagine what it was like growing up with a sewer rat for a sibling."

Lewis said something I couldn't hear, and Violet laughed. "She hates water? Well, in that case, I shall get myself a water pistol and keep her at arm's length. Would you like one? Yes? Unfortunately, I've agreed to let her on stage later, so we might need them." I chuckled to myself. I'd never seen Eli in drag, and he'd never given me any hints as to his persona. I'd been tempted to scour social media to find photos or videos, but I'd refrained because I wanted my first experience to be in person. Richard had always referred to it as Eli making a fool of himself on stage, but I didn't think that would be the case. Or, more likely, if Eli did make a fool of himself, it would be a deliberate choice.

When I tuned back in to what Violet was saying, she'd moved on and was wrapping up her introduction.

"Now we do have some wonderful talent for you this evening, and I hope you'll support them all. Our first queen this evening is the fabulous Bubblegum Galaxy, but I'm sure she's fibbing about her age because apparently she was born in 2002, which makes her nearly twenty, and I, of course, am only twenty-one, so one of us is clearly lying." She looked scandalised, the expression heightened by her lavish make-up. Someone in the crowd said something and she gasped. "You were born in 2003? Well, you clearly shouldn't be here because I'm sure you're only twelve. That better be apple juice in that pint glass."

There was a round of laughter, and I chuckled. "So," Violet continued, "without any further interruptions, I give you the one and only Bubblegum Galaxy."

Another queen bounced onto the stage, waving to Violet as she departed. Bubblegum Galaxy seemed to be aptly named in a wig that cascaded in varying shades of blue, purple, and pink with two enormous victory rolls at the front that were covered in stars. She was wearing a bright pink dress with a tutu-style skirt and enormous shoes that sparkled under the lights. In fact, everything about her sparkled. Her energy was like a live-wire, and she bounced through several popular songs, lip-syncing along with effortless style, even hopping down from the stage at one point to dance through the audience. I was in awe.

After her came a drag king named Robin Heartz, who strolled onto the stage in a glittering, pinstriped suit with a fedora perched casually on his head and spats that had the pride flag in rhinestones along the side. He told a couple of jokes, each dripping with wry humour and sarcasm that had everyone laughing before doing a couple of lip-syncs, including one to Weird Al's parody *Word Crimes*. His energy was different than Bubblegum Galaxy's, but I was no less in awe. They were both incredible performers.

Just the idea of getting up on stage was terrifying to me, but to really put themselves out there and craft such amazing looks and performances was something else entirely. I made note to follow them on social media and to come back to The Court more often. I'd never understood until now why so many people loved drag, but just one exposure had me desperate for more. It was art, pure and simple.

Robin strolled off the stage, throwing the audience a flirtatious wink as he did so.

Violet reappeared. She'd acquired an enormous feather boa from somewhere and now had it wrapped around her shoulders like a Hollywood starlet. "Are we all having a good time?" she asked. The audience cheered again. "I see you've been making good use of the bar. Well, keep drinking. I've got bills to pay." I laughed. Quite a few people had been up and down to the bar during the performances and during the slight break in between Bubblegum Galaxy and Robin Heartz. I'd finished my glass of wine but hadn't gotten another. It hadn't even occurred to me to get one because I'd been so transfixed by the performers.

"Are you ready for our main event?" Violet asked. "Tonight, we have our very own raccoon in residence, the one who is always picking fights, breaking hearts, and leaving a mess behind her. She's loud, she's mean, she's everyone's least favourite queen. She's the one and only Bitch Fit."

I clapped and cheered with everyone else, and then Eli, or rather Bitch Fit, stepped onto the stage, and I gasped. She was wearing a black-and-white skin-tight dress that was artfully ripped in places and clung to a new set of curves with fishnet tights and fingerless arm-warmers that were hung with ribbon. Her hair was white, hugely backcombed but with an artfully styled fringe, and her make-up was a dramatic mix of white, purple, and black. She looked almost like a heightened version of the emo style I'd seen everywhere in the late noughties, like one of those old MySpace emo girls come to life. It was wild and over the top and just… perfect.

I'd tried to imagine Eli in drag several times, but nothing I'd come up with had fit him. And now I realised why. I'd been trying to imagine Eli as some sparkling goddess or glamorous star, but Eli was neither of those things. Bitch Fit was an over-the-top personification of everything Eli loved, and she was fucking perfect.

"Hey, bitches," Bitch Fit said, holding up the microphone and grinning at everyone. "Oh my God, look at you all. You look worse than me."

"Not possible," Lewis shouted, and I snorted.

"Well, you can get the fuck out." Lewis laughed. Bitch Fit turned towards the bar and I saw a familiar glint in her eyes. "Davide? Darling, these hoes at table nineteen are cut off. No more drinks. They get nothing." Davide, a broad man in a dark t-shirt, called something and lifted a glass. Everyone in the room laughed.

"Thank you to Miss Bucket, for that charming introduction," Bitch Fit continued, casually strolling across the stage. She exuded a magnetising aura, and I couldn't take my eyes off her. She was Eli's confidence turned up to eleven. "My name is Bitch Fit, I'm Lincoln's resident emo trash goblin, and I'm here to annoy you all for the next forty minutes because you suckers apparently paid to see me, and I think that says more about your questionable taste than anything else." I laughed. A mischievous smiled played across Bitch Fit's lips that were painted with black lipstick. It was a smile I'd come to know quite well.

I settled into my seat, utterly entranced and hanging on her every word. There were stories and jokes that had me crying with laughter, including the pasta throwing family dinner, which she told in honour of Lewis's presence. There were a couple of parody Disney songs, most of which were delightfully rude about the government. I didn't know if Eli had written them himself, but I assumed he had. Yet another gorgeous hidden talent of his. Then a couple of lip-syncs to pop-punk and emo classics where Bitch Fit owned the stage like she was on the main stage at Download.

I couldn't see how anyone could think this was a waste of Eli's talents. Richard had been wrong. And so had I. Eli was born to perform. To be a drag queen. He belonged nowhere else but in that spotlight, and all I wanted to do was watch him, support him, and make him realise just how amazing he truly was.

Eli was a star. I was just a satellite in orbit.

Bitch Fit finished her uproarious set with a song from a musical television show called *Galavant*. I hadn't heard of it, but the song was called "Off with his Shirt" and involved Eli stripping down a couple of very delicious-looking back-up dancers while the audience cheered. I clapped along with them, but I couldn't stop the twisted knot of jealousy forming in the pit of my stomach. I didn't want to get on stage, but I did want Eli to rip my shirt off and run his fingers across my skin like he owned me.

At the end of the song, Bitch Fit did a dramatic curtsey and called on the others to take a bow with her. Everyone clapped and cheered, and Violet gave a little wrap-up reminding everyone about future shows.

The lights came back on slowly, and the spell that had been cast over me broke.

I'd been intending to sit and watch quietly then sneak out, but now I needed to see Eli. I needed to tell him how truly exceptional he was.

The crowd began to disperse slowly, the staff clearing away the tables for the night. I knew The Court transformed into a nightclub, and given that it was around ten, I guessed it was a quick turnaround between the show and them opening back up as a club. The three queens and king appeared from backstage and were instantly asked for photos and selfies. I debated leaving because if I headed for the door now there was no way Eli would see me. It would be my chance to escape like this was some secret rendezvous.

But that wasn't what I wanted.

I took a deep breath, steadied my resolve, grabbed my jacket, and began to head towards the little crowd that had formed. I wanted to linger near the back so I'd be one of the last ones. That way I'd be able to work out what I wanted to say before I reached the front. But then a group of people moved, and as I stepped to the side to avoid them, I suddenly found myself exposed. Bitch Fit turned her head, and I knew she'd spotted me because her mouth fell open. You couldn't fake her expression of shock.

"Tristan?"

"Hey," I said, giving her an awkward half wave and stepping forward. "You were amazing. Truly incredible."

"You came to see my show?" There was a soft note of incredulity in Eli's voice that I'd never heard before. For a second, Bitch Fit melted away to reveal a man who couldn't believe what he was seeing. She stepped closer to me, heels clacking on the floor. The rest of the world dissolved until it was only the pair of us—one lonely man half in love and one six-and-a-half-foot tall drag queen with black lipstick who couldn't seem to stop staring.

"Yeah," I said. "I did. I, er, I wasn't going to tell you, but I had to let you know how wonderful you are. Because you are. Wonderful that is."

And there it was. My first confession.

"You know, Mr. Rose, you're full of surprises."

Two hands found the front of my jacket and pulled me closer as our lips met in a crushing kiss.

CHAPTER TWELVE

Eli

I'D NEVER DREAMT about kissing Tristan Rose until that moment.

Fucking him? Yes. But kissing him? That had felt different. More intimate. Something I couldn't bring myself to think about because then the want would be real.

I hadn't meant to kiss him, but I was drained, both physically and mentally, and just seeing him there... hearing him talk about how much he'd loved my performance... something inside me had snapped, and I'd needed to give him tangible proof of what that meant to me. A kiss had seemed like the natural choice.

It was either that or a blow job, and Phil would kill me if I tried the second in the middle of the bar.

Tristan's lips were soft against mine, moving slowly as I drew out the kiss. I didn't want to let him go. I didn't want the moment to be over. But all good things had to come to an end. And it didn't mean it couldn't happen again. Not unless Tristan really hated it, and from the way his mouth pressed hungrily against mine, I didn't think that was going to be an issue.

I released him slowly and straightened up. A few people were staring, and some of them clapped. Tristan had my lipstick smeared across his mouth. It was a good look on him.

"Darling," said Violet before Tristan or I could say anything to each other, "as charming as it is to see you kissing a handsome young man, perhaps you and your beau would like to go elsewhere." She raised an eyebrow at me, a smile playing across her lips. I knew she wasn't upset. In fact, she'd probably put two and two together since I *might* have mentioned Tristan in a roundabout way once or twice over the past few weeks. "Your set starts at eleven, so make sure you're back by then."

"Okay." I couldn't think of anything sassy to say. Instead, I took Tristan's hand and towed him backstage where we could talk in private. He had a dreamy expression on his face like he'd had some sort of out of body experience. If it only took one kiss to do that, I was very interested to know what anything else would do to him.

I dragged Tristan into the little dressing room I shared with Bubblegum and Violet and locked the door behind me.

"So," I said, loosely caging him in against the door. "You liked my show?"

"I did." He grinned at me, fingers moving up to brush his lips, examining the traces of black lipstick that now stained his skin. "I've never kissed anyone wearing lipstick before."

"Never?"

"No. I've never kissed a drag queen either."

I smiled. Nobody in the world had the right to be as cute as Tristan was with his plush mouth, dreamy eyes, and swept-back hair. He was wearing dark jeans, a white shirt, a navy blazer, and sensible shoes and looked like a walking advertisement for those designer country brands. The handsome, sweet country boy that everyone was madly in love with. If this was a period drama, he'd be the kind, wealthy man everyone wanted their daughter to marry. Honestly, he was Mr. Fucking Bingley.

Did that make me Jane Bennet? I'd always considered myself more of a Lizzie. Or even a Lydia.

"Would you like to do it again?" I asked, stepping a tiny bit closer to him. In my shoes, I was several inches taller than Tristan. I liked looking down at him for once. Tristan's face tinted pink.

"Yes."

I reached my hand out to cup his jaw and bring him closer. Tristan came willingly, his hands wrapping around my waist as his lips found mine. It was another sweet, soft kiss. His lips moved gently, his tongue sliding between them, asking rather than taking. I'd rarely been kissed so softly. It was like he was trying to memorise the contours of my mouth. I wanted to live in this candyfloss-soaked moment forever.

My hands reached up to tangle in his hair, deepening the

kiss. Tristan let out a tiny moan, and a flare of desire sparked across my chest. I tugged gently on his hair just to see what would happen and was rewarded with another sweet moan. I deepened the kisses, letting my hunger flow into my touch. We didn't have much time, not today, but I fucking needed Tristan to know how much I wanted him. God, the rest of the night was going to be fucking impossible. How the fuck was I supposed to concentrate on work when all I could think about was the feel of Tristan's mouth against mine? I'd be replaying his little moans in my head until the end of time.

Tristan broke the kiss this time, gently releasing me even though it seemed painful for him to do it.

"Where are you going?" I asked quietly.

"Just here." He chuckled. "Are you working for the rest of the night?"

"Ugh, yes." I sighed. "They're just going to be getting fucking cheese and playlists at this point. Maybe I'll do all requests to save me from having to concentrate on anything."

"What about tomorrow?"

"It's Sunday, and my plans usually involve sleeping until noon."

"Come over to mine," he said, giving me an enchanting smile. Fucking hell, this man was literally a Disney prince. "I want to see you again."

"Okay."

"I'll make dinner, and you can meet Indy and Solo, and we can…" He trailed off like he couldn't think of a suitable word. I grinned, all sorts of delicious ideas popping into my head. But I decided to be kind to him. No need to make Tristan explode before I wanted him to.

"Hang out?" I suggested.

"Yeah. That. Just, er, come over whenever you're free. I'll message you my address."

"I can't wait." I trailed my fingers up the front of his shirt, casually imagining popping the buttons open to see what was underneath. I tried to remember if I'd ever seen Tristan shirtless at any of our family parties, but if I had any memories like that, they weren't recent. "It'll be fun."

There was a knock at the door, and I sighed. "Yeah?"

"You in there, hun?" It was Bubblegum. "Can I come in? I really need to get changed. These shoes are fucking killing me."

"Two minutes." Usually I'd give her some shit about suffering for her art, but my mind was otherwise preoccupied.

Tristan grimaced. "I better let you get back to work."

"You might want to wipe your face first," I said teasingly.

"That bad?" He peered over my shoulder, trying to look in the mirror behind me.

"I mean, I've seen worse." I grinned, then tottered over to the tiny station where I kept emergency make-up, some wipes, and my bag. I pulled out a make-up wipe and handed it to Tristan, then peered at my reflection to see what needed topping up. Someone really needed to make a good, long-lasting black lipstick that didn't rub off as soon as I kissed someone. I was sick of having to buy more of the stuff. Although I did like seeing people wearing my lipstick…

And now I was thinking about all the places I could leave marks all over Tristan.

That would be fun.

Tristan cleaned up his face and dropped the wipe in the bin. I saw him watching me out of the corner of my eye. Bubblegum knocked on the door again, but I ignored her. It wouldn't kill the bitch to wait a minute.

"Stop staring," I said. "I'll fuck up and make my lips uneven."

"Does that usually happen?" Tristan asked.

"No, but I'm not usually being stared at by someone like you."

"Like me?"

I turned and gave him a smile. He really was adorably clueless. On some people it would have been really fucking irritating, but on him it was just cute. "Someone so fucking sexy that if I didn't have Miss Sparkle Butt outside hammering on the door or a fucking set to do, I'd strip his ass naked and jump him right here, right now."

"Oh." Tristan's face flushed making him look like he'd gotten sunburn. "Maybe we can do that tomorrow instead?"

I stared at him for a moment, not sure whether he was being serious. Then I remembered it was Tristan, and he wasn't the sort to suggest something like that unless he meant it. I strode over to him, my fingers finding his jaw and tilting his face up to mine. "Of course we can." I leant down so I could press my lips to his ear. "You're going to be all mine."

He shivered under my touch, letting out a shuddering exhale. Something tightened in my chest. In my underwear, my cock strained painfully against the tape holding it tucked in place. Jesus fucking Christ, getting a hard-on while tucked was painful as fuck. I wanted to stick my hand up my dress and adjust myself, but that would have to wait until I'd finished with Tristan.

On a hunch, I whispered one more thing into his ear. "And you're not allowed to come between now and then either."

Tristan moaned softly, then nodded. "Okay."

"Good boy." I brushed my lips against his cheek. "I'll see you tomorrow."

I woke up late the next morning to a hammering on the front door.

I sat up blearily, wiping sleep and leftover mascara from my eyes, wondering who the fuck was trying to batter down the entrance to my sacred sanctum. Whoever it was could fuck off. My phone buzzed from somewhere under my pillow. I usually left it on vibrate in case Orlando needed me, but it wasn't him calling. It was Lewis.

"What do you want?" I asked, sounding like I'd been smoking forty a day for the past twenty years. I coughed and reached for the bottle of water beside my bed.

"Open the door," Lewis said.

"No."

"Yes."

"Fuck off and let me go back to sleep."

"If you don't, I'll call Orlando and make him let me in. I'll tell him you won't answer your phone and I'm worried."

"That's blackmail," I said, begrudgingly throwing back the duvet and looking for a t-shirt and some underwear. I always slept naked after shows. "Dirty, rotten blackmail."

"Just answer the fucking door." Lewis sighed. "You can't make out with Richard's best friend in public and not expect me to say something."

Bollocks. I hadn't been expecting that. I thought he'd left by then. I stumbled towards the front door, phone still in hand, and undid the chain and bolts. "How the fuck did you know about that?" I asked as I threw the door open. Lewis was alone at least, which was something. I'd been half expecting the whole bloody cavalry to turn up.

"You weren't exactly private about it," he said, raising an eyebrow and giving me his patented Lewis look of disapproval. It was the one that made all his clients quiver with fear and made him a rather effective personal assistant. "Can I come in, or do you want to have this conversation where half of Lincoln can hear you?"

"I'd rather not have it at all, but since I know you won't leave, you might as well come and be annoying in here instead."

Lewis grinned sweetly and slid past me, toeing off his pink hightops and heading towards the living room. I sighed and silently wondered what I was being punished for. Last night had been so much fun, and tonight promised to be even better. If I made it that far.

"I'm going to make coffee," I said.

"Can I have some too please?" Lewis asked from his new position on the sofa, curled up like a cat.

"Fine." At least making coffee would give me five minutes to work out what the bloody hell I was going to say to Lewis. It wasn't like I could deny what had happened. I'd just have to swear him to silence and threaten to NERF him if he breathed a word of it to anyone except Jason. I flicked our ancient kettle on and threw some instant coffee into a couple of mugs, then I dug the milk out of the fridge and reached for the sugar so I could dump Lewis's requisite five sugars into his mug. How the fuck he drank anything so sweet was beyond me. Then again, he was a walking ball of pastel sweetness with the cutest aesthetic with his pink hair, ripped jeans, and lavender tank top under a denim jacket covered in patches. Maybe he needed all the sugar to keep his sweetness levels so high.

I drank my coffee black because I was still an emo teen at heart.

I finished making the drinks and trudged back to the living room. Lewis was scrolling through his phone, but he looked up when he heard me approach, holding his hands out expectantly.

"So," he said before my butt had even touched the cushion. "You and Tristan?"

"It's nothing."

"It didn't look like nothing."

"Do all kisses look like something? Can't I just kiss

someone because they're hot and I want to fuck them?" I knew I was being overly touchy and defensive already, throwing my walls up before Lewis even had a chance to hatch a plan.

"You can, but if you just wanted to fuck him, you wouldn't have kissed him like that." Lewis raised his eyebrows again and looked at me scathingly over the rim of his mug.

"Like what?"

"Softly. That was a *relationship* kiss, Eli."

"It was not! Don't talk shit."

Lewis rolled his eyes. "Yes, it was. Don't lie to me, bitch. I've been out with you before. I've seen you pull. And you were completely different with him. So spill. What the hell is going on between you two? Does Richard know?"

"No! And don't you fucking tell him," I snapped. Just the mention of Richard was enough to have panic and anger flaring in my chest. Stupid Dick.

"I won't." Lewis held up a hand defensively. "Chill."

"Sorry." I took a sip of my coffee and exhaled. "I'm being a twat."

"Yeah, you are, but it's fine." He smiled gently. "Just talk to me. I won't tell anyone, not even Jason if you don't want me to. C'mon, Eli. We've always talked." That wasn't strictly true—we didn't tell each other every single messy detail of our lives, romantic or otherwise—but we'd always told each other the big things. And I guessed this counted as one of them.

"Fine. You know how I got an office job back in September?"

Lewis watched me closely as I spoke but refrained from reading me to filth any further. I decided it was easier just to tell him everything, so I included the lunches, the cocktails, the lolly sucking, *Mamma Mia!*, the office flirting and biscuits, and finally the fact I hadn't been expecting him to come to my show. "He just surprised me," I said. "And he was so sweet and looked so cute I couldn't resist."

Lewis's grin widened, a glint in his eyes. "And then you took him backstage."

"Yes, but nothing happened. Well, nothing interesting." That was going to happen later if I had my way. I wondered how soon I could kick Lewis out and what time would be considered too early to turn up at Tristan's.

Lewis's expression said he didn't believe me. "Are you dating then, or just hooking up?"

"I… I don't know." I didn't have an answer to that. Was I supposed to?

"What do you want it to be?"

The first. Definitely the first.

But I didn't say that. I just shrugged. "Not sure. I don't really know yet. We might just have some fun."

"Are you sure?" Lewis frowned. "You don't seem it."

"Of course I'm sure." Biggest lie ever.

"Really? Edward said you looked like you'd been dating forever," Lewis said. Edward was Lewis's boss, one of his best friends, and the most dramatic man I'd ever met. And that was coming from me.

"Yes, well, Edward has a tendency to over exaggerate. He's worse than I am."

"How do you know that?" Lewis asked, his expression

changing. I shrugged, then realised this was the perfect way to change the subject. I grinned.

"We fucked a few times a couple of years ago before he met his boyfriend. We met at a club." I took a long sip of my coffee and watched the chips fall.

"What the fuck? You fucked my boss? And you didn't think sharing that was relevant? How the hell could you not tell me? Why the fuck didn't *he* tell me he'd fucked my brother?" Lewis was already reaching for his phone, neatly distracted away from my personal life. "I can't believe neither of you told me!"

"I mean, if it helps," I said, lifting my mug to my mouth again, "he fucked me a few times too. It was fairly even in that regard."

"Oh my God. I hate both of you!"

CHAPTER THIRTEEN

Tristan

Why was it that when you wanted time to go fast, it slowed down to an agonising crawl that seemed to move at the pace of thick treacle in cold weather?

Usually, I liked the leisurely pace of my Sundays, but today, I felt like I was going to pull my hair out if things didn't get a move on. I'd woken up at six and stared at the ceiling, replaying every moment from the night before in high definition. My cock was achingly hard in my pyjamas just thinking about the way Eli had kissed me and whispered in my ear. I shivered, the ghost of his breath running over my skin. I clenched my fist, determined not to touch myself, even though it felt like I might explode if I didn't.

Eli had told me not to. And I was going to listen to him.

My brain kept concocting filthy fantasies about what might happen when he arrived that afternoon, and eventually, I had to throw myself out of bed to stop myself from desperately humping the mattress.

God, I'd never been so horny in my life. Not even when I was sixteen and managed to stumble across a couple of male nudes using our very slow dial-up internet.

I pulled on my clothes and went downstairs, wrapping up against the early October chill. Indy and Solo bounced around my feet, a little surprised to be going for a walk so early on a Sunday but pleased nonetheless. I piled them into my car and drove to some nearby woods, walking for miles in the watery morning light. I'd hoped the walk would distract me, but my brain was determined to follow its initial line of thought, and I was plagued by thoughts of Eli teasing me as I stomped through piles of leaves.

By the time I got back, it was barely nine, and I cursed myself for walking so fast. I managed to lose a bit of time to housework, but by lunchtime, I was bored. I was tempted to text Eli to ask if he was still coming over, but I didn't want to seem too desperate.

I tried to take my mind off the burning need under my skin by watching a film, but it was torture, and I resorted to moping around the house like some lovesick character from a period drama, gazing out the window into the grey, drizzly afternoon as I awaited the return of my beloved.

Eventually, I decided to go and shower, making sure every inch of me was clean. Perhaps it was unnecessary since Eli and I had done nothing more than kiss yesterday, but he had said he would have been up for a lot more if circumstances had allowed it. And I liked to be prepared for things. No harm ever came from being over-prepared.

The shower itself was hell. My cock had decided now that I was naked, it was time to rehash all my earlier fantasies and relieve the tension crawling over my skin. I turned the temperature down, hoping cold water would help. It did, but it made the entire experience very unpleasant. When I got out of the shower, I wrapped myself in a towel and trudged back to my room, flopping down on the bed with a sigh. I reached for my phone, silently begging for something, and was rewarded with two new messages from Eli, both sent while I'd been in the shower.

Eli *I'll be leaving in ten. I just had to get rid of Lewis first!*
Eli *I hope you were good for me ;)*

A soft moan escaped my lips as I read his words. At this rate, I was going to be throwing myself at him as soon as he walked through the door. Eli had sent the messages nearly twenty minutes ago, and a flare of panic flashed across my chest. I wasn't dressed at all, and the bed was a mess. I jumped up and began rummaging through my chest of drawers, wondering what I should wear. Neither of us had talked about what this was, but I presumed I could consider it some sort of date. I dug out some of my nicer boxers, the ones that clung to my skin and cupped my dick, then pulled on my jeans and grabbed a shirt out of the wardrobe. It might be a little formal, but I liked shirts. They looked good on me.

I'd just finished buttoning it when I heard a car pulling up outside. I glanced out the window to see a little red car and a familiar figure climbing out of the driver's side. I cursed under my breath, running my fingers through my hair as I quickly straightened the sheets and grabbed my towel. I threw it into the bathroom as I passed, clattering down the stairs as Eli knocked. Indy and Solo were barking already, bouncing around the front door like the excitable menaces they were.

"Go lie down," I said, shooing them out of the way. "You're not helping."

They ignored me. I pulled the door open a fraction, peering around it, my heart thudding in my chest at the sight of Eli on my doorstep. "Hello! I'm sorry. The dogs are rather excited. Are you okay with that? I can put them away."

Eli grinned. "It's fine. I'm here to be mauled."

"Indy, Solo, sit. Wait," I said, turning my head to look directly at them. To their credit, they both hovered in place, their fluffy behinds about six inches off the floor. It was as close as I was going to get. I chuckled and pulled the door open. "Come in."

Eli stepped inside and any restraint my monsters had displayed quickly went out the window. They didn't jump up, but they did bounce around Eli's feet, smacking everything in range with their tails. Solo was doing full-body wiggles, and Indy was doing funny little yowls, which was how he liked to greet new people. I laughed, watching them as Eli bent down and began to fuss at them.

"Watch out," I said, or at least started to say. One quick, enthusiastic jab to the backs of his knees from Solo had Eli staggering slightly and falling onto the floor. His laughter rang out as Indy and Solo descended on him, smothering him in licks and trying to climb into his lap.

"Oi, oi, oi. That's enough." I reached for Indy's collar, gently tugging him away. "Leave poor Eli alone."

"They're fine," he said, ruffling the fur around Solo's neck. "Look at them. They're just big babies who want lots of love and attention." He grinned up at me, then let out a groan as Solo flopped into his lap. Having a forty-kilogram dog drop onto you when you weren't expecting it was an experience at the best of times.

"Solo, please don't smother him." Solo huffed at me and leant on Eli's chest, tilting his head up to look pleadingly at him.

"I'm sorry," Eli said, rubbing Solo's ears. "Later. I will give you all the belly rubs later."

"He'll hold you to that." I gently nudged Indy in the direction of the kitchen, and then slowly pulled Solo upright. He'd decided Eli was his seat now, so it was like trying to move a brick wall. Solo grumbled under his breath once he'd been forced to resume a standing position and pottered off after his brother, undoubtedly to go and lie on his bed and sigh dramatically at his cruel fate.

"I like them," Eli said, climbing to his feet and dusting himself off. "They're adorable, just like you." He reached for the front of my shirt and pulled me in for a kiss, and I melted against him, willing to do whatever he wanted. "Hey," he murmured against my lips.

"Hey."

"I missed you this morning."

"You did?" Something tugged at that place in my abdomen, right above my stomach.

"I did." He grinned mischievously. "I wanted you in my bed so I could play with you all morning." He kissed me again, which was good because it meant he couldn't see the way my face flamed or the way my mouth wanted to hang open like a fish. My cock throbbed in my jeans, regaining its prior painful levels of hardness. Eli put his hand on my chest, turning us slightly, and I found myself backed up against the nearest wall. I groaned as his tongue pushed into my mouth, his fingers sliding under the bottom of my shirt to caress my hip. He pressed himself closer to me as the kisses grew more heated, and the flames that had engulfed my face began to spread across the rest of my body.

My hips gave an abortive thrust as Eli slid his hand down one side of me, and he pulled back slightly to chuckle darkly under his breath. His eyes glinted with a dark hunger that made me shiver. "My poor boy," he said softly as he traced his fingers slowly over my crotch, feeling my hard cock and stroking it lazily with one finger. I whimpered. "So needy and desperate. Have you been good for me?"

I nodded.

"Ah, ah, ah," Eli chided gently. "You have to use words. You have a mouth. Use it. I want to hear you."

"Yes." I swallowed. "I've been good."

"Were you thinking about me?" He rubbed my cock slowly, tracing the outline in the denim. "Dreaming about what I was going to do to you?"

"Y-yes."

He looked up at me, his expression so intense I felt I might combust from the heat. A wicked smile played across his lips as he continued to tease me with his fingers. My hip twitched, and he stopped. "Tell me what you've been thinking about."

"Um, I..." My tongue suddenly felt numb, my throat dry. I had so many fantasies, but I had no idea what to tell him. What if they were inappropriate or too much? I'd had boyfriends ask me to talk dirty, but they'd been satisfied with me just moaning and telling them I wanted their cock. And somehow, I got the feeling that wasn't going to be enough for Eli.

"Are you worried?" he asked, his eyes narrowing.

I nodded, looking somewhere over his shoulder instead of at him. "Yes."

"What about?"

"That I might get it wrong?" It came out as an unintended question. I exhaled. "I'm just worried I won't say the right things."

"Want me to go first?" Eli cupped my jaw, bringing my eyes back to his. I'd wondered for a moment if he'd be frustrated by my answer, but there was nothing in his expression but sweetness.

"You... you've been thinking about me?" I asked lamely.

"Of course. All fucking night." He kissed me again. "And all fucking day." Another kiss. "First rule, you never, ever have to do something you're uncomfortable with. Ever. And if you are unhappy or uncomfortable with *anything* I say, suggest, or do, you are to tell me." Another kiss. "And there will never be any repercussions from it. I want you to talk to me. I can't make this good for you if you don't tell me what you like and what you don't." Another kiss, soft and drawn out. "Promise me?"

"I promise."

"Good boy." I shivered again. "Would you like to go upstairs?"

"Yes." Eli gave me one final kiss and then stepped back. My heart was thundering in my chest, but my mind was surprisingly calm. There was one question lingering at the front of my mind, one I'd been pondering in the depths of my subconscious for the past eighteen hours or so. I debated delaying in asking it because it was the type that could easily derail the entire evening if we had opposing opinions, but it was one I needed the answer to. "Can I ask you something?"

"Of course," Eli said, reaching his hand out and inter-lacing it with mine. His fingers were warm, and his grip was solid and comforting.

"What is... What are..."

"What is going on between us, and what are we doing?" Eli grinned, once again appearing to read my mind.

"Yes. That."

"What do you want to be going on?" He squeezed my hand. "Do you just want us to be friends? In which case, we can stop now and go and watch a film. Or do you want to be friends with benefits? In which case, we're definitely still going upstairs. Or—"

"How do you feel about boyfriends?" I blurted out. My

face flamed again, my stomach twisting. I sounded like a teenager asking out their first crush. In fact, I sounded even more awkward than that. I didn't think I'd felt half as awkward asking Dylan Morris if he wanted to go out with me when we were sixteen.

Eli smiled and cupped my jaw, his thumb tracing my bottom lip. "Is that what you'd like?"

"Y-yes. What about you?"

"I think I'd like that too." He let go of my face and squeezed my hand again. "Come on. Let's go. I want to play with you."

CHAPTER FOURTEEN

Tristan

I LET Eli lead me upstairs. I was worried this might all be a dream, and any second the bubble was going to burst.

I still hadn't processed the idea of him being my boyfriend, and I knew I had questions for him. But they could wait. Everything could wait. Right now, there was only one thing I wanted.

Directing Eli to my bedroom, he gently pulled me across the threshold before letting go of my hand to shut the door behind us. A few scraps of pale, afternoon sunlight shone through the window, but they were soon covered up by a thick cloud. I wondered if I should pull the curtains closed just in case anyone saw us.

Eli's hands gripped my hips from behind, and I started slightly. He chuckled. "What are you thinking about?"

"Not much," I said. "Just wondering if I should close the curtains."

"You can if you want, baby, if it would make you feel more comfortable. But you're going to be spending all your time on the bed." I heard the smile in his voice. "Do you want to know what I've been thinking about?"

One hand reached around my hip, teasing the edge of my cock through the stiff fabric of my jeans. I moaned and nodded. "Yes. Please. I want to know."

"I've been thinking about slowly stripping you naked, making you do a little twirl for me in the middle of the floor so I can see just how beautiful every inch of you is." His voice was smoky and sweet, laced with heat and fire. "I want to watch you kneel in front of me while I pull out my hard cock and feed it to you, slowly fucking your face and seeing how much you can take before you choke. Letting you catch your breath before you take more." I groaned, forcing myself to hold still as Eli stroked my cock harder. "I want to paint your face with my cum and then feed it to you so you know you're mine. I know you'd look so pretty with cum dripping down your cheeks."

"What else?" I asked, forcing the words out because I had to know more.

"I want to lay you out on the bed and kiss every inch of you, sucking your nipples, teasing your cock, sucking marks into your thighs and making you spread them wide so I can play with your perfect ass." His other hand squeezed my ass cheek then spanked it, and I gasped. "I want to lick your hole until you're dripping and squirming, begging for me to fuck you. But I won't. Not yet. I'll just slide one finger into you and play with you until you beg for more. I'll edge you over and over until you can't think about anything but me and how much you need me to let you come. And then, if you're very good, I'll let you."

His hand gripped my cock almost painfully, and I groaned. "Y-yes, I want that."

"How much?"

"So much." I twisted my head, looking for his because I needed to feel his mouth on mine again. "Have... have you thought about fucking me?"

Eli chuckled, the sound sending shivers rippling across my skin. "Of course." He tilted his head up and kissed me. I was desperate, but Eli's mouth was controlling and firm. "I've thought about fucking you slowly, sliding inside your tight little hole and teasing you with my cock. Making you ride me and bounce on my dick, getting me off and making me come inside you." I groaned. Eli's fingers resumed their maddeningly slow stroking of my dick through my jeans. "But you'd have to keep your hands to yourself. You'd only be able to come if I let you."

Oh God, that was hotter than I'd ever anticipated it being. I'd thought about it before, once or twice, but I'd never considered suggesting it to anyone. And yet there was Eli, casually strolling into my bedroom with my darkest desires rolling off his tongue. My cock throbbed at the idea.

"You like that, don't you?" he asked.

"Yes. I... I'd never... I've never..."

"You've never told anyone that before?" his voice was gentle, but he hadn't let up stroking my cock. I couldn't think let alone focus long enough to string a coherent sentence together. But yes or no questions I could do.

"No."

"Would you like it if we did that? If sometimes you could only come when I let you."

"Yes."

Eli hummed under his breath. "I'll remember that. We can talk about it later." He kissed the back of my neck. "Will you strip for me please? I want to see what you look like under here." He squeezed my cock again, then released me. I felt him step away from me, and I mourned the sudden loss of contact.

"Tristan," Eli said, firmer this time. "I don't like waiting for what I want."

I jumped, not realising I'd been staring off into space. I turned to see Eli grinning, his arms folded across his chest. He'd lost the denim jacket and had draped it across the armchair in the corner. He was wearing another loose, dark tank top which meant I could see his broad shoulders and tanned arms. I wanted to reach out and run my fingers across his skin. I was taller than Eli, but I suspected he was stronger, and that opened up some delicious possibilities.

"Sorry," I said. "I was, er, thinking." I walked over to the curtains and pulled them closed, then I began to unbutton my shirt, my fingers fumbling over the tiny, blue buttons. It took me far longer than anticipated to get it undone, the burning heat of Eli's gaze distracting me at every turn.

"What were you thinking about?" Eli asked.

"What you said." I pulled my shirt off and moved to place it on the chair. Eli watched me carefully.

"Very nice. Now the jeans. Are you wearing underwear?"

I nodded. "Yes."

"Good. Leave it on. I want to take that off."

I reached for the button on my jeans, very glad I hadn't bothered putting on a belt or chosen ones with a button fly. It meant I only had one button to contend with. I pushed them off over my thighs, stepping out of them and adding them to the chair.

"Good boy," Eli said. "Come and stand here." He pointed at a spot on the carpet just in front of him. I did as I was told. My heart was racing, and my cock was straining against the fabric of my boxers. I was nought-point-two seconds away from begging for something... anything... and Eli had barely touched me. If this was what it was going to be like every time we were together, I was going to be dead in the next six months from anticipation.

I'd always thought I was a patient person. Current circumstances were proving otherwise.

Eli walked forward, reaching his hand out to stroke my chest. He ran his fingers down my stomach, then trailed his hand around my waist as he moved around me. "You're very fucking sexy," he said when he returned to stand in front of me. "You have a beautiful body."

I opened my mouth to politely disagree. My body was on the nice side of average at best. I could do with getting some more exercise and not relying on the genetics I'd been gifted to keep me in shape.

Eli raised an eyebrow. "No arguing. You're beautiful. Accept the compliment, and say thank you."

"Thank you."

"Good boy."

He reached for the waistband of my boxers. "I don't want you in these anymore." He tugged them gently, pulling them over my cock and down my thighs, tapping my leg to make me step out of them. He placed my underwear on the chair, and I was astounded by his control. "Gorgeous," he said. "You have a nice cock."

"Thank you." I couldn't stop my voice from shaking, especially when Eli stepped closer. His finger ghosted over the head of my dick, making my breath catch in my throat. Eli smirked.

"You're so good, Tristan," he said. It sounded like it should be a good thing, but the mischievous look on his face said otherwise. I bit back a moan as he sank to his knees in front of me, still dressed in his jeans and tank top, although he'd kicked off his shoes. "Second rule. If you want me to stop at any point, for any reason, say red. If you want me to slow down or you're unsure, say yellow. And if I ask you if you're okay and you're happy and want to keep going, say green. I'll ask for your colour periodically, and you must always be honest with me. I'll never be upset with you if you say red or yellow. Do you understand?"

"Yes. I understand."

"Good boy." He stroked my thigh, then winked at me. "You're still not allowed to come until I say so."

I opened my mouth, but the question I'd been going to ask was lost to space and time as Eli leant forward and brushed his tongue across my leaking slit. I gasped, my hips threatening to buck forward, seeking the warm, wet heat of his mouth. But Eli's hand on my thigh kept me in place, stroking up and down and grounding me. Reminding me to do as I was told.

I wasn't allowed to come. Not yet. I wasn't… Fuck!

Eli wrapped his mouth around the head of my cock and sucked. I moaned, the sound morphing into a whine as Eli pulled off a second later. I glanced down to see his dark eyes looking up at me, full of desire.

"Would you like more?" he asked.

I nodded, my head moving so fast it almost made me dizzy. "Please. I need more. Please, Eli." He rewarded me by returning his mouth to my dick, but it barely lasted a fraction longer than the last time. "No! Please. Don't stop."

Eli chuckled, the sound melting my insides. "You seem to have forgotten I'm in charge here. You're just my pretty plaything." He ran his finger up the underside of my cock. "Unless you want to stop?"

"No!" I didn't want that at all. Fuck, Eli could play with me for as long as he wanted. Being the focus of his attention, taking whatever he gave me, was doing ridiculous things to my chest and my mind. I never wanted him to stop. "Please don't."

I never wanted Eli to stop touching me the way he was… looking at me the way he was…

Like I was special. Important. Precious.

Like I meant something to him.

"Then you're going to be good for me and let me play with your cock." He stroked my thigh again, and I felt the muscle twitch under his touch. "But first, you're going to lie down. On the bed, on your back with your head on the pillows and your hands wherever they're comfortable. You may not touch yourself though. What's your colour, Tristan?"

The sudden use of my name pulled me up short. I smiled at him. "I'm green. Very green."

"Thank you." He rose to his feet and pressed a gentle kiss to my lips. "Lie down for me. I want you to be comfortable."

"That sounds ominous," I said.

Eli chuckled. "It might be." He put his hand on the small of my back and gave me a gentle nudge towards the bed. "Would you like me to tell you what I'm going to do to you?"

I thought for a second as I climbed onto the bed, stacking the pillows in the middle and making myself comfortable. "No," I said. "I'd like it to be a surprise this time." I trusted Eli to take care of me. And this was already turning into the best sexual encounter of my life. Which at thirty-two years old might have been considered sad.

Maybe I just hadn't been having the right kind of sex. Or the right kind of sex for me.

"Okay," Eli said. He pulled off his tank top and draped it across the chair with his jacket, then followed it with his jeans. His underwear was black and very close fitting. I swallowed hard, realising I could see the outline of his cock in perfect detail. God, I wanted it inside me.

Eli moved around the side of the bed. "Where is your lube? I'm not going to fuck you, but lube makes everything better."

"Er, it's in the drawer over there." I pointed at the large

chest of drawers on the other side of the bed. "In the top drawer with my underwear."

I didn't use it that often, so I knew the bottle was nearly full. Eli moved around the bed to fish it out, humming to himself as he looked inside the drawer. "Do you have any toys?"

"No." I shook my head and stared up at the ceiling. My sex life matched the rest of my life—quiet and boring. "I've thought about getting one," I continued, still not looking at Eli. "But I never got around to it. I wasn't really sure what to get…"

"We'll have to rectify that," Eli said. "Don't worry. I have some ideas for you."

I wanted to tell him he didn't need to do that, but somehow I didn't think Eli would believe me. He seemed to be able to see right through me, down to the little details and secrets I kept hidden from everyone else. Even myself.

The bed dipped as he slid onto the mattress next to me. His hand traced slowly up my thigh again, and I relaxed under his touch. My cock twitched needily as Eli's fingers skirted around it and down my other thigh. I knew he was going to keep teasing me, and the thought had desperate want surging under my skin.

The bottle of lube clicked when Eli opened it, and I glanced over to see him drizzling some onto his fingers. He smiled at me, soft and hungry.

"Remind me, Tristan. What are you not allowed to do?"

"I'm not allowed to come."

"Good boy."

Those words echoed around in my head as Eli took me apart.

Time stretched out, slowing to the most perfect crawl. I couldn't focus on anything except Eli's voice, the touch of his hands, and the occasional heat of his mouth. His fingers teased my cock, wrapping around it and pumping it slowly, thumbing his head over the slit until I was breathless and gasping and so close to the edge. Then he let go and sat back while I moaned and whined, writhing on the bed. My cock was red and aching, and I wanted to come, but I already knew Eli wasn't going to make it easy.

Eli seemed to know just how to play with my body to get the reaction he wanted, and when my potential orgasm had subsided, he began again. He rolled my balls in his hands, skimming a finger down my taint while his other hand stroked my cock in a loose grip. I spread my legs wide, desperate for Eli to give me more. He chuckled again and moved so I could bend my knees with my feet on the bed, laying myself out in front of him.

He stroked my cock slowly, his fingers trailing up and down my thighs, my taint, and my balls. He leant forward to press a couple of kisses to my heated skin, and I gasped. My whole body felt electrified and on edge.

"Please," I begged. "Please, Eli."

"Please what? What do you want?"

I knew I couldn't ask to come, but there were so many other things I wanted. I just had to find the words to ask for them. "Touch me."

"I am touching you," Eli said, tightening his fist around

my cock for a second to prove his point. I moaned, my head twisting in the pillows.

"Please. I want…" I gasped, panting for air as he began to jack my dick again, rolling my balls in his hand. I already felt my orgasm starting to build again, but I knew I wasn't going to be allowed over the edge. "Oh God, Eli."

Eli took his hands off me again, sitting back on the bed and gently stroking my calf. "Good boy, Tristan. You're doing so well for me. Such a good boy for me, baby."

"P-please," I said, knowing I was begging. "Please, Eli. I need it."

"Need what?"

To fucking come wasn't going to get me anything, except maybe more edging. I tried to think, but my brain had already shut down. Cognitive reasoning was going to have to wait until later. I lifted my head up an inch, gazing down at my painfully hard cock that was almost burgundy in colour. Eli sat between my legs still stroking my calf and looking ridiculously calm, but I also saw the way his dick was straining at his underwear. How or why he wasn't jerking himself off was something I couldn't currently comprehend.

Eli had already made it clear he wasn't going to fuck me, but maybe…

"Will… Please will you play with my hole?"

Eli smiled at me, the warmth of it lighting up my chest. "Of course." He reached for the bottle of lube next to his foot. "Put a couple of pillows under your ass."

I did as I was told even though my whole body felt like jelly. Eli pressed another kiss to my leg. "Good boy." His wet fingers circled my hole while his other hand caressed my thigh. "Relax for me. That's it. When was the last time you played with this pretty hole?"

My face prickled. "A while," I said, attempting to be vague.

Eli raised an eyebrow. "How long is a while?"

I groaned as he ran one finger over the furled skin. "A couple of months. Maybe longer. I don't… I don't tend to when I'm…"

"Jacking off?" Eli supplied helpfully, a grin playing about his mouth.

"Yes. That."

"Is that because you don't like it?" He teased the sensitive skin, sending ripples of pleasure through me. I'd forgotten how good it could feel.

"No, it's… it's not that." I wasn't sure why we had to have this conversation now. Eli's other hand ran up my thigh and then he trailed a leisurely finger down my cock. "I just… don't."

"That's okay," Eli said. "We can talk about this later. Thank you for being honest with me."

I went to reply, but my words melted into a deep moan as Eli slowly pressed the tip of one finger into me. It burned slightly, the sensation unfamiliar. Eli's other finger teased the head of my dick, rubbing the slit and the vein at the back of the head. Pleasure hummed through my body, alleviating the burn.

Eli continued to tease my cock as he worked his finger into me. His pace was achingly slow, but for once, I was grateful. He paused, giving me a moment to adjust and reminding me to breathe, before he began to pump it in and out of me. I moaned again. The heat under my skin returned full force. I wasn't going to last much longer.

Eli leant forward, hovering over me. His eyes met mine. "You've been so good for me. I think you deserve a reward."

"Th-thank you."

His grip tightened around my cock. He lowered his head, his tongue darting out. He looked up at me and winked. "You can come whenever you want to."

Then he wrapped his lips around my dick, sucking me into his mouth as his finger pumped in and out of my ass.

Sensations overwhelmed me, my body going taut like a stretched-out rubber band. Then it snapped.

I came with a shout, my cock exploding in Eli's mouth as pleasure overtook me and I sank into oblivion.

CHAPTER FIFTEEN

Eli

TRISTAN'S CHEST WAS HEAVING, his eyes were closed, and his mouth hung open as the last of his orgasm rocked through him. His spent cock twitched in my mouth, and I gently released it, licking off the last drops of cum as I slowly eased my finger out of his twitching hole.

My heart ached for this beautiful man, so desperate and eager to please. All I wanted was to spoil him rotten and make him melt in front of me.

I hadn't even touched my own dick, and it was now aching and pissed at being ignored. But it was going to have to wait. Poor Tristan had clearly not experienced something so intense in a long time, if ever, and I needed to take care of him.

Orlando had been right when he'd said Tristan needed better sex.

"Tristan," I said softly, gently sliding my hand up his thigh, "are you still with me?"

His eyes fluttered open, taking a moment to focus on me. There was a glassy sheen to the blue-grey like a settling sea under a stormy sky. "Hey. That was… Wow."

"Did you have fun?"

He nodded, his tongue darting out to wet his lips. I needed to get him a drink and something to eat. "I did. Thank you."

I grinned. God, he was so fucking polite. It was adorable as fuck. One day I was going to fuck his brains out, and he'd probably write me a thank you note for it. "Good." I slid up the bed so I was beside him, leaning down to give him a soft kiss. "I'm going to get you a drink and a snack. Get into bed for me, and I'll be back in a minute."

"Okay," he said after considering my words. "There are glasses in the cupboard above the kettle."

I kissed him again. "I'll find them. You stay here. You were very good for me."

Tristan smiled softly, and my heart fucking melted. I'd only agreed to date this man a couple of hours ago, but he already owned my fucking soul. If anything happened to him, I would fucking murder whoever was responsible. I'd shove one of my heels through their eye or something.

I kissed his forehead, then slid off the bed. Tristan extricated the duvet from underneath him and pulled it over his body. I watched him for a moment, then grabbed my tank top off the chair and pulled it on before heading for the door.

I padded downstairs, finding my way to the kitchen at

the back of the cottage. Indy and Solo came pottering out of another room when they heard me, and I froze for a moment, thinking they might start barking. But all they did was wander over and nudge my hands. Ah crap, hands. I washed them in the sink, then rubbed Indy and Solo's ears since it was worth keeping them on my side.

I rummaged through the cupboards and found some glasses, which I filled with water, and a couple of peanut butter and chocolate cereal bars. They'd do for now, and we could sort dinner later. I wasn't even sure what time it was. Tucking the cereal bars into my hands behind the glasses, I headed back upstairs. It was a little tricky to close and open doors, but I managed it.

Tristan was right where I'd left him, curled up in the middle of the bed.

"Hey, can you sit up for me please?" I asked, putting my scavenged supplies on his bedside table. Tristan's eyes opened slowly, a smile creeping onto his face. I desperately wanted to kiss him.

"Hello," he said. "It's you."

"It's me." I pulled back the duvet, threw my tank top off, and slid in beside him. Tristan pulled himself into a sitting position, and I propped the pillows up behind him. "How're you feeling?"

"Amazing."

"Good." I handed him a glass of water, watching as he sipped it slowly. When he'd downed half of it, I opened a cereal bar and broke off a chunk for him. "Eat this for me."

He looked at me quizzically but didn't say anything. He took the cereal bar and dutifully began to chew. I wondered if I needed to explain things like his potential drop in blood sugar from the intense orgasm or that sub-drop might come later. It wasn't as if we'd really strolled far down the yellow kink road, but I highly suspected Tristan had never even visited the outskirts of whatever vanilla-sex-ville he'd been residing in.

I leant over and pressed a kiss to his temple, handing him the second half of the bar and gently sweeping his hair back. "You were so good for me. Thank you," I said. "I had a lot of fun playing with you. You were amazing, and I'm so proud of you for being open and honest with me about what you wanted."

"You are?" Tristan looked astounded, and I chuckled.

"Of course."

"I... I had fun too," he said softly. "I've never done anything like that before, but I, er, I'd like to do it again."

"Me too." I took his now empty glass from him and set it down before sliding down the bed and opening my arms so he could cuddle into me. Tristan hesitated for half a second then attached himself to me like an enthusiastic giant squid. I wrapped my arm around him and pulled him close. "We can talk about things you want to do and try," I said, stroking the back of his shoulder. "And what your limits are."

"That sounds good." He was quiet for a second. "I might need some help with ideas. I've always been quite boring."

"I'm sure I can help," I teased. "There are so many things I want to do to you."

Tristan looked up at me. "I'd like that."

We lay together for a while just enjoying being close to each other. His skin was warm and soft, and I loved feeling him pressed against me, wrapped in my arms.

"So," Tristan said eventually, giving me a teasing smile. "We're dating then?"

"Yeah. I guess we are." The whole agreement had happened so quickly I hadn't really given it any thought. I'd been too busy quickly putting together plans for playing with Tristan. I liked the idea though. I liked it a lot.

"Are you okay with that?"

"Very much so." I looked down at him as Tristan tilted his head up to look at me. "You're so cute. And definitely not boring."

"We'll see about that."

I raised an eyebrow, giving him my best unimpressed stare. "Stop being so down on yourself. I won't allow it. You're not allowed to be mean to my Tristan."

"Your Tristan?"

"Mine." I rolled him gently until he was lying half-underneath me. I leant down and kissed him slowly. "All mine."

Tristan hummed happily. "I like that idea."

"Good." The temptation to keep kissing him was very real, but there were other things I wanted to talk about first. Then maybe we could look at dealing with the resurging erection in my underwear. I moved so I was lying on my side beside him, my head propped up on my hand. My curls were starting to fall out of place, and I kept having to huff them out of my face.

"What are you thinking?" Tristan asked, looking over at me with a curious expression.

"Who do you want to tell? Do Holly and Andrew have policies against staff dating? I mean technically you're not staff, but I don't know whether they'd consider it crossing a boundary or a conflict of interest." I tried to rack my brains for long-forgotten details of employment law. It had been a while since I'd had to dig out any mental files related to my degree, and they were all covered in a thick layer of dust and cobwebs.

"I don't think so," Tristan said. He looked suddenly serious like a switch had flipped, and I realised there were three main parts to Tristan's personality: the absolute professional with the brilliant financial mind, the sweet nerd who loved history and his dogs, and the soft, needy man who just wanted to be cherished. I didn't think many people had gotten to see the third part, and it made something possessive burn in my chest. A desire to keep that part of him for myself and to spoil him with love and orgasms.

Except not love. Definitely not love. Lust only.

Lust and my darkly possessive need to make him squirm and beg for me and to look at me like I was everything.

But not love.

Because... well... just because.

"We can tell Holly privately if you want," Tristan continued. "I know she wouldn't tell anyone, but it would probably be polite to give her a heads up. I can tell her tomorrow if you want."

"Okay. Let me know if you need me to come too. Although, if you tell her, I'll probably be summoned to the office to explain myself." I grinned. "I've not even been at Green & Wodehouse for two months, and I'm already seducing the staff. Naughty me."

Tristan laughed. "We're definitely not the first ones."

"Oh? Do tell." I grinned, completely intrigued. "You cannot tempt me with such tantalising gossip and then withhold information. They have laws against that."

"Do they?"

"Yes. Spill."

"Well, I know Rebecca and Alistair have definitely had an on-and-off thing going for years," Tristan said. "And the only reason I know is because I stayed late one night because I had a meeting with a guy in LA who was buying a house here, and I caught them fucking in the sales office."

I cackled. "Oh my God, that's amazing. Does anyone else know?"

"Pamela might. She knows everything."

"Too fucking right," I muttered. She'd know as soon as I arrived tomorrow that something had happened. That woman should have been an interrogator for MI6. "What did they say when they saw you?"

Tristan flushed. "I'm not sure they did. They, er, were rather preoccupied, and I didn't make my presence known."

"I don't think I'd have stuck around either," I said with a shudder. "I definitely don't need to know what Alistair's *O* face looks like considering the man looks like a frog normally." Tristan laughed. "If Holly says our relationship is inappropriate, you can drop hints that at least we're not banging in the offices. And anyway, Holly can't really say shit, considering she's married to the company's owner."

"Very true. Holly's fun when she's not in business mode. I've known her for a long time."

"I'll take your word for it," I said. Holly definitely wasn't the worst manager I'd ever had, but she did seem a little cold at times. I'd only been there since September though, so maybe she'd warm up to me.

"What do you want to do about your family?" Tristan asked. I blinked, trying to wrap my head around the change in conversation. Shit. I hadn't even thought about them.

"Let's not tell them for now," I said. "I don't tend to tell them about my relationships unless they get serious. Nobody does unless they're Dick. We only found out about Lewis and Jason when Jason came out on fucking Instagram and posted a photo of them together. I mean, it was pretty fucking awesome of Jason to stick it to the network like that, but it would have been nice to know." I smiled. I'd teased Lewis about hiding Jason, but I'd understood why. Our family could be a handful, especially me, and dating an actor was bound to have caused chaos.

"I remember that," Tristan said. "Richard told me."

"On the subject of Dick, I'd rather he didn't know. I know he's your best friend, but—"

"But it's also you that I'm dating." Tristan nodded, his smile faltering. I reached for his hand, interlacing our fingers together. I hated the idea of causing him pain and making him hide something so big from someone he was so close to, even if I thought that someone was a complete wanker. There was a new level of complexity there I'd not considered before, and I'd have to navigate it with care.

"I don't want Richard to think I'm just messing with you for fun," I said. "Because that's immediately what he'll think."

"I know." Tristan sighed. "He'd probably stage some sort of intervention to tell me this is a horrible idea while listing your many faults."

"I do have a lot of them."

"I don't think you have any," Tristan said, leaning across to kiss me. "And if you do, I'm willing to overlook them."

"That's probably because I just melted your brain."

"Probably." He grinned. "I don't care though."

He kissed me again, a new heat simmering under his touch.

"There is one thing you should know though before we get distracted," I said. "Lewis knows. And Jason will too by now. He saw us kissing last night. It's why the little shit was hammering on my door at noon."

"Oh…"

"It's fine. He promised he wouldn't tell anyone. Not even Jules or Finn. His friends might know, but they don't know my family, so it's fine." I pulled him close against me. "But since he knows, you should tell your sister. You're close, right?"

"Yes. And she has this habit of randomly coming into my house, so I should probably let her know."

I laughed. "Definitely. Can I tell Orlando too?"

"Sure," Tristan said. "He sounds really sweet."

"He is. And he'll be dying to meet you, so be prepared for that."

"Maybe we can all get drinks sometime?"

I cupped his face and kissed him again. "You, Tristan Rose, are too sweet. Far too sweet."

"Thank you." He smiled at me, pressing himself close against me. My cock twitched against his hip, reminding both of us I hadn't come that afternoon. Not that I needed to. Tristan licked his lips. "You know," he said, "you were so nice to me earlier. You really spoilt me, and I haven't even attempted to return the favour."

"Do you want to?"

"I do." The next kiss was deeper, the simmering heat beginning to turn into new need. "Can I suck your dick?"

"Baby, you can do whatever you want to me."

CHAPTER SIXTEEN

Eli

"HAVE you put an entry in for *It's a Drag!* yet?" Orlando asked as the front door clicked shut behind me. I'd barely set foot in the door, and I was already being nagged. It felt like being at work. Orlando was looking at me over the arm of our battered sofa like a large, fluffy kitten.

"Good evening to you too," I said, toeing off my shoes, shrugging off my jacket, and loosening my tie. It had been a hellish start to the week, and all I really wanted at that moment was to eat my weight in pasta and cheese. Alistair had been on my case all day about some email a client had sent, and even though I'd forwarded the fucking thing to him twenty bloody times, he kept claiming he didn't have it. I had been this close to marching up to his office and shoving his head through his monitor.

"Have you put your entry in?"

"You know," I said, ignoring Orlando's question and

heading through to the kitchen, "it's customary to ask someone about their day when they come home instead of pelting them with questions as soon as they step through the bloody door." I grabbed the plastic tub I'd shoved some sandwiches into this morning out of my bag and dumped it into the sink. Then I flicked the kettle on.

Orlando sighed dramatically. "Fine. How was your day? Now, stop avoiding my question! Applications close on Friday, and you need to enter."

"Oh, do I now? Says who?"

"Says me. And Daddy and Sir." Orlando wandered into the kitchen and pulled himself onto the counter. "You're really good, and everyone deserves to see that."

"Honey, I am a two-bit trash goblin with cheap shoes and cheaper wigs."

"Yes, and you've built a whole fucking act around it," Orlando said scathingly. "Don't knock yourself. You spent the whole of last year trying to do drag full-time. I don't know why you're not using this to put yourself out there."

He had a point. I had to give him that. I'd looked up the competition, and it had looked like fun. The only reason I hadn't done it so far was the self-doubt gnawing away at my chest. Not being able to make money with my drag had knocked my self-confidence a little, even though I'd known it was a distinct possibility from the start. Drag, like all art forms, did not pay well. Most people did it for the love of it. But having to go back to work had put an insidious worm in my head that sometimes whispered that maybe I wasn't more than a cheap imitation of someone better. I had a good life at The Court. I did well there. And entering a competition, no matter how small, took me outside that world and outside my comfort zone. The Court loved me, but that didn't mean anyone else would.

I'd been starting to wonder whether being The Court's weekend darling was enough. It was the realistic option, but I hated myself for thinking like that. That was Richard thinking, not Eli thinking.

"I'll help you put it together," Orlando continued, taking my silence as a sign that he should continue. "We can film something this week. I bet Phil would let us into The Court one night. Or I've got some stuff from your shows. It doesn't have to be long. Oh, and I think you have to do a little two-minute video in drag introducing yourself."

I looked over at Orlando. There was an earnest look in his eyes, a sparkling confidence in my abilities that I'd started to lack. I sighed, knowing I wasn't going to win. And maybe I didn't want to. I might not believe in myself, so I'd have to let Orlando do it for me. It would be enough for now. "Fine. I'll do it. But you'll have to help."

"Yes!" Orlando punched the air, wiggling his bottom and nearly falling off the counter.

"Yeah, yeah, don't celebrate too much." I poured myself a cup of tea. "They'll probably hate it."

"You know," Orlando said, a gleeful note in his voice, "if I doubted myself the way you did, my Daddy would give me a spanking."

"Well, luckily I'm not in possession of such a mean boyfriend."

"When do I get to meet Tristan?"

"When I decide I no longer want a boyfriend," I teased. "I know you. You'll scare him off."

"I won't! I'll be on my best behaviour." He grinned. "And I promise not to compare notes with him about what you're like in bed. Or what he might like to try. Even though I'm sure he'd find the information useful."

"I'm so grateful." I stared at him, my voice deadpan. Orlando laughed.

"Don't worry. I'll keep my lips sealed. And it's not like you've told me much anyway." He gave me a soft smile. "I'm happy for you though. You deserve someone like this."

"Like what?"

Orlando shrugged. "Someone who gets you. Who intrigues you. Someone who"—he thought for a second —"someone who isn't dramatic or needs to be the centre of attention. You have enough of that. You need someone who's going to balance you out, and Tristan sounds like that kind of person."

"Thanks." I finished making my tea, turning his words over in my head. "I think you might be right there."

"I always am! Besides," Orlando said, "you'll be good for him too. Tristan sounds like a tiny, scared bunny rabbit, and you'll be able to bring him to life a bit."

I laughed. "Bunny rabbit?"

"I mean, I thought tortoise, but bunnies are cuter. And Tristan is cute."

"He really is." I thought back to that afternoon when he'd come out of a client meeting looking smart but tired. Then he'd seen me watching, and he'd smiled, his weary face crinkling. That little smile had made my whole day better.

"I bet Tristan could help us film your entry for *It's a Drag!* He's probably got a very steady hand. And I bet he'd love to help," Orlando said in a tone that suggested nothing but trouble.

"You're just trying to get me to bring him over so you can meet him." I looked at Orlando pointedly over my mug. "It won't work. You're not going to win."

Orlando smiled in a way that told me I was very wrong.

Two days later, I found myself in full drag, sitting in the tiny dressing room of The Court while Phil, Orlando, and Tristan stood in front of me, adjusting a ring light and talking quietly amongst themselves about angles.

Apparently, I got zero fucking say in my own application.

I'd made the mistake of mentioning to Phil that I was putting an entry together, and he'd insisted on helping. He'd had some very good footage from one of my most recent shows, which he'd sent across, and then he'd volunteered the dressing room—with a sneakily placed piece of branding for The Court in the background—as the backdrop for my mini-introduction.

Tristan had been a last-minute addition because I'd *umm*ed and *ahh*ed about telling him until it was almost too late. Eventually, I'd told him right at the end of our lunch date earlier in the day, and he'd happily volunteered his time. We'd decided to try to keep things low-key in the office, so although Pamela and Holly knew, nobody else did, and we were attempting to maintain some level of professionalism in our relationship. Which was why we'd decided to get lunch together several times a week—so we could get out of the office and I could drag him into the nearest hidden side street and kiss him. I'd never been as desperate to keep kissing someone as I was with Tristan.

Orlando had pinky sworn he'd be on his best behaviour, and so far, all he'd done was give Tristan a delighted hug, tell him he was very handsome, and then spend twenty-minutes obsessing over my wig. I'd told him it was fine, but Orlando had threatened to hit me with a hairbrush and declared that "fine didn't win competitions".

I'd debated arguing with him but decided the effort wasn't worth it.

"Can we perhaps start filming this shit?" I asked, read-justing my skirt for the umpteenth time and being very glad I'd been allowed to sit down. One day, I was just going to start performing in trainers. Although… a battered pair of Converse or Vans would be perfect for my look. I had an old pair of Converse in my wardrobe I'd stopped wearing because they had holes, but they'd be fine to perform in. They were a limited-edition pair where one was black with a white pattern and the other shoe was white with a black pattern. They'd been a twenty-first birthday present, and I'd worn them for years.

"Two minutes," Orlando said, not looking at me.

"Do you know what you're going to say?" Tristan asked. He turned his head and gave me a smile. "Orlando said they provided entrants with some guidelines and potential topics. Would you like one of us to ask you the questions? We can edit them out afterwards."

"That's not a bad shout," Phil said. "We can film the topics in snippets. Makes it easier to put together afterwards."

"Fine." I sighed. "Let's just get it the fuck done." I was tired and hungry, and it was making me cranky. "Who's putting this together anyway?"

"I am." Orlando raised his hand. "I can do it tomorrow night. It'll be tight, but you'll make the deadline."

"Whatever."

"You're so grumpy today!" Orlando pouted. "Tristan, do you have any snacks? Your boyfriend is hangry, and it's making him mean."

"I might have a cereal bar," Tristan said, looking for his bag.

"Don't worry," Phil said, grabbing a Snickers out of the basket of snacks he usually left in the dressing room on a nearby table and throwing it at my head. It bounced off my chest and into my lap. "Eat that and stop being such a bitch. I've dealt with enough dramatic queens in my lifetime, and you're not good enough to be one of them."

I laughed, ripping the wrapper open. "You're so charming."

"Honey, you haven't seen anything." Phil raised an eyebrow as I bit into the chocolate. "Tip from an old pro," Phil continued, looking at Tristan and Orlando. "Always feed your drag queens. Having your dick taped to your taint for hours tends to make you cranky. Not to mention the shoes."

"Thanks," Tristan said. "I'll make sure I pack snacks in future."

"Make sure it's chocolate," I said, unwrapping more of my Snickers. I wondered if Phil would let me have another. "Or those peanut butter and chocolate cereal things you've got. I like those."

Tristan laughed. "Any more demands, your majesty?"

"Yes. Stop being so sassy. It's too cute." I stuffed the rest of the Snickers into my mouth.

"You know we should just film you like that," Orlando said. "It kinda goes with the whole raccoon thing."

"I'm going to ignore that," I said as I dumped the wrapper into the nearest bin. I glanced in the mirror to check my lipstick. I did feel better now that I'd eaten something. "Okay. Tristan can ask me the questions, and Orlando can film. That way if Tristan ends up in a shot, we can keep it and use his handsome face to distract the judges."

Tristan's cheeks flushed, but he didn't say anything. Phil laughed and grabbed him a chair.

"You sit there then," he said, directing Tristan to a spot a couple of feet in front of me and just to the left. "That way we can get all of Bitch in the shot."

"This is why you made me get in full drag, then?"

"Yes. Now zip it and do as your told, or I'll tell Bubblegum you want to do that lip-sync duet she's been dying to organise with you."

"Low blow, bitch." I laughed. It could be fun though. Bubblegum was a bouncing baby in heels with way too much glitter and enthusiasm, but her heart was more or less in the right place. "Tell you what, if I get in to *It's a Drag!*

you can tell Miss Sparkle Butt I'll do a routine with her at Christmas. Her choice." I grinned. "Oooh, unless she wants to grab Eva and the three of us can do the *Mean Girls* 'Jingle Bell Rock' routine. I'll even wear latex."

Eva Nessence was another local drag queen who I got on with very well. She was a couple of years younger than me and tended to do more shows in Nottingham than Lincoln, but she still came back to visit The Court and take the piss out of me on Twitter whenever she had time. Dragging her into a sexy Christmas routine would be hilarious. She'd hate me for it. Which was obviously why I was going to do it.

"If you do that, I'll definitely come watch," Orlando said with a wink and a cheeky grin. "And I'm sure Tristan would *love* to see you in a teeny-tiny latex dress and thigh high boots. Wouldn't you, Tristan?"

To my surprise, Tristan didn't go pink or clam up. Instead, he laughed. "I mean, it would definitely be something I hadn't seen before."

That settled it. I was going to Regina George my ass off.

"Right, ho-bags, let's get this over with," I said. "Make me look pretty."

Orlando winked, slotting two phones in behind the ring light. "There are some miracles even I can't work, babe."

CHAPTER SEVENTEEN

Tristan

"IF YOU CAN JUST SIGN and date at the bottom, I'll be able to get the formal application started for you. It should take about three to four weeks." I slid a small stack of papers and a pen across the polished meeting room table towards Mr. and Mrs. Shipley, my last clients for the afternoon. They were an older couple moving up from Cheltenham to be nearer to their adult daughter and her family, who were just in the process of purchasing a very beautiful Grade II–listed house in a village north of Lincoln. The house had some beautiful original features, and I'd spent several hours staring longingly at the pictures on the Green & Wodehouse website.

Not that I didn't have a very nice house already, but I'd always liked beautiful old houses.

"Thank you so much for your help," said Mrs. Shipley as she took the pen from her husband and began to print her name in neat letters. "We haven't moved house in such a long time."

"My pleasure." In all truth, they hadn't needed a lot of help or a large mortgage, given how much their old house had been worth. But they'd been extremely pleasant to deal with, which made everything so much easier. I took the finished paperwork, double-checked everything, then returned one copy to them for their records and slid one inside a paper folder for myself. "That's you all sorted then. I'll let you get on with your weekend, and I'll give you a call as soon as I hear anything."

I shook their hands, then directed them out of the meeting room. Eli's head turned as I walked out, giving me a little smile as I answered Mr. Shipley's question about liaising with their solicitor.

"Go well?" Eli asked as the front door closed behind the Shipleys. It was already dark outside, thick clouds darkening the late afternoon and threatening more rain. I was glad I'd brought my umbrella.

"It did," I said, walking back to the conference room to collect my laptop and papers. "And that's my last meeting done for the week."

"Congratulations. Would you like a celebratory biscuit?"

"If there's one going."

"Pamela," Eli said, rolling his chair away from his desk and leaning back in it, craning his neck. "Can Mr. Rose have a biscuit?"

Pamela rolled her eyes and grinned, reaching under her desk for the teddy bear tin. "I don't know why you're asking me. I think Tristan's been indoctrinated into the secret biscuit club by now."

"You are a darling and an angel." He took the tin and popped open the lid, holding it out to me.

"Don't worry. I won't tell a soul," I said, crossing my heart. "And I'll bring more biscuits for the tin on Monday. What sort do you like?"

"Anything chocolate," said Eli, picking out a bourbon biscuit.

"I wasn't asking you, monster."

"So rude. And after I introduced you to the secret biscuits." He grinned mischievously. "What terrible things are you going to tell Dick about me tonight?"

"I'm not going to say anything," I said.

Eli twirled his chair and handed the tin back to Pamela. "Tristan is having dinner with my brother this evening and leaving me all alone. I've suggested he tell Richard all sorts of delightful lies about me just to annoy him." Pamela raised an eyebrow at Eli over her glasses. "What? It's fun."

"Don't listen to him," Pamela said to me. "This one is nothing but trouble."

"One hundred percent, but that's what makes life interesting." Eli laughed.

"I wasn't going to," I said to Pamela, ignoring Eli.

"Harsh. But a good life lesson. You shouldn't listen to me." Eli shrugged, but the gleam in his eye caught my attention. We both knew what it meant: here I didn't have to listen to Eli at all, but when we were alone, in my bedroom, things were very different. I coughed. Fuck, I wished it was tomorrow already. Eli was coming to mine to spend the day relaxing before he had another show at The Court. I wasn't sure what his plans were, but I knew they were going to be fun. We'd hardly had any time together since last Sunday, and I was feeling the separation. It was one thing to see each other at work, but we had to be professional there. I couldn't just sink to my knees and beg him to use my throat like I was some pretty fuck toy.

"What time are you meeting Dick?" Eli asked, derailing my train of thought just in time.

"About seven."

"Good, that gives me three hours to come up with some spectacular lies."

"And where will I have heard these ridiculous rumours?" I asked, shaking my head with a smile. "I don't know your family that well. None of them would have told me."

"Oh, I'll think of something. A friend of a friend." He winked. "By the way, what are you doing for Halloween?"

"Nothing. When is it this year?"

"Thirty-first, same as always," Eli said. I raised my eyebrow. "It's a Monday, sadly, but the Saturday before The Court is holding its annual Halloween show and party. You should come. I'll be performing, obviously, and then I'm DJing for a while, but I can escape to see you."

"Er, sure. I don't know what I'd wear though." I couldn't remember the last time I'd done a Halloween party. I didn't know if I'd ever been to one. Maybe when I was in London? Some of the guys in my department liked to go out because it meant lots of girls in barely there costumes, but that had never appealed to me. They'd taken me to a strip club once and had bought me a lap dance as a joke to help me loosen up. I'd just given the girl a very generous tip and we'd talked about the stock market for twenty minutes. Then she'd given me the number of her brother, a history teacher, in case I fancied meeting someone who I might be interested in.

"I'll find you something." Eli turned to Pamela. "Want to come, Pamela?"

She laughed. "I think I'm a bit too old for that now."

"Nonsense."

"You let me know next time you do one of your variety shows, and I'll bring the girls down. We haven't been in a while."

"I shall, and I shall get you a good table reserved too," Eli said. Then he did a slight double take. "Pamela, do you mean to tell me you've been to The Court before and never told me?"

"Of course I have." She gave Eli a mischievous smile of her own. "I was the one who helped Phil buy it back in 2004 when he moved back from Manchester. He'd been dreaming about opening his own place instead of running someone else's, and that old place was perfect for it. He's been telling me about you for years, although not as Eli. Took me a while to figure that one out, but I didn't want to say anything in case you wanted to keep it a secret. Some queens are quite protective of their privacy outside of work since not all employers are so good about it. But Holly and Andrew won't give you any trouble. I'm sure Holly would try and work a positive angle on it for the business."

"How... What..." Eli stared, struck speechless. I

chuckled quietly to myself. Then Eli seemed to do some mental calculations and looked shrewdly at Pamela. "Brother?"

"Cousin. But we're very close. I introduced him to his husband. He was my neighbour's son when I was growing up." Pamela grinned. "We used to go to all the parties back in the day. The stories I could tell you would make your hair curl."

Eli smiled. "One day, I'm going to need to buy you a drink."

Several hours and one slightly exhilarating drive in the pelting rain later, I found myself sitting opposite Richard at our usual table at The Red Lion.

"How was your week?" I asked, taking a sip of the large pint of Coke I'd ordered.

"Not too bad. Had parents' evening for the year eights." Richard sighed. "Had one mum complain at me for forty minutes because she thinks her son should be in the top set, and I had to explain to her that if he actually bothered to pay attention and stopped trying to light shit on fire with a Bunsen burner, then he might spend more time in the classroom and less in detention. But she thinks he's an angel, so what the hell do I know."

Sometimes I didn't know how Richard did it. Teaching teenagers seemed like an absolute nightmare, especially when there were chemicals involved.

"But," he continued, a soft smile coming onto his face, "one of my year thirteens applied to Oxford for chemistry, and she's got an interview. First in her family to think about university, and I'm so proud of her. Just got to get her there now. Apparently her Nan gave her fifty quid for some new interview clothes—she'd been saving just in case. They're going to hit town at the weekend."

"That's amazing. It's been a while since I did mine, and it was for a totally different subject, but if you need any pointers about the interview process then just say. It's probably changed a lot though."

"Cheers," Richard said. The waitress appeared and slid our food onto the table. Today I'd gone for their homemade lasagne that oozed cheese and sauce and a bowl of thick cut chips I could dip in it. It had been one of those weeks. "Bad week?" Richard asked, grinning and nodding at my food.

"Just very long." I gave him a short summary of work, minus the details of lunch with Eli, the secret biscuits, and my evening helping him with his drag competition application at The Court. The video had turned out really well. Eli had forwarded it to me after Orlando had finished it. I'd saved it on my phone and had re-watched it several times, enchanted by Eli's personality.

"What are you doing this weekend?" Richard asked when I'd finished.

"Er, not too much." Except spending as much time as possible in bed with your brother. "What about you?"

Richard smiled broadly. "Ruby and I are going down to Burghley House for a food festival. You should come with us! You can stay at mine if you don't want to drive all the way back, and Indy and Solo can come too since it's all outside. I know it's a bit short notice, but it'll be fun. And we haven't spent any time together in ages."

Buggeration. What on earth could I tell him? I couldn't exactly say I didn't want to go because I'd rather spend my time getting my mind melted by his little brother. The very same brother he couldn't stand. I supposed I could see Eli tomorrow and Richard on Sunday. That might work at a push. I could tell Richard I was seeing someone, but then he'd want to know all the details, and it would be so awkward to tell him I didn't want to share. I couldn't even tell him Eli's name.

"Um." I speared a chip with my fork and dipped it into the lasagne, trying to buy myself some time. "Are you going both days or just tomorrow?"

"Think we were just planning on tomorrow. Why?"

"I promised Alexis I'd give her a hand moving some bits around. She wants to experiment with the layout of her sitting room, and I've been roped in to help with the furniture." It was a reasonable lie, and something Alexis would get me to do. "She's got this big new client she's starting work for next week, some Hollywood star, and I think she's nervous."

Richard nodded. "She does this every time she's anxious. Do you remember the time she made you move everything around in her craft room?" he said. "But that's great for her business. Maybe she'll get some more recommendations out of it. Not that it sounds like she needs them."

"Yes. It really is." I breathed a tiny sigh of relief. Now I thought about it, this was something Alexis had done before. Last time she'd had a big job to do, she'd made me repaint her bedroom with her, and the time before that, we'd spent the whole weekend re-organising her kitchen and dining room. It was like she had to get all her nerves out on her own house first as if it were a test run of her abilities. But I'd seen her finished work, and it was always amazing. She didn't need to be worried. "Maybe we could do Sunday instead? We should be done by then. Her sitting room isn't that big."

"Perfect," Richard said before launching into an explanation about the event and what time we could go.

I speared another chip on my fork, only half listening. At some point I wasn't going to be able to keep my relationship with Eli a secret, and I didn't know how I was going to begin to explain it. I just hoped when we got there Richard would be willing to listen in the same way he always did when I needed him.

CHAPTER EIGHTEEN
OCTOBER

Eli

"ELI. WHAT'S THAT?" Tristan asked, staring down at the clothes I'd laid out on my bed for him to wear to The Court's Halloween party.

"Your costume." I grinned, reaching for the bottom of the fleece he was wearing so I could start undressing him. I hadn't seen him naked in six days, and that was far, far too long. Honestly, trying to juggle a relationship and two jobs was harder than I'd anticipated, especially a relationship that wasn't just a good fuck whenever one of us needed to get laid.

Rehearsals at The Court for this fucking Halloween Spooktacular show had eaten up a horrible amount of my time and energy over the past few weeks, and then we both had day jobs, family commitments, friends, chores, and the need to get some sleep. It was killing me.

But seeing Tristan naked would make things at least sixty-nine percent better.

"What am I supposed to be?" Tristan shrugged the fleece off, then leant down to run his finger over the very tight, dark trousers I'd laid out for him.

"You're going to be my fallen angel," I said.

"In a harness and leather trousers?"

"Technically, they're not leather, but yes." I grinned at the slightly stunned expression on Tristan's face as he turned to look at me. "I've got you some wings too, and I'd like to style your hair and do your make-up. I know it's a cheesy costume, but I couldn't resist." I leant forward to kiss him. "You're so sexy, and I'm dying to show you off. Please?"

I'd spent hours trawling websites in my spare time trying to think of ideas, but my limited budget had left me with few options. I could have told Tristan what to buy, but this was more fun. "If you really hate it, you can wear the shirt you brought under the harness. In fact, you can do that for the show and then take it off for the party. You can leave the shirt in my dressing room. I promise to make it worth your while."

Tristan considered for a second, clearly turning the possibilities for a little dressing room fun over in his head. "Okay," he said. "For you."

"You spoil me." I kissed him again, running my hands under his t-shirt to caress his soft skin, sliding them around to his ass to squeeze it. "You're going to look so sexy for me."

"Thank you." His cheeks tinted slightly. He was getting

more used to the compliments. I was going to have to turn things up a notch. One day, I was going to whisper such delicious things in his ear that his face would probably melt. I couldn't wait. "Strip for me please."

Tristan reached for his t-shirt and shrugged it off, and I sighed happily. The temptation to delay getting ready by just a few minutes to play with him was very strong. And we did have the flat to ourselves for the time being...

Tristan pushed his jeans down. Temptation won.

After all, it had been a very long week, and I deserved a reward.

I walked over to the bedroom door and flicked the lock into place just in case Orlando decided he'd forgotten something and came home. It hadn't happened before, but there was a first time for everything. Not that I cared about being seen, but I wasn't sure how Tristan would cope if Orlando barged in. Knowing the little brat, he'd start giving us pointers instead of just getting the fuck out.

Orlando's heart might be in the right place, but that didn't mean his mouth always was.

Tristan heard the lock click and turned towards me. "I thought we were getting dressed?"

Bless. "We are," I said as I walked towards him. I put my hand on his chest, trailing a finger down his sternum. "But first, I want to have a little fun. Otherwise I'm going to have to go the whole evening looking at you shirtless in a harness, and a hard-on is absolutely going to ruin the lines of my costume." I was going full-emo, slutty zombie Alice in Wonderland, so I'd have to tuck anyway, but the point still stood.

Tristan grinned, wrapping his arms around me and pulling me in for a kiss. "I'm down for some fun. Tell me what you want."

"That's a dangerous question." I thought for a second, kissing Tristan languidly as I did so. We didn't have a lot of time, so some of my ideas were automatically thrown out the window, but that still left plenty of options. I pressed my tongue into Tristan's mouth while flicking one of his nipples with my nail. He moaned, leaning into my touch. I fucking loved how responsive he was for me.

"Get on your knees for me, baby. I want to fuck that pretty mouth of yours," I said, taking a tiny step back. Tristan whined, then sank to his knees in front of me, his hands resting on his thighs. His lips were soft pink and slick and so utterly fuckable. He'd blown me a couple of times over the past couple of weeks, and every time his enthusiasm had had me shooting down his throat faster than I'd intended. But it was hard to hold back when I looked at his face and saw the sheer want and joy in his eyes as I told him how good he was, how handsome he was, how pretty he looked with my dick in his mouth. Clearly, Tristan thrived on praise, and I was happy to pour it over him.

"You look so good for me like this." I popped open my jeans and shoved them off, kicking them across the room before doing the same with my boxers. I wrapped my fingers around my cock, stroking myself slowly. Tristan licked his lips, tilting forward on his knees. "Do you want my cock?" I asked, stepping close to him and rubbing the leaking head across his bottom lip.

"Yes. Please. I want it."

"Good boy. Open your mouth for me." Tristan did as he was told, and I gently pressed my cock into his waiting mouth. I ran my fingers through his hair, tugging on the blond strands and encouraging him to take me as deep as he could. "That's it. So good for me. Take it all."

Tristan moaned, his eyes looking up at me earnestly.

I grinned, stroking his hair. "Is that good? Do you like my cock?" Tristan moaned again, and I sighed, biting my lip at the delicious sensations running through my dick. "You look so good like this. So pretty on your knees for me, taking my dick like a good boy." He groaned, eyes fluttering shut for a moment. "Ah-ah, eyes on me. I want you to watch me as I fuck your beautiful face." I waited until he opened them again, the stormy blue fixed on me with such intensity I thought my heart might explode.

This man did things to me nobody else had managed before, and it was exhilarating. I just hoped it would last. That he wouldn't find my schedule, or my personality, so intense that he fled at the first sign of trouble. So many of my exes had walked the moment they realised they weren't always going to get one hundred percent of my attention all the time. I was busy, and I liked it that way. But not everyone wanted a partner who spent every weekend on stage or his weeknights practising, sewing, spray-painting shoes, or attempting to write parody lyrics to Disney songs. At one point or another, they all wanted someone to go out to dinner with, or to take them away for a spontaneous weekend getaway, or to drop everything for a Saturday night out. And I couldn't do that. Getaways had to be planned. Dinners had to be scheduled. Nights out were a thing of the past unless it was during the week or they wanted to party while I worked.

But now was *definitely* not the time to get lost down that rabbit hole. Not when I had Tristan's perfect mouth around my cock, waiting patiently for me to fuck it.

"I'm sorry, baby," I said, stroking his hair. "I was just thinking about how extraordinary you are." Tristan's face tinted, and he hummed around my cock. I groaned, slowly starting to move my hips, thrusting my dick in and out of his perfect mouth. "So... fucking... extraordinary. Fucking perfect for me. God, your mouth. Such a fucking perfect mouth." Tristan's eyes were shining, and saliva ran from the corner of his mouth. "Play with my balls. That's it. So good for me." I groaned, thrusting a little deeper as Tristan's fingers caressed my sack. "Fuck. Do you want to come too? Yeah? Gonna come for me like the good boy I know you are. Touch yourself for me." I tugged on Tristan's hair, loving the way he gasped and moaned. The wet, sloppy sounds of the blow job were suddenly accompanied by the slapping noise of his hand on his cock as he jerked himself hard and fast. I wasn't going to tell him to slow down because I was already way too fucking close to the edge. Curtain call and scene, bitch.

"Fuck! That's it. Take it. So fucking good like this. Gonna make me come." Tristan moaned, his lips tightening around my cock. "Oh fuck. Yeah. You want it, don't you? You want my load." Tristan nodded as best he could, letting me fuck deeper into his mouth, desperation etched across his face. "Don't worry, baby. Gonna fill your pretty fucking mouth." Tristan's groans reverberated through me, and the burning heat under my skin ignited into an inferno. "Fuck! Fuck! Gonna come."

I gripped Tristan's hair, holding him on my cock as my orgasm rocketed through me, shooting cum down his throat. Tristan swallowed greedily, a tiny bit of stray cum dribbling out of his mouth. Bloody fucking hell, the man was perfect. I loosened my fingers as the last vestiges of my orgasm rippled through my muscles. I stepped back, easing my cock from Tristan's plush lips.

"So good for me," I said, stroking the side of his face. I dropped to my knees and leant forward to kiss him, licking the last of my cum off his lips. Tristan still hadn't come, and his fingers were still wrapped around his cock, which was dark red and leaking. I smiled and reached out to put my hand on top of his, squeezing his cock in both our fists. I began to jack him, moving Tristan's hand with mine. "Are you going to come for me?"

"Y-yes." Tristan's voice was hoarse and desperate. I moved my hand a little faster, squeezing a little tighter, making Tristan gasp. "Please. Can I… can I come?"

"Yes, baby," I said, leaning forward to take his mouth. "Come for me."

Tristan let out a deep, sweet gasp as his cock pumped ribbons of cum over our fists, his fingers stroking out his orgasm for as long as possible. He panted against me as we traded slow kisses, pausing now and then so he could catch his breath.

"Was that good?" I asked, bringing my other hand up to cup his face, tracing my thumb over his cheek.

Tristan nodded, a wide smile spreading across his face. "Amazing."

"God, you're so fucking perfect." I kissed him again, trying to pour everything I felt in that moment into it. I wasn't even sure I knew what I felt, but it was heady and beautiful and seeping into my bones so I couldn't escape it, even if I'd wanted to.

"We, er, we should probably get dressed now," Tristan said, chuckling. "Or you're going to be late."

"See? I should be annoyed at you for being sensible, but I don't currently have a brain, and I'm going to get to see you in a harness, so I can't launch any objections."

Tristan snorted, and the pair of us climbed slowly to our feet. I headed for the bedroom door, unlocking it and doing a quick check for sneaky roommates with no boundaries before directing Tristan to our bathroom to clean up. I needed to wash my hands too, then do my make-up, put my underwear on, and start the laborious process of transformation. Drag would be so much easier if it came with a Sailor Moon-style magical transformation where I could say something like "Emo goblin power. Make-up!" and have the universe do it for me.

When Tristan returned, he kissed me again slowly, wrapping his arms around me and pulling me flush against his warm chest. It just made me want to get into bed and snuggle the shit out of him. We hadn't even managed to get to the sharing a bed part of dating yet, and it was making me grumpy. I missed having someone to cuddle.

"What time do you finish tonight?" Tristan asked.

"About three, three thirty." I sighed. It was going to be a long fucking night. "Why?"

"I just wondered if you'd want company afterwards. But you'd probably rather just sleep." I glanced up at him, staring.

"You serious?" I mean, it made sense for Tristan to come back here. And we probably should have talked about our post-party plans before this point. But still.

"I mean, I can get a taxi back to mine if you'd rather be alone," he said quickly. "I'm sure you'll be exhausted from working and all the people, and the last thing you'll want is me hanging around."

"Tristan." I put my hand on his lips. It was a cheesy but effective gesture. "I want you to come back here. And if you get tired, I'll give you my keys, and you can come back early. I'll just knock when I need you to let me in. Might get you to order me a kebab too." I was always knackered and starving by the time I'd finished, and having a tiny bit of disposable income to spend on greasy takeaway was dangerous.

Tristan frowned. "I'm not coming back without you. I'll just wait, and if you're hungry while you're working, I'll nip out and get you something to eat. I'm sure the McDonald's in town is open twenty-four hours."

"If you bring me a McFlurry and fries, I will blow you right there in the DJ booth," I said, kissing him again. Tristan laughed.

"Fries and a McFlurry it is then."

CHAPTER NINETEEN

Tristan

ELI and I had gotten to The Court while it was still being set up, so I'd lurked backstage with him while he finished getting ready. I'd felt a bit awkward, but the other queens in the dressing room hadn't minded, and most of them had flirted outrageously with me until Eli had snarled at them to keep their paws off.

As a result, I now had a very distinctive lipstick mark on my neck. It was virtually a stamp that said *Eli's.*

He'd handed me a make-up wipe and said I could get rid of it, but I kind of liked it. It was hot. And it fit with the costume I was wearing.

I'd been a bit dubious about the outfit at first, but when I'd finished squeezing myself into the very tight trousers Eli had handed me and buckled the leather harness over my shirt, Eli had sat me down and started running product through my hair before lining up various bits of make-up.

The eyeliner had felt a bit weird going on, but afterwards I'd looked in his mirror and barely recognised myself. My hair had been artfully tousled, and my eyes were surrounded by dark, smoky make-up and a little bit of silver glitter scattered across the outside that made them pop. Eli had added a soft gloss to my lips, and the whole thing made me look incredibly sexy.

I'd stared at myself in the mirror, not sure how to process what I was seeing.

I'd never thought of myself as sexy before.

But in dark make-up, a white shirt with the sleeves rolled up, a leather harness with shining buckles, and skin-tight trousers, I couldn't see myself as anything less. It was a heady sensation, and it made me want to kiss Eli senseless for giving it to me.

When we'd arrived at The Court, Eli had attached a pair of dark angel's wings to the harness. "If I had a simple one, I'd have given you a collar as well," he joked. "Then everyone would know you were mine."

I laughed, but the knotted feeling in my stomach made it hard to deny I'd found that idea interesting.

Eventually, I'd had to leave the dressing room, giving Eli one final kiss before I left.

I made my way out onto the main floor, scanning the busy room for an empty table. The Court was fully made up for the occasion with cobwebs adorned with large plastic spiders draped from the rafters and skeletons hanging on the wall along with a ghostly mirror with smoked glass. There were fake pumpkins everywhere and candles with electric flames flickered on the tables. The bar staff were all dressed in their usual black, but most of them were also wearing elaborate skeleton make-up that shimmered under the lights, and there were smoking cauldrons placed at various points along the bar with glittering poisoned apples tucked around them.

It was already packed to the rafters with people in costumes—everything from the simple, the sexy, and the elaborate on display. I cursed myself for not having come through earlier because it didn't look like there was going to be anywhere for me to sit without intruding on someone else's table.

"Tristan! Over here!" I turned, frowning, in the direction I'd heard my name. "Tristan!"

Lewis was frantically waving at me from the other side of the room where he stood next to the same group of friends he'd been with last time. He was wearing a tiny nurse's hat perched on top of his head and a short pink dress with a white apron over the top with a little round pin on the shoulder. It was a costume that was familiar, but I couldn't place it.

I walked towards him, picking my way through the crowd.

"I thought it was you," Lewis said, beaming at me. "I'm glad it was otherwise I would have looked like a right banana. Are you here by yourself?"

"Sort of. My date's backstage." Eli had said Lewis knew, so there was no point denying it. And I didn't mind Lewis knowing. He'd always seemed very sweet.

"I figured. Do you want to sit with us?" He gestured

around. Everyone at the table was smiling at me. "I promise we're all very nice!"

"Thanks, that would be great."

Lewis grinned and indicated the chair next to him. "Let me introduce you to everyone. This is my boyfriend Jason." He pointed to the man in the chair on his other side, who was wearing a beautifully tailored suit, dark make-up, and silver rings. "He's a late addition because he didn't have a show this week, and he cheated by just dressing up as his own character from his last TV show."

"Hey," Jason said with an indignant chuckle. "Nobody's recognised me yet. They just said it was a good Ameus costume."

"It's still cheating." Lewis grinned and shook his head fondly. "And this is Edward and his partner, Izzy. They're my PA clients."

"Charmed," said Edward, the fae man I'd seen before, as he shook my hand. He was currently wearing a spectacular pirate costume complete with a red-and-gold frock coat and tricorn with an enormous feather sweeping out the side. "It's so nice to meet you."

"Nice to meet you too."

Izzy, who was the possessor of the curled moustache and flaming hair, grinned as he gave me a crushing handshake. He was wearing a white shirt, an embroidered waistcoat under a red-and-gold coat similar to Edward's, except Izzy was also in possession of a spectacular top hat—the very picture of a vintage ringmaster. He also had a toy lion perched in his lap, which made me chuckle.

"And this is Jay and Leo," Lewis said, gesturing to the

last two men at the table. "Jay runs The Lost World bookshop on Steep Hill, and Leo owns Wild Things."

"I've had some flowers from you before," I said. "They're always gorgeous."

"Thanks," Leo said, giving me a gruff smile. He was wearing chef's whites, which had a restaurant name embroidered on the breast. He must have seen me staring because he grinned. "I pinched them off my brother. He runs a restaurant over near Nottingham."

"I think that's probably cheating too," said Jay with a wry grin, straightening his top hat. He'd gone for something that resembled a Victorian adventurer with a steampunk flare.

"No, it's called being resourceful."

I laughed. "Well, I can't say anything because I just brought a shirt and Eli did the rest."

"That sounds like him," Lewis said. "Did you get any choice?"

"None whatsoever."

Lewis laughed, and I felt myself relax. The group conversation slowly dissolved into smaller ones, and then Izzy procured a couple of bottles of wine before drawing me into a very interesting conversation about history and steampunk with Jay. We'd gotten so sidetracked I barely noticed the lights dimming until an unearthly howl filled the air, nearly making me jump out of my seat.

"Welcome, darlings, to this year's Halloween Spooktacular," said Violet, sweeping onto the stage as the Bride of Frankenstein with an enormous black and white wig and a white, sequined gown. Everyone cheered and clapped.

"And may I just say, you all look hideous. Are you ready to have some fun? Well then, you're in for the perfect treat…"

The show was incredible.

A full on two-and-a-half-hour spectacular complete with dancing, lip-syncing, singing and circus acts, including a man who twirled fire fans and breathed fire across the stage. Eli was amazing, as always, doing a couple of amazing lip-syncs and then singing several songs from various films, including a wonderful re-enactment of "Remains of the Day" from *Corpse Bride* with himself as the skeleton singer, a queen called Eva Nessence as the Bride, and Robin Heartz as the mysterious stranger who murdered her, followed by a rock version of "This is Halloween" from *The Nightmare Before Christmas*.

My voice was hoarse by the end of the show, my hands ached from non-stop clapping, and my wallet was significantly lighter. There'd been a couple of charity buckets passed around, which we'd all donated generously to. We'd also drunk quite a few bottles of wine, although I was the most sober of the party alongside Jason. He currently had Lewis perched in his lap, his hand resting on his thigh. The only reason I wasn't completely wasted was because I wanted to stay up all night with Eli, and alcohol tended to make me sleepy. I normally got quite excitable for about half an hour, then I fizzled out and crashed like a damp firework.

The performers came onto the stage to do a final bow, and we all cheered again. Eli stood on our end of the stage, and when he saw me, he winked and blew me a kiss. I grinned, another knot twisting in my stomach.

The lights lifted slightly, and the staff began to swarm the floor to clear the tables away, but this time there was still music playing. They were doing a straight transition from show into club night. A dance floor quickly formed with a couple of blocks being dragged out to make platforms for people to dance on.

"Come on," said Lewis, grabbing Jason's hand. "Let's dance." He pulled his boyfriend towards the dance floor and growing crowd, pressing himself flush against Jason's chest. Edward dragged Izzy onto the floor near them, and Leo and Jay stood quietly off to one side, Leo's arms wrapped around his boyfriend almost protectively.

"Is my brother grinding on his boyfriend in public again?" Eli appeared behind me, peering over my shoulder to watch Lewis. "Typical. And I'm always the one who's accused of making a spectacle of myself in public." He wrapped his arm around my waist, leaning in close to brush his lips against my ear. "You look spectacular, but I think it's time to lose the shirt."

I turned my head, kissing him. "Your wish is my command."

"Good. Come with me."

Eli led me backstage where there were still a few people getting changed and wandering around. "Typical," he muttered. "Fucking typical."

"It's okay," I said, realising any plans Eli had for dressing room fun had been derailed by the fact that

Bubblegum sat there in her underwear bitching to Eva about some guy on Grindr. "I can change later."

He grinned at me. "You're so fucking cute, but that's not what I meant."

"I know." I kissed him and raised an eyebrow in what I hoped was a suggestive manner. "But we've got all day tomorrow."

"Good." He reached for the harness, helping me carefully remove it along with the wings. "Now, take off your shirt."

"You realise," I said with a smirk, "that I can't go to McDonald's dressed like this."

"Pfft. I've been in there in less. It's Halloween. Nobody'll care."

"It's true," said Eva from her chair on the other side of the room. "I went in there once in booty shorts, Pleasers, and body glitter. The boy behind the counter gave me a free McFlurry."

"Proof you've always been a ho," Eli said, blowing her a kiss.

"You should know."

"Hey," I said as I unbuttoned my shirt, "I'm not knocking a free McFlurry. Especially if it's one of the Galaxy ones."

Eva laughed. "I like this one, babe. He's fun."

"He is." Eli leant forward to kiss me, and I felt warmth flood my chest.

"So are you," I whispered. "I'm very lucky." I'd never felt like this with anyone before. Eli made me feel things I'd never felt before, cheesy as it sounded. All my previous relationships had been safe, steady, and predictable. I'd even go so far as to label them boring. Eli still made me feel safe, but he also made me feel more alive than I had at any point in my existence. He was funny, and clever, and sexy, and I couldn't see life with him ever being dull.

My thoughts screeched to a halt. *Life with him*. It was too soon to be thinking like that, wasn't it? After all, it wasn't as if we'd been together for that long. And relationships were meant to take time.

But there was just something about Eli, something that told me that deep down I would never find anyone else quite like him. That it was always going to be Eli because nobody else would ever come close.

"Aww, you two are adorable," Bubblegum said, clapping her hands, then sighing dramatically. "Why the fuck can't I have that?"

"Because you send strangers photos of your butthole and think it's a romantic gesture," Eva said acerbically. "Your butt might be cute, but it's not that cute."

"Hey, don't knock it," Eli said, reaching for the wings and harness to slide them on over my shoulders. "That's how my roommate met his boyfriends."

"Are they coming tonight?" I asked. "Orlando and company."

"Not sure, but I hope so." Eli grinned. "He hasn't let me meet them yet. Can't imagine why."

"If I see them, I'll message you so you can come and annoy them."

"You truly are the best." He kissed my cheek dramatically, then stepped back. "And you look fucking gorgeous."

"Thanks," I said quietly. "Do you want to come dance for a bit? Or have you got to set up?" I wasn't the best dancer in the world, but even I could manage a little bit of club dancing. Especially if it involved Eli.

Eli looked me up and down, heat burning in his eyes. "I think I can spare ten minutes. Just for you."

He took my hand and said goodbye to the others before we headed back out to the dance floor. The party was in full swing, and we found the others, not far from where we'd left them.

Lewis launched himself at Eli when he saw him, drunkenly chattering nineteen to the dozen and then gesturing at me. Eli laughed and said something that sounded like "Calm down, Nurse Joy." The rest of the group appeared, and we all danced together for a while. Eli grumbled a bit about the music, saying it was monotonous, but there was a wicked glint in his eye that suggested he had something planned for his time in the booth.

When he left, he kissed me deeply. "See you later," he murmured. "Be good for me."

The kiss left me dizzy, my head spinning, and when I recovered, he was already gone. A few minutes later, when the song ended, a familiar voice flooded the speaker system.

"Hey, bitches! Let's cut that crap. It's time to have some fun." The familiar first notes of "Livin' on a Prayer" burst through the air, and the whole crowd cheered. I'd never heard a club perfectly harmonise the entire song while drunk, but it was amazing. But then Eli followed it with "Bohemian Rhapsody" and nothing would ever top that.

I couldn't remember the last time a night out had ever been this fun. Maybe one never had been.

Lewis and his friends were incredibly welcoming, adopting me into their circle as if I'd known them for years.

We danced, we drank, we sang, and we danced some more. Time passed, but I wasn't marking it.

"Hey," Jay said at one point when we were all taking a quick break and drinking the glasses of water Jason had pressed into our hands. "Is anyone else starting to get hungry?"

"You know what we should do," I said, thinking about what Eli and I had talked about earlier and Eva's comments about freebies. "We should go to McDonald's!"

"That," Lewis said, "is the best idea I've ever heard."

CHAPTER TWENTY

Eli

WAKING UP ON SUNDAY, snuggled in Tristan's arms, took the edge off the exhaustion. I wasn't sure what time we'd finally climbed into bed, but it was closer to dawn than midnight.

My lip twitched, remembering how Tristan had been when he'd come back to mine—tipsy as fuck but with an adorable puppy energy as he'd insisted on trying to help me get undressed. It had made the whole process more difficult, but I hadn't had the energy to resist. When I'd finally convinced him to let me take his make-up off, he'd sat very still, then given me an enthusiastic kiss, climbed into bed, and crashed.

My sweet, beautiful man.

"Good morning," he said quietly, his arm pulling me tighter to his side. I glanced up to see him looking at me sleepily through long, dark lashes, his blond hair all askew. "Or afternoon. I'm not sure what time it is."

"Me either."

"Does it matter? Did you have anything to do today?"

"No." I grinned and rolled until I was half on top of him, one leg slotted between his. "Well, you. But that's about it."

"Mmm, I like that plan."

I kissed him slowly, rocking our bodies together. We had nowhere to be and nothing to do, so I had no desire to rush. And no desire to get out of bed until absolutely necessary. Tristan groaned, his cock filling against mine. His hands came up to tangle in my hair, pulling me closer to him. His tongue slid into my mouth, our kisses turning heated. Would he let me fuck him? Because I really wanted to fuck him. I wanted to watch his face when I pushed my cock inside his perfect ass, hear him beg for me to touch him, and listen to his sweet moans as I fucked him slowly and stroked his cock until he covered us both in his cum.

"Fuck," Tristan groaned, throwing his head back into the pillow. I trailed kisses down his neck, finding the smudged lipstick mark from last night. Seeing it there made my cock throb, something deep and possessive twisting in my chest. More and more I was realising just how special Tristan was. And I wanted everyone to know. I wanted to fucking paint it all over the sky that Tristan was mine, and I was the luckiest fucking bitch in the universe. We'd said we would keep this a secret, but God, I wanted everyone to know.

"I want to fuck you," I said, running my tongue over his

collarbone. Tristan moaned. I chuckled, thinking we might need to revisit our previous conversations about giving me answers. "What's the first rule?"

"U-use my words."

"Good boy." I slid down his body, flicking his nipple with my tongue. "So, what did you actually mean? Can I fuck you? Or would you just like to keep doing what we were doing?"

"The first one," Tristan said, his voice hitched as I gently pinched his nipple between my teeth and tugged. "I want you to fuck me. Please, Eli." He looked down at me. "Fuck me. I want you to fill me up."

I released his nipple and moved up his body, taking his mouth again. "You say the sexiest things. You turn me on so fucking much." I ground my cock against him, loving the way Tristan moaned. With one final kiss, I rolled off him so I could rummage in the bedside table for some lube and a condom.

"How do you want me?" Tristan asked, leaning up on one elbow and watching me.

"Just like you were." I tossed the bottle of lube onto the sheets along with a condom. "Spread your legs for me and just relax." I moved between his thighs, kissing the inside of his knee where he'd drawn his legs up. I'd played with Tristan's ass a few times, and he obviously loved it, but I wasn't sure when he'd actually taken dick last, and I wanted to take things slowly.

I'd have to get him a dildo to practice with when he was home alone. Then get him to send me pictures because he'd look hot as fuck playing with toys.

"Stroke your cock," I said, pouring lube onto my fingers. Then I grinned. "And Tristan... you're still not allowed to come until I say so."

Tristan chuckled, then groaned as he wrapped his hand around his hard cock, spreading precum across the swollen head. "I-I didn't think I'd be allowed to anyway."

"You're a fast learner." I rubbed a wet finger over the sensitive, puckered skin of his hole, loving the way Tristan sighed out a little moan, his eyes fluttering. "So good for me," I said, pressing another kiss to his knee. "So fucking good. Can't wait to be inside this pretty hole. Can't wait to fill you up with my cum."

"Y-yes. Want that." Tristan gasped as I pressed a finger inside him, jerking his cock a little harder. "W-want... want to feel it dripping out of me."

"Fuck, baby," I said, leaning over him so I could press a kiss to his beautiful, filthy mouth. "That's so fucking hot."

"Yeah?"

"Yeah." I kissed him again, wanting to kiss away all his uncertainty. "I want that too. Want to watch my cum leak out of your ass. Want to lick it out of you until you're squirming and begging because it's too much. Want to put a plug in your hole to keep my cum inside you so you know you're mine." Tristan groaned, nodding desperately. I slid another finger inside him. "Then I could pull it out and you'd be all ready for me to fuck you again. Ready for me to dump another load in your tight little ass." My cock throbbed, and fuck, did I like that idea. Tristan clearly did too. "Yeah? You want that? Want me to just fill you up again and again? Wreck this pretty hole."

"Y-yes, fuck. Please, I want... Fuck, I want that. Want it so much."

"God, you're so fucking perfect, Tristan." We were absolutely ringing someone tomorrow to get tests sorted because I fucking needed to make this fantasy come true for both of us.

I pushed three fingers inside him, working Tristan's ass open while he stroked his cock until he was whimpering and writhing underneath me. I already knew him well enough to know he was close, and I wasn't going to let him come until I was balls deep inside him.

"Hands off your cock." I grinned. "I know you're close, and you know you're not allowed to come."

"B-but..."

"No buts," I said, giving him my sternest look and sliding my hand down the inside of his thigh to gently tap his cheek. It definitely *wasn't* a spank, but the way Tristan moaned made me want to add that idea to the long list of things I wanted to try with him. "Hands off. Now. Or I won't let you come at all."

Tristan's eyes widened like he couldn't believe I'd even suggest such cruelty. His hands flew to the sheets, gripping them so tightly his knuckles turned white. I chuckled to myself.

"Good boy. See? You can do as you're told." I slowly withdrew my fingers from his hole, then reached for a condom. My poor cock was aching from neglect, and I gave it a few strokes before rolling the condom onto it. I definitely did not have the biggest dick in the world—there were no beer can cocks or porn-star nine-inchers here—but

I'd spent my entire life learning how to use what I had. And I'd never had any complaints.

"Spread your legs for me," I said, lining up my cock. "Relax. And if you need me to stop, just say. Okay?"

"Okay." Tristan nodded, his eyes focused on mine.

He gasped as I pressed my cock inside him, moaning as I slowly filled him, giving him a moment to adjust as I slid deep inside. The tight, velvet heat felt amazing around my shaft, and I leant down to kiss Tristan slowly, whispering against his mouth.

"You okay?"

"Y-yeah. Feels so good."

"Want me to fuck you now?" I asked, giving him another teasing kiss.

Tristan nodded again, his legs coming up to brush against my ass, pulling me into him. The hair on his calves scratched against my skin. "Fuck me, Eli. Please."

I began to move, rocking my hips deep and slow and giving little teasing thrusts just to see how Tristan responded. He moaned, his ankles digging into the small of my back. I grinned and kissed him again, starting to fuck him harder.

"Oh God, yes! Just like that." Tristan gasped as I pulled back and slammed into him. "Fuck me!"

If I'd expected this to be something slow and sensual, I'd definitely gotten the wrong end of the stick. Tristan wanted it hard, and I was very happy to oblige. At least this time. One day, I'd spread him wide and fuck him slowly and teasingly until he begged for more, but it wasn't going to be today.

I slowed for a second, sitting back onto my heels and unwrapping Tristan's legs from around me. I put my hands on his thighs, pressing them open and spreading him wide so I could pound deep into his ass and watch my cock move in and out of his perfect hole.

"Let me know if it's too much," I said. "I... I don't want you to pull a muscle or some shit."

Tristan nodded and then grinned slyly. "I... Fuck... I feel like this might... inspire me to, er, to start doing yoga again."

I snorted and shook my head, giving him a wry smile. "I might too."

Tristan moaned as I fucked him, then gasped as I changed the angle slightly, thrusting deeper in the hopes I'd hit his prostate. His reaction told me I hadn't missed. Tristan's hands were fisting the sheets by his head, his cock red and leaking onto his abs. God, he looked so fucking amazing like this—all spread out for me, moaning desperately as broken words filled the air. His dick throbbed, more precum spilling onto his skin. I reached down and wrapped my hand around his cock, stroking it fast as I fucked him.

"Fuck, Eli... I... Fuck!"

"Are you going to come for me?" I asked, gripping his thigh with my other hand so I could pound into him. My own orgasm was barrelling down on me with increasing speed, heat spreading down my spine and into my balls. "Go on, baby. Come for me. Want to watch you come."

I jacked his cock again, twisting my fingers across the swollen head, and I thrust deep into him. Tristan howled, his body going stiff underneath me and his ass tightening around my dick as he came, drenching my hand and his stomach in ribbons of cum.

I stroked him through it slowly, my heart pounding for a moment as Tristan panted and gazed up at the ceiling. "You still with me?"

"I-I think so…" Tristan grinned at me. "Not sure, to be honest. Ask… ask me again in a minute."

I laughed. Then I lifted my fingers that were dripping with his cum to my mouth and slowly licked them clean. Tristan watched me with wide eyes.

"No…" he panted. "Nope, I think I'm dead now." He gave me another smile, his thighs starting to shake under my fingers. I sat back and slowly eased my cock out of his ass. Tristan groaned, looking at me desperately. "What…"

I grinned, stripping the condom off and pumping my cock hard and fast. "I'm going to make you mine," I said, my words coming out in a low growl. Tristan moaned, watching me with heated eyes.

"Yes. Please. Come on me… I want it."

I wanted to say something to him, something about good boys always getting what they wanted… but I was too close to do anything but moan and curse as my orgasm rushed through me, sending a wave of pleasurable heat through my muscles. I painted Tristan with my release, the knot in my chest swelling at the sight of him covered in my cum. God, he looked so hot like that. He looked like mine.

I leant down, a possessive snarl escaping as I pressed a deep kiss to his mouth, pulling his lip between my teeth. I should have been embarrassed by my outburst, and I probably would have been… except Tristan moaned and wrapped his arms around me to pull me deeper into the kiss.

We lay there in a tangled heap, smeared with cum and trading lazy kisses.

"Are you still dead?" I asked eventually.

"Maybe." Tristan smirked. "Maybe you should kiss me some more? Just in case. You know, kiss of life and all that."

I snorted. "Not sure that's how it works."

"How do you know if you don't try?" Tristan asked, his fingers carding through my hair and brushing a stray curl out of my eyes. "You wouldn't want me to die."

"You make a good point." I kissed him again. "Very persuasive."

We kissed for a bit longer, time slipping away. I knew we'd have to get up and shower eventually, but right then, I just wanted to stay there, in that moment, with Tristan. I wanted it to sink into my memory so I'd remember it forever.

I already knew Tristan was special, that I'd never meet anyone quite like him ever again, no matter how hard I looked. I knew I was falling for him so fast and hard that the landing was probably going to hurt. But I couldn't bring myself to care. Because Tristan had given me wings, and I was learning how to soar.

CHAPTER TWENTY-ONE

Tristan

IT WAS AROUND three o'clock in the afternoon by the time Eli and I finally extricated ourselves from his bed and made our way to the shower to scrub off the remnants of last night's make-up and sweat and today's cum. Despite our best efforts, there wasn't room for both of us under the shower head, so Eli sat on the end and watched me.

I'd asked him if he was cold, but he'd just said he didn't mind because he got to keep looking at me naked. It had made something clench inside my chest because I didn't think I'd ever had a boyfriend who was so enthusiastic about my body. Or me in general.

Afterwards, when we'd gotten dressed and were sitting on the sofa debating what to eat, there was a heavy knock at the front door.

"Expecting anyone?" I asked.

"Not unless Deliveroo suddenly takes psychic orders,"

Eli grumbled. He glanced at his phone and sighed. "For fucks sake."

"Everything okay?"

"Do you remember taking selfies with Lewis last night?" I thought back. There was definitely a possibility that had happened. I groaned, running my hands through my still damp hair.

"Yeah, I think so. We took a group photo at McDonald's," I said. Lewis and his friends had adopted me into their group with open arms, and he had insisted on including me in all the photos, even though I'd only met most of them a couple of hours beforehand. "There were a group of girls there, and they all said Lewis was really cute. And then he asked if they'd take a picture of us. And I think we took some selfies while we were dancing." There was a sudden sinking feeling in my stomach like a ball of hot lead had settled inside it. "Why? Did Richard see them?"

"No, not Dick. It's fine." Eli chuckled, shaking his head. The sinking feeling inside me levelled out. "But Lewis sent them to Finn and Jules with the caption: *Look at Eli's new boyfriend! Isn't he fucking cute? 10/10. Much sexy.*" He laughed. "There were a lot of emojis too apparently. Jules just forwarded it to me." He looked at me. "How, er, how do you feel about seeing them again?"

"They're outside, aren't they?"

"Yeah. Lewis told them you were staying at mine last night," he said. "Why the fuck can't my family mind their own fucking business for once?"

"Would you want them to?"

"Sometimes it might be nice. Might get to keep some

secrets for once." He stood up, his expression tight. "Are you sure you don't mind? You never actually said."

"It's fine. It's not like I've never met them before," I said. "I just haven't seen them in a while."

"Okay. I'll go let the vultures in, then I'm ordering some bloody food." Eli headed to the door, and I tried to push down the swell of panic rising inside me. I wasn't sure why I was so nervous. It wasn't like I didn't know Eli's family. But then again, how well did I really know them? I was Richard's friend, not theirs, and although I'd been around since I was fourteen and had seen all the ups and downs that went along with being a teenager, I wasn't sure how they'd feel about me dating their brother.

Their brother who I *wasn't* best friends with. Or at least, hadn't been three months ago.

Now, though… my feelings for Eli were very different. Richard would always be my best friend, and nothing could change what we'd been through together, but my feelings for Eli were growing into something far bigger than I'd ever imagined. They were so bright and hot I was afraid to look directly at them because the intensity might kill me. It would be like trying to look directly at the sun during the middle of summer. If there came a moment where I had to choose between my relationship with Eli and my friendship with Richard, I knew I'd choose the former.

I didn't want to choose though, which was why we'd agreed to keep it a secret. But secrets were always hard to keep when family was involved, especially one as nosy as Eli's. It was almost inevitable that the rest of his family were going to find out, and that scared me, mostly because I wanted to protect Eli from any backlash Richard might throw his way. I hoped Richard would understand because they were brothers, but Eli had always been a sore spot for him, and involving me in that tangled mess of emotions was unlikely to produce a good result. I just hoped it wouldn't end in violence.

I heard the click of the front door and a swell of voices. I swallowed, pushing down my worries and fixing a smile on my face.

Lewis was the first to appear through the door, looking distinctly hungover in an enormous pale blue hoodie and a pair of grey joggers. He flopped onto the sofa, sprawling out next to me, and smiled. "I'm sorry. I didn't mean to expose your secret. Drunk me got a little carried away."

"And hopefully your hungover ass is paying for it," Eli said, walking up to the sofa and shooing Lewis towards the other end so he'd be able to sit between us.

"Yes. I am," Lewis said. "Take pity on me."

"No."

From behind Eli, a voice laughed, and Jules appeared in the doorway with Finn just behind her. She leant against the door frame, a wry grin on her face. "This is what you get for going out without me," she said.

"You didn't want to come when I asked you," Lewis retorted. "Neither did Finn, and they're sort of his friends too."

"You said it was all couples," Jules said.

"It was! Tristan's other half just happened to be in the DJ booth." Lewis stuck his tongue out, then pulled his knees up to his chest.

"Gem and I already had plans," Finn said, sticking his head over Jules's shoulder. "And he'd already agreed to open for Jay today, so he didn't want to be too exhausted. It's also not fun going out when everyone else is getting wasted and you're not."

"I wish I hadn't," Lewis mumbled, now looking slightly green around the gills. "I've never felt worse. Can I go back to bed now?"

"No," Jules said, walking into the room, grabbing one of Eli's dining chairs, and turning it so she could straddle the seat and lean on the back. "Hey, Tristan. Nice to see you again." She sounded a little cool like she was still sizing me up and wondering whose side I was on—whether I was fully committed to Eli or whether I'd sell him out to Richard. That was fair enough. I hadn't expected anything less.

"Nice to see you again too," I said. "And you too, Finn."

Finn gave me a little smile and a nod, sitting himself on another of the dining chairs. Eli had disappeared into the kitchen, and I heard the hum of the kettle and the clatter of mugs on the side. "Do you want a hand?" I called.

"Nah, I've got it," Eli said. Then his head appeared, a frown on his face as he peered at his siblings. "If we get food are you fuckers going to steal it?"

"Yes," said Jules.

"No," said Finn.

"Depends what it is," added Lewis, looking like he might be sick. He sighed mournfully. "I can't believe you turfed me out of bed for this. I could be at home with Jason."

"Suck it up," said Jules with another grin. She turned to Eli. "Guess you're ordering food then."

"Assholes."

"I'll order some pizza," I said, opening up my web browser to find Domino's. If anything would make Eli feel better it would be a stuffed crust pizza laden with barbecue sauce, chicken, pepperoni, and sweetcorn. "What would you like?" I asked, looking at the other three.

It didn't take long to get an order in, and my stomach was already growling at the thought. Probably because I hadn't eaten anything since the twenty-piece box of chicken nuggets Jason and I had shared at half one that morning. Or maybe it was the fries and McFlurry's I'd taken back to The Court for Eli and me to eat. That would have been it. We'd sat on the floor and shared the enormous bag of fries, dipping them into the ice cream like we were seventeen all over again. My thirty-three-year-old insides were now reminding me how much of a bad idea that had been. They were probably not going to agree with the pizza either. I'd feel like shit tomorrow and have to spend the rest of the week living on cold chicken, salads, and vegetables in an attempt to pacify my stomach.

But it had been fun to let loose for the evening. I hadn't done that in... well... at least thirteen years. I couldn't remember the last time I'd gone out for the night and actually enjoyed myself.

Not that I'd be doing it regularly, but I thought I'd be up for doing it once in a while.

Eli reappeared with various mugs, thrusting one into Lewis's hands and muttering "Drink this. It'll help."

Lewis wrinkled his nose at the acerbic lemon smell wafting out of it, but dutifully sipped it slowly. Eli had made me tea, trading the mug for a soft kiss. Once he'd passed Finn and Jules theirs, he wedged himself between Lewis and me on the sofa, leaning against me.

"So," Eli said, taking a sip of his black coffee and staring at his siblings. "Are you here to interrogate my boyfriend or just to be nosy?"

Jules grinned. "Can it be both?"

"We were just... curious," Finn said quietly. He was looking at me with clever eyes, and I fought the urge to shiver. It felt like he was peering into my very soul. It was similar to the way Eli looked at me but with an intensity that Eli would never master. Finn had always been the quiet one, ever since I'd known him, and I got the impression that had given him the chance to learn how to read people with a deep certainty. "You and Tristan are, or at least always seemed to be, very different."

"That's not a bad thing though," Lewis added, more to Finn than Eli and me. "Lots of people are in relationships with their opposites. Look at Mum and Mimbles."

Finn nodded and sipped his drink. "That's very true. Opposites attract for a reason, and they can bring balance, but too much opposition can cause problems because you disagree on the fundamentals. What seems like a cute quirk at the start of a relationship can quickly become irritating in the long run."

"Look at you." Jules grinned. "Laying down wisdom like fucking Obi-Wan."

"Just because you're a useless lesbian, doesn't mean the

rest of us are," Eli said with a grin. "And when are you going to let me introduce you to my friend Elle."

"I told you. Masc lesbians can't be friends until we're like… thirty-five. Too many similarities." Jules waved her hand.

"Pfft, Elle is like a fucking Disney princess," Eli said. "She could pass for Aurora if you gave her the right dress. Except she's got a mouth like a sailor and once raced a man down Lincoln high street while wearing six-inch heels because he said he could run faster than her. She won." He clicked his fingers excitedly. "Oh, and she does fencing too. She's like a fucking sword lesbian but like one who'd kick ass in a pink ballgown."

"Oh, she's the one you showed me the picture of," I said, thinking back to a conversation from a couple of weeks ago when Eli and I had been eating lunch outside the castle, and he'd shown me a picture on his phone of a beautiful woman with shimmering golden hair holding a fencing foil. She really had looked like a Disney princess.

"Yes! You used to fence, right? You should start going again. Elle could get you in," Eli said. "You'd look hot with a sword."

I chuckled. "I doubt I'd be much good anymore." I hadn't fenced since university, but I'd enjoyed it in the past. It was something I'd meant to take up when I moved back to Lincoln, but I'd only ever gotten as far as looking up a local group. I'd never gotten around to emailing them. Life had always seemed to get in the way. "But it might be fun to try again."

"I'm going to hold you to that," Eli said with a grin, leaning over to kiss me.

"What? My vague mutterings about fencing again?"

"Yeah. Something like that." I kissed him again, not really caring if anyone was watching.

"Wow," Jules said. "You two are gross. You were right, Lew. They're perfect for each other."

"I told you." Lewis's voice sounded a little strained. "But you just had to see for yourself."

"Obviously."

There was another knock on the door, which turned out to be our food. We spread the pizza boxes out, and the conversation turned to last night's antics, family gossip, and random anecdotes. The four siblings were so fun to watch, falling into their natural, easy dynamic as they talked over each other, bickered, and laughed. I might have felt like an outsider if it weren't for the fact that they kept dragging me into their debates, telling me little stories, and including me in in-jokes and family traditions.

"You know," Finn said, during a momentary lull in the conversation. "Richard is going to have to be told about this at some point. What are you going to do?"

"Way to ruin the mood," Jules said, shaking her head and reaching for another slice of the enormous veggie feast pizza with extra cheese and jalapeños she and Finn were sharing.

"Sorry." He grinned. "But we all know it's the elephant in the room. And you're going to have to deal with it sooner rather than later."

"I know," Eli said with a sigh. "But I don't want to. Dick

can fuck off if he thinks he's dictating my relationship. We all know he's going to throw an epic shit fit about it."

"It might not be that bad," Finn said.

"Finn, darling, I love you, but I cannot deal with your unrelenting optimism right now." Eli waved his hand at Finn, then reached for another slice of pizza, slowly picking the pieces of chicken and pepperoni off and eating them individually.

"Finn's got a point," Lewis said. "None of you were *that* bad when I brought Jason home. I was expecting it to be a thousand times worse."

"That's because we were all threatened to be on our best behaviour," Eli said.

"Hey! Not all of us needed threats," Jules said.

"Says the woman who had to be forced to put on a clean t-shirt and wash her face just before they arrived because she turned up looking like she'd just climbed out of an engine."

"Not my fault Dad's car is a piece of shit. It'd be better as scrap."

"I can tell him," I said, interjecting before Jules and Eli started another full-blown, albeit loving, debate. "If, or I guess when, we decide to tell the rest of your family, I can talk to Richard." I reached out and squeezed Eli's thigh. "He's one of my best friends, and he'll listen to me." I grinned. "And if not, I'll just remind him about every single dating failure, disaster, and near miss he's had over the years."

"See? I knew I liked you for a reason."

"Because I'll stoop to petty blackmail?"

"Exactly." Eli laughed, then frowned as his phone buzzed in the pocket of his hoodie. Frowning, he pulled it out, tapped on the screen, and read something.

"Everything okay?" I asked. "Does Orlando need picking up?"

"No. It's not that." Eli's voice was surprisingly quiet and distant. He was staring at the screen like he couldn't quite believe what he was reading. "I... I got in. To *It's a Drag!* They've offered me a place in the final."

CHAPTER TWENTY-TWO

Eli

NEVER IN MY wildest dreams had I expected to get into *It's a Drag!*.

Not that I wanted to be down on myself, but I'd been trying to be realistic. The video Orlando had made for me had been spectacular, but it was almost impossible to tell what the selection committee had in mind. I'd given myself a stern talking to in my moments of doubt, telling myself I was just as fabulous and amazing as everyone else, but the worries had still lingered.

But now I had proof. I had an email inviting me to the final, which was enough to banish all my doubts, fears, and misgivings—at least for now. Okay, so, performing at *It's a Drag!* wasn't likely to launch an international career or even a national one. It might get me a few more gigs though, and it was a sign I wasn't just a one-trick bitch who needed to stay in her lane and her very small pond.

It did mean I needed a new routine though. A truly spectacular one.

I'd replied to the organisers with my acceptance while Jules, Finn, Lewis, and Tristan had all been celebrating, and they'd promised to send me all the necessary details in the next few days. I had a vague idea of what I'd need though because Orlando had spent last night recapping the details from the previous year... once he'd finished squealing and jumping up and down like a rabbit on ecstasy.

"You okay in here?" Tristan asked from somewhere behind me, snapping me out of my thoughts. "You've been staring at that coffee machine for ten minutes."

"Have I?" I blinked rapidly, focusing on the machine in front of me. I'd apparently pressed the button for coffee at some point because my mug was three-quarters full. "Sorry, my mind was elsewhere."

"Thinking about yesterday?" Tristan stepped into the kitchen and examined the kettle, checking to see whether it needed filling before he flicked it on.

"Yes. Sort of." I picked up my coffee, inhaling the rich scent. God, I needed a machine like this at home. They cost an arm and a leg though, and I currently had neither to spare. "Just thinking about what I need to do now since I'll need a new routine and probably a new look."

Thank God I'd just been paid. Everyone was going to be getting very small Christmas presents from me this year.

"Just remember they picked you for you," Tristan said, giving me a stern look. "Don't go and change what they loved because you think you need to be different. They wanted Bitch Fit, so give them Bitch Fit."

"Thank you." I smiled at him, that fuzzy warm feeling I got when I was around Tristan intensifying to a new level. It was like my chest was full of tribbles. "I'll do my best."

"And if you need anything, just let me know." He began making his cup of tea. "I might not be any good with hair… or make-up, but I can sort of sew, and I'm pretty good with painting." He smiled. "And if all else fails, I make excellent cups of tea and can provide dog snuggles."

"My babies," I said. "I miss them. I need to come and see them again."

Tristan chuckled. "Your babies?"

"We're dating now. Everything that's yours is now mine."

"Figures. I think they view me as a glorified butler."

"Aww. You'd look very cute in a butler's uniform," I said. "We'd be like Jeeves and Wooster—only I'm much smarter than Bertie."

"That you are." Tristan shook his head, smiling at me fondly. "If you want you can come round tomorrow or tonight. Or any day this week. Bring a bag and stay."

"I'd love that." We still hadn't done a lot of the staying over thing, but now that we'd started I didn't think we'd stop. I now knew what it was like to wake up next to Tristan, and it was something I wanted to experience every single day. "Tomorrow?"

"Tomorrow." He leant towards me slightly, tilting his head as if he were going to kiss me. There was a cough behind us, and we sprang apart. Pamela stood in the doorway with a raised eyebrow.

"Busy day today, Mr. Rose?" she asked.

"Er… yes?" Tristan picked up his mug and headed for the door, sliding past her with a sheepish smile.

"Good answer." She looked at me over her glasses. "You two are going to get caught. I thought you wanted to be subtle."

"We're trying."

"Honey, if that's subtle, then I am the Duchess of Cambridge."

"You'd make a good duchess."

Pamela laughed. "You're trouble."

"Yes, but I am also irresistibly charming." I winked at her, taking another sip of my coffee. From somewhere out in reception, I heard the clattering of feet on the stairs.

"Eli?" Alistair's angry bark made me sigh heavily.

"Duty calls," I said, schooling my face into the most neutral expression I could muster. One day, I was going to tell that man exactly what I thought of him, but it was not that day. I needed at least another paycheck to afford *It's a Drag!*. The problem was I'd never met anyone so incompetent, and it was getting very hard to keep the snark at bay.

I strolled out to find Alistair, whose face was an interesting shade of puce, with my coffee in hand. "Yes? Can I help you?"

"Why haven't you answered my email? I need the list of viewings for the rectory in Cherry Willingham."

"I sent you the list this morning along with everyone's details."

"I haven't seen it."

"Well, maybe if you use your eyes that will help." I smiled. "I realise that Outlook is a little advanced for a man of your skill set, but I'm sure if you revisit the top of your inbox, you'll find it."

"How dare you," Alistair growled. "I've never been so insulted."

"I highly doubt that."

"Do you know who I am?"

"Another middle-aged, white man with an overinflated sense of entitlement?" I knew I was starting to push my luck, but I was having far too much fun. It was just like dealing with Richard, which made it very easy to know which buttons to push.

"I... I..." he spluttered. "No wonder you're no more than a glorified secretary. Useless—"

"I think that's quite enough from you," Pamela said from behind me. Her voice was ice cold. I smiled. I didn't need rescuing, but Pamela had a level of clout I didn't. Besides, it was amusing to watch Alistair's face change colour rapidly. I didn't think he'd expected Pamela to hear him. "Eli has sent you all the details you need as he does every morning. And I will not have you slandering my colleague or my profession just because you haven't worked out how to read your emails."

"I... All I meant was..."

"Yes?" I asked sweetly. "I believe you were going to say something after the word *useless*. Would you like to continue? Because if I were a betting man, which I'm not normally but I'll make an exception on this occasion, I'd say you were about to add some sort of slur regarding my gender or sexuality. Probably the latter. After all, can't have useless gay boys like me running around in public."

"I… I…" Alistair had gone very pale. I wanted to laugh. I'd taken a pot shot and hit the nail on the head. Sadly, I wasn't surprised.

"But I'm not sure if you realise that both my gender and sexuality are protected characteristics under the equality act, so please do open your mouth and allow me to provide you with some legal education," I said. "Just in case you weren't aware, I have a first-class law degree from the University of Leeds. So I may be a glorified secretary, but I'm a glorified secretary with a law degree and enough of an attitude to take you to school. You won't win if you argue with me, by the way. I'm just putting that out there. All my lecturers thought I'd make an excellent barrister."

"Well… I didn't mean it like that," Alistair said, suddenly looking like he wished he could take back the last five minutes.

"I'm sure you didn't." My voice was cool. "And I'm sure you won't do it again. Because I may be just the bitch in administration, but I'm the bitch who makes you look good and gets you clients. So if I were you, I'd think very, *very* carefully about how you treat me and my colleagues in future." I gave him a cold smile. "Oh, and Alistair? The next time you want to make assumptions about someone's sexuality, I'd suggest you don't. Because I will not make your life pleasant if you do. After all, we wouldn't want Holly and Andrew to know you hold these… views since we definitely have some clients who are full-fledged members of the alphabet mafia. The current owners of the rectory in Cherry Willingham for example."

I enjoyed watching Alistair's expression go through a

mix of anger, fear, loathing, and disgust before settling on begrudging acceptance of his position. I doubted this would be the end of the conversation, but for now, I was going to take the win. I took a victory sip of my coffee.

"I'll go and check my emails," Alistair said, his voice clipped. "Thank you."

He turned and walked towards the stairs at a slightly faster pace than usual. I smirked. "Don't cross me bitch," I muttered quietly.

"That was exciting," said Pamela as she returned to her desk.

"What's Halloween without banishing a few frogs." I pretended to wave a magic wand. "Bippity-boppity back the fuck up, bitch. I have the magical powers of a law degree and too much self-confidence, and I'm not afraid to use them."

She gave me a wry grin. "You know, you really would make a good barrister."

"I would," I agreed, "but powdered wigs are so not my style."

The rest of the afternoon passed in typical fashion with no more excitement. I spent most of it doing busy work and occasionally poking Tristan on Microsoft Teams because I was bored. In the back of my mind, I was turning over potential routine ideas and dismissing ninety percent of them. I definitely wasn't going to do anything Christmas themed—that was cliché and so not my style—but doing something Halloween-esque felt similar.

Bitch Fit looked like a stereotypical, walking Halloween

fantasy but she was so much more, and I wanted people to see that.

As Tristan had said, I didn't need to change who I was. I needed to be quintessentially me, only with the dial turned up a notch.

I was also going to need to get the date in everyone's diaries ASAP if I wanted them to come. The show had been selling tickets and tables for months, and if my family wanted to be there, they'd need at least one table. Probably two.

I sighed to myself, tapping my pen on the notepad beside me, pretending to be making memos for Holly.

If I did want my family to come, I was going to have to tell them about Tristan because there was no way in hell I was going to do this without him. And I wasn't going to pretend for a whole evening that I had no clue who he was beyond a friend of Richard's. That wasn't fair to me, and it wasn't fair to Tristan. We were grown-ass adults in a consenting relationship—who the fuck cared if he was my asshat older brother's best friend? I lov—had very strong feelings for Tristan. And I was going to own them. Fuck Richard, and fuck anyone else who kicked up a stink. They could be happy for us, or they could get the fuck out of my life.

Besides, if we got a couple of bottles of wine down Lewis, he'd tell everyone anyway. Might has well tell it my way.

By the time Tristan came downstairs again, I'd made up my mind.

"I've been thinking," I said as I reached for my coat, "about my family and *It's a Drag!*."

"We should tell them," Tristan said, pulling on his own dark peacoat. I'd never considered men in suits particularly sexy until I'd met Tristan, but he carried them effortlessly. "I mean, I'd like to because, selfishly, I don't think I can pretend we're just friends for the evening."

"You read my mind." I grinned. "You should stop stealing my thoughts. I need them."

"Maybe you're stealing mine?"

"Outrageous." I stepped in close to steal a quick kiss. "The nerve, Mr. Rose, the nerve."

He chuckled, the sound resonating through my chest like a church bell. "I heard you really pissed off Alistair this afternoon."

"Yes, well, Alistair should learn to read his emails and think before he speaks."

"I wish Pamela hadn't banished me. I'd have liked to have seen that."

"Don't worry," I said, straightening the lapels of Tristan's coat simply because I wanted to touch him. "I'm sure it'll happen again."

"Next time, please get Pamela to buzz me. It'll break up my workday."

"Of course. Wouldn't want you getting bored. It's not like you have work to do."

"It's not like you don't have work either," Tristan said, poking me gently in the chest. We both laughed, and he leant down for another kiss. God, this man... this man. He'd changed everything.

"A dead hamster could do my job, and nobody would notice I'd been replaced."

"I'd notice." Tristan pulled a sad face, but his eyes were twinkling. "Who else is going to give me secret biscuits?"

"I knew you had an ulterior motive for dating me."

"Ah yes, how else would I get biscuits?" he said with a deadpan expression, then he reached out his hand and interlaced his fingers with mine. "Want to come get dinner at mine? We can plan how to tell your family. I can drop you back later if you want. Or did you have Halloween plans with Orlando?"

"Not really. I think we were just going to watch silly horror movies and eat sweets," I said. "Our plans have somewhat mellowed as we've gotten older." Once upon a time we'd have gone out partying, getting drunk and hooking up with whoever looked cute in their costume. But I was too old for that now. I'd spent half the weekend on my feet, and now I just wanted to sleep and maybe eat some Tangfastics and a mini Milky Way.

"Will he mind if I steal you?"

"If he does, he'll just ring his boyfriends and say he's alone and scared. They'll come running and fuck him sense-less instead." Tristan snorted, and I grinned.

"Okay, so dinner at mine it is," Tristan said. "But if you want to watch a horror movie, you'll have to protect me."

"I'm sure I can do that." I stole another kiss. Three was a magic number. "If you want, we can divert via mine so I can grab something for tomorrow and then I can stay the night?" I suggested. "I know we said tomorrow, but—"

"Sounds good to me," Tristan said, cutting me off before I could finish. "Let's go."

He pulled open the front door and led me out into the darkness of Halloween night, his hand wrapped tightly around mine.

CHAPTER TWENTY-THREE

Tristan

THE JOURNEY to Miranda and Eleanor's house on the following Sunday seemed to take far longer than the usual hour, and yet it also felt like no time at all. By the time we pulled into the driveway, I still wasn't prepared for what we were doing.

Eli had said the best way to do this was to rip the plaster off and bring me to a family dinner. That way we'd get it all over and done with at once. We'd also have allies there in the form of Lewis, Finn, and Jules, but not Jason, as he was back in London for work.

"Still," Eli had said, "that's five of us against Richard, so that's pretty good odds."

I wanted to ask him if he was expecting a punch up, but I wasn't sure I wanted to know the answer. Telling my family hadn't been nearly so dramatic. Alexis had just given me an enormous hug and asked to meet Eli as soon as she returned from her trip to London where she was doing a consultation for a footballer and his partner. My parents had had the same reaction as usual—a vaguely disinterested "That's nice darling"—but I had taken great delight in pointedly telling my father that Eli was a drag queen instead of the usual banker or lawyer I usually brought home. I sadly hadn't been able to see his face, but his silence and strained voice had been enough. I knew they'd be polite to Eli if they ever met him because they were just those sort of people, but I doubted I'd see them any more than I already did.

It wasn't like they were falling over themselves to spend time with me anyway.

"Well," said Eli, making the sign of the cross. "If there was ever a time to pray, it's now."

I laughed. "It won't be that bad. Richard isn't that much of an asshole." At least, I prayed he wasn't. We'd been friends for long enough that I hoped he'd be happy for me. "And if all else fails, we can appeal to Ruby. She's very sweet."

"Which really does beg the question of why she's with my brother, but I suppose we'll have to chalk that up to being one of the great mysteries of life." Eli unbuckled his seatbelt and reached for the door. "Come on. Let's go and introduce you. If it goes horribly, we can go back to mine and drown our sorrows in tequila."

"Don't be so overdramatic," I said, climbing out of the car and straightening my jumper. I'd gone for my nicest knitted one, which was also one of the only jumpers I had that wasn't covered in dog hair, and a pair of dark jeans. I'd known Eli's parents for years, but I still wanted to make a good impression. I wanted them to know this was serious. Even Eli had pulled out a nice pair of jeans and wore a dark t-shirt under an old shearling aviator jacket he'd found at a vintage store. "It'll be fine."

I reached for his hand and laced our fingers together, squeezing gently.

We began to walk towards the front door, which swung open before we reached it. Richard appeared with a confused expression on his face. Maybe he'd seen my car and wondered what I was doing there. Then he caught sight of our hands linked together, and his face dropped.

"Hey," I called, trying to sound relaxed, but I couldn't stop myself from gripping Eli's hand a little tighter.

"What the hell? What's going on?"

"Didn't anyone tell you I was bringing my boyfriend?" Eli asked.

"Your boyfriend?" Richard stared at us. Behind him I saw a few of his family members congregating.

"Surprise." I smiled and lifted our hands slightly. There was a pause—a split second where everything seemed to slow down, and I thought maybe that would be it. Then Richard, stupid, hot-headed twit that he was, barged out the front door towards us.

"Eli! This is low even for you," he snarled. "Why do you have to ruin everything?"

"Hey! This has nothing to do with you," Eli said. He let go of my hand, despite my attempts to hold it tight.

"Eli, please," I said. "Richard, calm down."

"Jesus fucking Christ," Richard said. "Do you hate me

so much you decided to fuck with my best friend just to get back at me?"

"I'm not an object," I said, but they both ignored me. The situation was escalating rapidly, and I could only see it getting worse.

"Rich." Ruby appeared behind Richard and put a hand on his shoulder, but he shrugged her off. "It's okay."

"No, it's not fucking okay. Once again, everything has to be all about Eli!"

"Fuck you, you pretentious asshole," Eli snapped. "Not everything is about you. Boo fucking hoo. I'm dating your best friend. Do you really think I'm that much of a twat that I'd fuck Tristan just to get back at you? What kind of small-minded, conniving—"

Eli's sentence was cut off as Richard punched him in the face.

Everyone stared.

Eli staggered.

I opened my mouth, putting my hand out to pull him away, but Eli just grinned, wiping his mouth on the back of his hand.

"Is that all you've got, Dick?"

When I looked back at the moment, I'd never be able to give an accurate representation of what happened next. Eli leapt at Richard with the unrepentant fury of a honey badger while Richard lashed out with wounded anger. The resulting brawl had ended up with the pair of them on the front lawn, trying to beat the shit out of each other like two teenage boys in the middle of the schoolyard.

Ruby was watching and screaming at Richard, her

moment of calm forgotten. Lewis and Jules, who'd appeared behind them, were chuckling darkly and filming with their phones like they'd been expecting this to happen. Finn didn't seem to know what to do with himself. And I was just staring... wondering how on earth it had come to this. I wanted to be angry at both of them, and I was, but I was also astounded they'd stoop to this level and hurt they were so wrapped up in their hatred for each other they couldn't look past that for one minute.

It felt like this had been a long time coming though. The final explosion of years of repressed emotions.

A piercing whistle split the air. The bystanders all turned. Lewis hurriedly put his phone away. Standing in the doorway was Miranda, crackling with fury. Her soft, ethereal demeanour was gone, and her pastel-tinted hair seemed to stand out like a halo. I'd never seen her look so angry. I didn't think it was possible. Miranda was the gentle hippie with bangles, bracelets, and tie-dyed skirts. But every parent had a breaking point, and it appeared she'd finally reached hers.

"That's enough!" she said, marching straight up to the heap on the floor that was now Richard and Eli. "Get up."

"But—" Richard tried to protest. He was already sporting the start of a black eye.

"Be quiet. I am not interested in your excuses. You are two grown adults, and neither of you should be acting like this."

"Sorry, Mum," Eli muttered as he climbed to his feet. His lip was split, and there was a thin line of blood trickling down his chin.

"Sorry."

"It's not me you should be apologising to. Get in the house now. One upstairs, one down. You're in time out until you calm down," Miranda said, glaring at them and pointing at the front door. "If you're going to act like children, I'm going to treat you like children. You can both sit and think about what you've done. And you will both give me your phones. That is not a request."

Eli fished his phone out of his jacket pocket, checking it wasn't cracked before handing it over. Richard pulled his out of his jeans. Miranda raised an eyebrow, and they both headed wordlessly for the house. I stared. Out of the corner of my eye I saw Jules and Lewis trying to stifle their giggles. Ruby just looked exasperated.

Miranda turned to me, her demeanour softening again. She beamed at me. "Hello, Tristan darling. I'm so sorry for the kerfuffle." She walked over to me and pulled me into a hug that smelt like a summer meadow. "You look very well. It's so nice that you're joining us," she said. "You'll have to tell us all about you and Eli. Why don't you come inside and get a drink while they calm down?"

"Er, that would be lovely. Thank you."

"Come on then," she said, steering me gently towards the house. "Ruby, sweetheart, would you like a drink?"

"I think I need one," Ruby said. She gave me a weary smile. "I'm sorry, Tristan."

"Don't apologise," I said. "It's fine."

"It's not. Rich's being a twat."

I laughed. "Well, yeah."

"Just leave them to cool off," Miranda said with a sigh.

"Men. So ridiculous." Ruby laughed, and we all traipsed into the house. "By the way," Miranda said, turning to Lewis as we entered the kitchen. "If I see that footage anywhere but your phone, there will be consequences."

"Mum! I'm twenty-seven," Lewis said.

"And you're still my baby. Now delete that video and go and see if either of our prize fighters need an ice pack."

"What on earth is going on?" asked Mimbles, appearing from the dining room. "Why is Eli in my dining room with a split lip?"

"You see, Mum," Lewis said, gleefully pulling out his phone. "This is where videos are useful."

After we'd had a drink, I'd decided I needed to talk to Richard. I needed to talk to Eli too, but Richard was the more difficult of the pair, and I wanted to try to talk some sense into him.

I found him upstairs, sitting on a chair in the room he'd once shared with Eli. He was holding a bag of frozen peas wrapped in a tea towel against his eye.

"Is this where I start singing the *Rocky* theme?" I asked, leaning against the door and folding my arms.

"Maybe," he said, wincing as he tried to smile. "But I don't think Rocky was as much of a prize twat."

"Oh, undoubtedly not."

"If I said I'm sorry, would that be a good start?" he asked, lowering the peas for a second. He was going to have a lovely black eye at school tomorrow. The kids would love it.

"It would," I said. "But I'm not really the one you should be apologising to."

"Yeah, I know."

"Jesus Christ, Richard. What the fuck were you thinking? Do you genuinely think Eli is dating me to get back at you? Do you think I'm so stupid that I have zero agency in this? Because right now, you're treating me like a fucking object. I'm not some prize for you two to compete over." I glared at him. Richard winced again.

"That makes it sound even worse."

"Good," I said. "I love you, Richard, but you're being an asshole."

"I know. And I'm sorry." He sighed. "Ruby has made it abundantly clear I'm in the wrong here. God, I hope she forgives me."

"You better hope so because you're fucked if she breaks up with you."

"Christ." He rubbed the unbruised side of his face. "I've been such a twat."

"At least you know it." I moved from the door frame to perch on the end of one of the twin beds, resting my elbows on my knees. We sat in silence for a moment.

"I'm sorry," Richard said, sounding genuine this time. "I let my frustration with Eli boil over, and I saw red. It's not an excuse, and I need to be better about not letting him get to me. But you're my best friend, and I just... I don't ever want to see you get hurt, and I was scared for a moment that Eli was just using you for fun and would break your heart. I'm still not completely convinced he won't, but that shouldn't stop me from supporting you. If you're happy with him, then I'm happy for you. Because you deserve to be happy."

"Thanks." I reached out and patted his knee. "You're my best friend too, but Eli... There's just something about him that makes me feel alive. We balance each other, I think. He's funny and outgoing and so fucking talented. Seriously, Richard, you're missing out. Your brother is amazing, and I know he's been a dick to you too, but maybe... maybe you could try to meet each other halfway."

"Maybe." He didn't sound sure, but it was better than an outright no. "Where did you two even meet?"

"At work. He's temping at Green & Wodehouse for a year. He's far too good for it, but Eli doesn't care about that. I don't think he wants a high-powered career. He just wants to get by so he can perform, and having seen him, I understand why."

"Seriously? He's been working with you the whole time." Richard stared at me, and I saw the hurt on his face. "Why didn't you say anything? Why didn't he?"

"Well, firstly, it wasn't my place," I said. "That's Eli's choice. And secondly, I don't think he told you because he knew you'd spend the whole time either telling him he was too good for the job or that it was good to see him finally getting his act together. He's not like you, Rich, and you can't keep treating him like a disappointment." I stared at him. "Eli has different dreams than you, and that's not a bad thing. Stop punishing him because you want him to be different. Eli is always going to be Eli, and if you push him, he's going to push back. As you now have proof."

Richard grimaced and nodded. "Okay… I can't promise I'll always understand him, but I can try."

"It's not me you need to tell," I said. "It's him."

"Yeah, I know. Just give me ten minutes, and I'll come down."

"Good plan." I gave him a wry smile. "You know, you're going to need a good excuse for tomorrow. Or some great make-up."

Richard groaned and then laughed. "God, the kids are going to rip the shit out of me for months."

I patted his knee. "Let's face it, you probably deserve it."

CHAPTER TWENTY-FOUR

Eli

SITTING in Mum and Mimbles's dining room with some crushed ice cubes wrapped in a unicorn tea towel pressed to my lip was not the plan I'd had for my Sunday. Mimbles had looked at my lip and said the swelling would go down in a day or two before giving me some baking soda paste to rub on it. It tasted disgusting, but apparently that was my punishment for getting smacked in the face by my dickhead older brother.

We hadn't had a bust up this bad in years. The last time had been when I was about thirteen and Richard was seventeen, which in hindsight hadn't been a good move on my part. I'd still kicked him in the nuts though, even if he had handed me my ass. After that, Mum had quietly threatened death and destruction if we ever tried something like that again. We'd believed her.

It was why we'd moved on to verbally sniping at each

other. But I guessed showing up with his best friend in tow had been a step too far for Dick.

"Knock, knock." Tristan's head appeared around the door. He looked at me and smiled softly, shaking his head. "How's the lip?"

"You know," I said, putting the tea towel on the table next to me, "I think my ribs actually hurt more where the bastard smacked me in the side a couple of times. I'm going to be beautifully bruised tomorrow, like a banana." I winced slightly as I uncrossed my legs and swapped them over, something pulling in my side.

"Oh dear." Tristan walked over to me and leant down to press a kiss to my forehead. "Will you live?"

"I suppose but mostly out of spite. I can't believe he hit me!"

"Me either," Tristan said, pulling out a chair next to me and sitting down. "Although you did antagonise him."

"I was defending my honour. And yours."

"I don't need defending." Tristan's expression could only be described as withering. "I'm not some prize for the two of you to compete over."

"I'm sorry," I said, thinking back to what I'd said. It hadn't been my finest hour. "I just didn't want him to think I'm fucking with you. That's just insulting. To you and me."

"I know. Richard knows that too."

"Did you speak to him?"

"Yes. And you need to."

"No thanks," I said, waving my hand. "I'd rather have another fight."

Tristan chuckled. "That's definitely not happening."

I sighed. "I just don't get it. Why the fuck are you two friends? You're the most amazing person ever, and he's well... him." It was the politest way I could think to phrase it. I picked up my ice again, flinching as I pressed it back on my lip. Thank God I didn't have a show tomorrow, otherwise I'd be fucked. Although I could definitely work this into a routine somewhere...

"We're friends because Richard has always been there for me," Tristan said. He gave me a soft smile. "He was the first person I ever told I was gay, and he just... didn't care. It wasn't a thing to him, whereas every dickhead in our year thought *gay* was the best insult around. I was so nervous because I was fifteen and terrified, and Richard just said it was cool. Then he started bringing me around here so I could see that I could be gay and have a good life—considering nobody else had told me that was possible."

"I didn't know that."

Tristan shrugged. "It doesn't matter. I only figured it out later." He shook his head as if remembering something funny. "Then there was the time Richard punched Adrian Belper in the face because he called me a cocksucker. I've never seen anyone looked so shocked—Adrian and Richard."

"When was that?" I stared at him. I'd never known any of this about Richard. He'd never seemed to care, but then again, I'd never wanted him to. And I'd never had any problems at school. I'd been one of those lucky ones who flitted between groups of people, flirted outrageously, and managed to get on with everyone.

"I don't know. When we were in sixth form? About seventeen."

I rummaged around in my memories, seeing if I could remember anything. I frowned. "I think I remember that. I didn't know it was about you, but I remember Mimbles being very angry that Richard had been punished for fighting. I'd never asked why. I think I was just happy Richard got grounded."

Tristan chuckled. "He did. He spent the whole month texting me like he was writing from prison. You drove him nuts the entire time."

"That sounds about right." I grinned.

"And after we left school, he was just always there," Tristan continued. "He was there when I got my first boyfriend at Oxford and was panicking because I didn't know anything about gay sex." He chuckled. "Not sure why I turned to Richard, but he'd had a string of girlfriends by then, so I think eighteen-year-old me figured he might know something."

"I don't think I need to know that."

Tristan laughed. "Don't worry. I figured it out."

"And for that, I am very grateful." I wanted to lean forward and kiss him, but my lip was still painful, and the taste of the baking powder paste smeared on the cut was bound to ruin the moment.

"Richard might be a dick, at least to you, but he cares," Tristan said. "When I was in London on my ill-advised banking adventure back when I was trying to get my dad's approval, I was so fucking miserable. But Richard was just there, on the other end of the phone, whenever I needed him. He was the one I'd call at two in the morning when they'd dragged me out clubbing and bought me strippers and were all off their faces on coke. Or when I was so stressed and tired from the long hours I could barely stand up, when I just wanted to lie down and not get back up again because the thought of going back to work made it hard to breathe. He was the one who finally convinced me to quit and move back here." His lip twitched in a tiny smile. "I remember it so clearly. He came down to London one Friday night, took me to the pub, looked me dead in the eye, and said 'You have to quit your job. If you don't, it's going to kill you'. He's just always been there to protect me. I know it's stupid, but your brother has always looked out for me, and I don't think my life would be the same without him."

I sat there for a moment, staring at Tristan, lost for words for the first time in my life. "I'm sorry," I said, lamely. "I didn't know."

"You didn't have to," he said, reaching out and taking my hand, squeezing it tightly before lifting it to his mouth to kiss my grazed knuckles. "I'm just telling you so you know now. None of this changes your relationship with Richard or what's happened between you over the years, but I wanted you to know he's not always a complete twat. Misguided? Yes. But most of the time his heart's in the right place."

I squeezed his hand, taking comfort from the warmth of his skin against mine. There was still a lot about Tristan I didn't know, and so much of that was tangled up in his friendship with Richard. But this felt like a step forward, and now I just wanted him to tell me everything—the good, the bad, and the ugly. I'd tell him the same.

There was something I had to do first though, and it was the one thing I'd avoided for as long as possible. I was going to have to have an honest-to-God conversation with my brother.

"I have to talk to him, don't I?" I asked. Tristan nodded.

"Yes, you do." He grinned. "Don't worry. I've already told him he's a twat and that I'm not some damsel in distress who needs him to rescue me, so you don't need to remind him."

"Curses. Foiled at the first hurdle."

Tristan chuckled and leant forward to press another kiss to the top of my head. "I know you too well already."

"You do." I smiled, lowering my now soggy tea towel and tilting my head up to beg for a kiss—split lip be damned. I needed him to kiss me because I was rapidly coming to the realisation that I needed Tristan more than I needed anything or anyone else. Now probably wasn't the right time or place to tell him though. It would be memorable, but I couldn't bring myself to tell him I loved him right after my brother had punched me in the face. Because I did... love him. I loved Tristan Rose more than life itself. It should have shocked me, but it didn't. It just felt right, like something I'd been missing my whole life had finally slotted into place.

"What?" Tristan asked, looking at me with a raised eyebrow and a confused expression.

"Nothing," I said. "Just thinking about how ridiculous this whole thing is."

I could tell him later when it was just us. When I could lay him down and whisper the words against his skin like a prayer, sinking them into every kiss, every touch, like a spell.

There was a gentle tap on the dining room door, and Richard's voice filtered in from the other side. "Can I come in?"

I sighed. It was now or never. "Yeah."

The door creaked open—Mimbles really needed to oil the hinges—and Richard's face appeared. I wanted to laugh at the spectacular black eye he was sporting, but I knew it would be best not to mention it. Not unless I wanted to start round two, and for Tristan's sake I was going to try for civility.

"I'll give you two some space," Tristan said, standing up and giving me another kiss. He took the tea towel out of my hand. "I'll get you some more ice."

I watched him go, wishing I could convince him to stay. Richard shuffled through the door, closing it after Tristan but not coming much farther into the room. The awkwardness between us was palpable. I wanted to say something to cut the tension, but once again, I was convinced my mouth would get me into more trouble than it could handle. I could only take being punched in the face once a day.

"So," I said.

"So…"

"I hear you once punched a guy called Adrian Belper in the face." Richard stared at me for a second and then burst out laughing.

"Yeah, because he was being a knob," he said. "He

didn't give me a black eye though." He reached up to touch the swelling gingerly. "But I might have deserved this one."

"You might." I gestured to the chair Tristan had vacated. "You can sit down you know. I'm not going to bite."

Richard opened his mouth as if he was going to say something but then thought better of it. He walked over to the chair and sat down. "So… you and Tristan."

"Me and Tristan."

"He says you met at work?"

"Yes," I said slowly, wondering where this line of questioning was going. "I'm temping there for a year. Just covering someone's maternity leave."

"Cool. Is that the job you didn't want to tell me about?" I squinted at him suspiciously, but Richard looked more hurt than anything.

"Yes."

"Okay." He paused. "Why didn't you say anything? Or want to say anything I guess would be the better question. Nobody else seemed that surprised. Did everyone know about you and Tristan?" He'd muddled a couple of questions together there, so I considered them for a second before starting to unpick them.

"Not everyone," I said. "Lewis knew because he saw us together at one of my shows. Finn and Jules found out last week after Lewis sent them pictures of him and Tristan at the Halloween show I did."

"Oh… okay."

"But yes, everyone knew about the job, I think. I'm surprised nobody told you though. I thought they would."

"Mum said she had to respect your wishes. Mimbles

and Paul said they weren't getting involved, and Dad said we needed to sort it out between us." I hummed in surprise. I hadn't expected that. "Am I... am I that bad that you didn't want to tell me?"

"Richard," I said, raising my eyebrows at him, "you know exactly what you're like. I only took this job as a temporary thing, and I knew if you found out you'd go on and on about how I was finally growing up and settling down, or you'd start lecturing me about how admin work wasn't good enough and how I should really make some-thing of myself. And you'd definitely find a way to throw in how pleased you were I'd finally stopped prancing about on stage like a fool."

Richard winced. I wondered if he'd ever thought through what he'd said to me and really considered how it came across. I guessed not.

"I know you think you have my best interests at heart, but it just makes you look like a dickhead. I mean, I know you think the root of all happiness is a stable career that contributes to society, but it's not for everyone. You're a fucking teacher for Christ's sake. You've got to know everyone has different dreams. And mine is to not be a capitalist slave. Money is useful and all, but working an office job for the rest of my life sounds like pure hell. You'd never tell any of your students the shit you tell me."

"Point taken," he said. "I just... You're my brother, and I want the best for you."

"I know." I smiled. "And for me, the best is strutting around on stage in seven-inch heels and a dress, wearing more make-up than the entire cast of *Love Island*. It's what makes me happy, and I'm not gonna lie, I'm pretty fucking good at it."

"Tristan said you're amazing," Richard said. "I'm sorry I've never seen one of your shows. I'm sorry for a lot of things."

"Well, have no fear. There's plenty of time yet. I'm not dead."

Richard chuckled and then sighed. We still hadn't really addressed the elephant in the room; we'd just tiptoed around the edge of it and pacified it with some sugar cane.

"What?" I asked. "Come on. Tell me. Since we're being all honest and shit. What do you want to say? Or better yet, what is it about me that bothers you? There's got to be something. And what is it about me and Tristan that makes you so upset? Because if you seriously think I'm with him just to hurt you, I will punch you again. I'm not that much of a bitch."

"I don't think that. At least, not anymore," he said. "Tristan made it abundantly clear that train of thought makes me look like a knob."

"Tristan is a smart cookie."

"It's… Things have always been so easy for you… at least from where I stood. You were smart and popular and charismatic. You could do anything. I mean, you got a fucking first-class law degree like you were picking apples off a tree. That's something most people would kill for. And to me, it just seemed like you were throwing it all away, and I guess I never understood it." He looked almost sad. I grimaced. I wanted to be angry with him, but I just couldn't bring myself to be. From where Richard was standing, my life probably had looked easy, especially considering what I knew now about Tristan's time at school.

"It must have hurt," I said, attempting to extend an olive branch, "to see me skipping through school untouched, knowing Tristan had been bullied for being gay."

"A little. That didn't mean I wanted you to get hurt though."

"No, but that doesn't mean you don't resent me a little. And I always accused you of not caring when deep down you did. Only your method of caring is different than mine, and mixing them together is like..." I tried to think of something explosive, but my days of GCSE Chemistry were so long ago I'd disposed of the information.

"It's like putting alkali metals in water," Richard said.

"Are they the ones that explode?"

"Yeah." He grinned. "One of my professors at Reading once said that when he was a student, he stole a load of potassium from the chemistry labs and threw it in the water fountain on campus. I'm not sure how he managed it or avoided getting caught, but the resulting explosion destroyed the fountain and left a crater in the ground."

"That's us then." I chuckled.

"Yeah, it is."

"If it helps," I said, "I think part of the reason I got angry with you was because I just wished you'd see me for the person I am, not the person you want me to be. You're not my parent. I've got enough of those. You're my brother, and it always irked me that you saw me as nothing but a disappointment."

"It doesn't help. I'm sorry though." He sounded genuine, and for the first time in my life, I believed him.

"I'm sorry too." I looked at him, trying—for the first time—not to see him as my enemy. As Tristan had said, Richard wasn't deliberately a twat all the time. He was just misguided. He wanted the best for me, but he'd gone about it all wrong, and instead of talking to him, I'd just pushed his buttons because it was fun, which had just confirmed everything he thought he knew. I didn't think we were ever going to be close, not like I was with Finn, Lewis, and Jules, or even Oscar, but maybe this was the first step towards a begrudging truce.

"What now?" Richard asked.

"Hopefully dinner," I said. "I'm starving. But after that, who knows. I guess we just try not to kill each other." Richard nodded. "Don't worry, I'm not going to completely steal Tristan away, and I have no intention of gate-crashing your dinners together. He'll still be your best friend. He'll just be mine too."

"Okay then." Richard looked at me, a small smile crossing his lips. "I feel like I'd usually have to tell Tristan this since you're my brother, but this is different."

"Oooh, is this where I get the scary talking to? Don't hurt your best friend, or they'll never find my body?"

"Something like that." He chuckled. "Take care of him. You'll never find anyone else like him."

My heart raced as I thought about Tristan, all my feelings exploding like a never-ending parade of fireworks. "For once, Richard, you're actually right about something."

CHAPTER TWENTY-FIVE

Tristan

AFTER THE DRAMA OF SUNDAY, I thought I'd be ready to go back to the office for a quiet week at work. Then Monday arrived, and I realised I'd made a mistake.

I wasn't sure what was in the water, but everyone seemed to suddenly want to move house, and I'd been flooded with mortgage appointments, financial planning meetings, emails, and phone calls. December was looming large on the calendar with Christmas just over six weeks away, and the words *We'd like to get this sorted before Christmas* were now playing on a loop in my brain.

No matter how much I explained to people that waiting times were waiting times and *everyone* was busy, I'd still been subjected to several irate calls from various buyers. One man had even demanded I ring the bank every hour to see where his application was, and another wanted me to physically drive to their solicitor's office in Norwich to see where their contracts were despite the fact that part of the process had nothing to do with me. By Wednesday, I was debating asking Eli to screen my calls in return for cocktails and the opportunity to be snarky to people. He'd have a wonderful time politely telling people to get fucked, and I'd get some space to think. But I wasn't sure Holly would go for it.

I needed to have a conversation with her anyway. Eli had said *It's a Drag!* was looking for sponsors, and Holly was always talking about how she liked the company to raise money for charity. I had my suspicions Holly's motivations were less altruistic and more appearance driven, but this would be a good opportunity for her to put her money where her mouth was. Especially as the charities the competition was supporting this year weren't the type Holly usually suggested we fundraise for.

Shaking my head, I reached for the mug on my desk then sighed. It was mostly empty except for some cold, congealing coffee dregs stuck at the bottom. I only drank coffee when I needed an extra caffeine hit, and it had been one of those days. I wasn't even sure what time it was. I glanced down at the clock on my monitor then blinked several times. It was twenty past eight.

Where the fuck had the day gone? And why the hell was I still at the office?

I groaned, stretching my arms out and feeling all the muscles in my torso pull and strain. I'd clearly been sitting in one position for too long. It was definitely too late for more coffee. The dogs were going to go mad when I got home, and I felt a pang of guilt because this was far too late to leave them. It didn't happen very often, but once was still too much for my liking. I really needed to get things in order so if I had things I had to finish, I could take them home and do them there. At least then I could sit on the sofa with Indy and Solo snoring beside me.

Reaching for my phone, I saw a couple of different message threads, first from my sister and then from Eli.

ALEXIS *I assume you are working late AGAIN, so I'm going to yours to feed the boys.*
ALEXIS *I'm taking this bag of Peanut M&Ms out of the cupboard as payment.*
ALEXIS *Also, you know I can make you a home office? Your spare room would make a very nice one if we tidied it up and painted it. You could have a painting desk for your minis and another for work. Or maybe a combo one. Will come up with ideas! xx*

I chuckled to myself and muttered, "Guess I'm getting an office then." I wasn't going to argue with Alexis because she had a point. I closed the thread with my sister and opened the string of messages from Eli.

ELI *Don't forget I'm off to The Court this evening to practice x*
ELI *I'm leaving! Don't stay too late x*
ELI *Since you're not responding, I'm going to assume you are being very busy and important x*
ELI *Are you still working?? x*
TRISTAN *Sorry, lost track of time! I'm leaving now.*
ELI *Are you STILL at the office? x*
TRISTAN *Maybe?*

Eli *Stay there. I'll be ten minutes ;) x*

I frowned, wondering what he could have planned. Knowing Eli, it would either be something sweet, like stopping by to say goodnight, or it would be something dirty. I swallowed, heat flooding my chest. I'd fantasised about something happening in the office in the past, but there was a difference between fantasy and reality. My brain murmured something about this being a bad idea, but the thought was quickly squashed by more enthusiastic parts of my anatomy.

Standing up, I strode over to the door, deciding to do a quick sweep of the building just in case there was anyone else lurking. The last thing I wanted was for Eli and me to get caught. The risk was fun but only up to a certain point.

All the offices were empty, their residents having gone home a long time ago.

I went back to my office to wait, hurriedly clearing papers off the desk and shoving them into drawers—I'd sort them in the morning—and closing the blinds over the window. I'd just finished when I heard the door opening downstairs, and Eli locking it behind him. My heart kicked up a notch, thundering in my chest like a drum and bass line. Was I really considering this? Technically, Eli hadn't suggested anything. It was my brain that had gone straight to office sex. I wanted it though. Even if it was just a quick, messy blow job with me half-under the desk and Eli sitting in my office chair, his fingers pulling my hair as he fucked my face.

My cock throbbed and started to fill, straining against the confines of my underwear and my suit trousers.

I heard feet on the stairs. I wasn't sure what to do. Was I supposed to be waiting for him? Would it look odd if I stood? God, why did I have to be so fucking awkward? My office door was still open where I'd rushed back inside after my sweep of the building, and I turned from my spot by my desk to see Eli at the top of the stairs. He was wearing his shearling jacket and ripped jeans tucked into a pair of old Nikes. His artfully styled curls were windswept, his face was pink from the brisk wind that had blown in this week, and his customary wry smile curled across his lips when he saw me.

"Tut, tut, Mr. Rose," he said, strolling towards me and pushing the door shut behind him. "Working so late." He leant against the door until it clicked, then flicked the lock across with one hand all without taking his eyes off me. "What am I going to do with you?"

I tried to school my face into a serious expression, but I couldn't stop myself from grinning wildly. It had only been a couple of hours since I'd last seen him, but it felt like forever. "I don't know," I said. "But we are here all by ourselves."

"Oh, are we?" Eli walked across to me, his fingers reaching out to wrap themselves around my tie and tug me close until we were nose to nose. "How convenient."

"It's a miracle." I let my lips brush against his. A spark jumped across our skin. Whatever resistance either of us had been planning to put up disappeared in a puff of smoke.

Eli's kiss was fierce, his tongue pushing into my mouth and taking. His fingers fisted the front of my shirt while his other hand tightened around my tie, keeping me close. I loved it when he did this, when he put me wherever he wanted me and took what he needed. Eli stepped towards me, moving me backwards one step at a time until I found myself pushed up against the desk. I groaned into his mouth as he pressed against me. My cock strained against the painfully tight confines of my trousers. I gasped, breaking the kiss as Eli ran his hand down my chest to slowly rub my erection through the material.

"Look at you," he said. "So desperate for me already. It's a good thing I stopped on my way to get supplies."

"You stopped?" I stared at him. Eli reached into his coat pocket and pulled out a small bottle of lube.

"Good thing Tesco is open late. I can't keep you like this." He smirked, setting the bottle down on the desk and shrugging off his coat. "Although you do look so cute when you're needy. Like you need my cock but also like you're afraid I won't let you come." I swallowed. "Don't worry. I will…"

"Thank you," I said, even though I was sure there was a "but" at the end of Eli's sentence. I didn't want to know what it was. Eli palmed himself through his jeans.

"Undo your trousers, then bend over the desk." His voice was firm, and his eyes were full of heat as he watched me. I hurriedly did as I was told, unbuttoning my trousers then turning to bend over. I was glad I'd cleared my desk now. Anticipation flooded my body, heightening every sensation. I heard the sounds of a zipper being lowered and the soft slap of skin on skin.

I groaned, glancing over my shoulder to see him jerking himself as he watched me. Eli saw me staring and winked.

"Do you want my cock?" he asked, stroking it slowly. "Want me to fuck you?"

"Yes." I nodded. "I want it."

"Are you sure? You don't sound sure."

"Please, Eli. I need it. I need you inside me." I bit back a moan as my fantasies resurged. "I... I've thought about this for so long."

"Oh?" He grinned. "Have you been thinking about me fucking you like this? Bending you over your desk and giving you my cock, making you come all over the surface so whenever you're here you think about me." He stepped closer, his hand twisting my head towards him as his cock pressed into my ass. "Is that what you want?"

"Y-yes, please." Heat pooled in my muscles, and I wondered if Eli had thought about this as well. He leant forward and kissed me again, nipping at my lip. Then he shoved me down onto the desk and yanked my trousers and boxers down to expose my ass. I moaned at the sudden roughness and then again when Eli smacked my ass twice —not hard but enough to send a fresh spark of pleasure through my nerves. I twisted my head slightly, watching him pick up the lube. I heard a click and felt a cold drizzle of wetness between my cheeks. Eli pressed his fingers to my hole, pushing two inside me and making me squirm. The burn was intense, but it faded quickly. Eli worked his fingers in and out until I was a writhing mess. My own hands tried to find some purchase on the smooth desk surface, but all I could do was grasp the far side and cling on for dear life.

Then I felt the blunt press of Eli's cock against my hole.

"Are you ready?" he asked. "Still want it?"

I wanted to tell him to stop fucking teasing me, but I knew if I said that he'd just draw it out even further. "Yes, yes… Please, Eli, fuck me!"

His fingers gripped my hip, and I moaned as he pushed inside me. It felt like I had barely any time to breathe before Eli started to move. His thrusts were slow at first—slow and deliberate and teasing—until all I could do was beg for more, looking wildly over my shoulder at his heated gaze and plush, smirking mouth. He knew exactly what he was doing to me, and I both loved and hated it. I needed more, but I wasn't going to get it until Eli decided to give it to me. It was almost like I was a toy, a warm hole for him to use, and that thought made my cock leak against the desk. I loved it when he used me like this.

"Fuck, your ass feels so good," Eli said, slamming his cock deep inside me. "You look so fucking perfect bent over for me. Dreamt about fucking you like this!"

"Y-yeah?"

"Fuck. Yes." He groaned, his fingers tightening on my hips. "Except you usually have a tie in your mouth and the office is busy."

I laughed breathlessly. "Yes to the first part. No to the second."

"That's fair enough." He slowed his thrusts for a

moment, teasing me. "I'd never want you to feel uncomfortable."

Something swelled in my chest, hot and sweet. Then Eli reached around to start jacking my cock, and my thoughts fell away.

"I want you to come for me," he said. "I want you to paint the desk with your cum." He gripped the back of my shirt, pulling me half-up. "Stroke your cock, Tristan. Make a mess for me."

I groaned, nodding my head as I reached for my cock. I began to stroke myself hard and fast as Eli fucked me, pleasure burning under my skin. My orgasm caught me by surprise, hitting me with the force of a rocket as I came, shooting hot cum all over my desk. I gasped out Eli's name, my ass tightening around his dick. Eli swore, pounding into me until he grunted out his release. I knew I'd be going home full of his cum, and a shiver of delight ran down my spine.

He pulled out of me slowly, and I straightened, feeling a tiny trickle of cum leak out of me. I tried to find the words to summarise how I felt. I wasn't sure I knew any, though, since my grasp of the English language seemed to have ceased to exist. Eli grinned at me, looking at the streaks of cum on the desk. He moved beside me and ran his fingers through the mess, scooping some up and holding his fingers out to me.

I leant forward and wrapped my lips around them, sucking my cum off his skin. Eli's eyes flared. He surged forward and kissed me, thrusting his tongue against mine as if he wanted to taste me. I groaned, my spent cock twitching.

"Fuck, you're sexy," Eli murmured.

"Thanks." I grinned then sighed, a perfect post-orgasm high making me feel more relaxed than I had all week. "What are you doing now?"

"Hmmm," Eli said, kissing me again. "I don't think I have any plans."

"Do you want to come back to mine?"

"Is that an invitation for round two?"

I laughed. "I mean, it wasn't… but I…"

"Wouldn't say no?" Eli raised an eyebrow. I felt my face heat, then nodded. "Let's do that then."

I reached for my trousers, then glanced at the mess all over the desk and sighed. "Probably should clean that up first though… y'know, so I don't have to scrub it off in the morning or give the cleaner a heart attack."

"Probably best." Eli laughed. "Where the fuck are your tissues?"

CHAPTER TWENTY-SIX

Eli

"How about this one?" Orlando asked, leaning over the back of the sofa and thrusting his iPad under my nose, gesturing at the cosplay wig in the middle of the screen. "That would be cute."

I hummed, zooming in on the picture. It was a long, Lolita-style wig in a pretty grey gradient with a side-swept fringe. It probably wouldn't be too hard to style into what I wanted, and it was only twenty-four pounds, which was definitely a bonus.

"Or this one?" Orlando leant over my shoulder and tapped the screen a couple of times, pulling up a black and white wig with long curls and various additional styling pieces that could be attached. "That's really cute. Very you."

"Is it? I'm wondering if it looks more E-girl than noughties emo," I said, scrolling through the pictures and pulling at my lip. This was turning out to be much harder than I'd anticipated. I'd decided I needed a new wig for *It's a Drag!* but nothing I'd found so far was calling my name. I'd asked Orlando for some suggestions, and he'd taken to the task with gusto, but nothing he'd found was appealing either. Maybe I was just being too picky.

"I can see that," Orlando said, taking back the iPad and climbing over the back of the sofa. I lifted my pile of blankets so he could slide in next to me. "Don't worry. We'll find something."

"You sure? Maybe I should just stick with what I've got."

"Nope! I'm finding you a new one." He began scrolling, giving the screen a piercing stare. "What are you going to wear?"

I hadn't even gotten that far yet. The past two weeks I'd been attempting to write and perfect a new routine, which meant I spent most of my time staring at blank pieces of paper, scrolling endlessly through YouTube, and walking about on The Court's empty stage, moaning to Phil and hoping inspiration would strike. The routine only had to be five minutes long at most, but I still had nothing. Every time I attempted to be funny, it fell flatter than a pancake. My ability to write parodies had apparently gone the way of the dodo, and I seemed to have forgotten the lyrics to every song ever written.

I'd never had a case of nerves so bad, and it was starting to gnaw away at me like an insidious rodent. What if I couldn't think of anything? It was seventeen days until the competition, and I was supposed to turn my music in no later than five days beforehand. At this rate, I was fucked and not in a fun way.

"Don't know," I said, finally answering Orlando's question. "Haven't gotten that far yet either, babe."

I was trying to play it off as nonchalant, but I'd evidently failed when I found myself being kicked in the shin. "Ow!"

"That didn't hurt." He rolled his eyes. "Stop being melodramatic."

"Can't. It's my livelihood."

Orlando huffed. "Don't be a banana! Why haven't you thought about your outfit yet? What if you need to order something?"

"That's why there's next day shipping," I said, brushing him off. "And there's always the goth shop in town."

"Don't avoid the question." He jabbed me in the ribs. "Talk to me!"

"I am." I grinned, knowing I was winding him up. His face wrinkled cutely as his lips formed into his customary pout. "Don't pout at me. It won't work." Orlando made a soft, sad noise like a distressed kitten. I sighed. "Fine. I'm just stressed as fuck! I still haven't gotten a routine together, and I have no fucking clue what I'm doing! I've got seventeen days, babe. How the hell can I pick a fucking wig when I can't even pick a fucking song to sing?"

"It's okay," Orlando said, leaning against me. "You'll find something. And I bet half the reason you can't focus is because you're overthinking it. I know you. You'll want it to be perfect and the best thing they've ever seen, but that's not possible." He looked up at me and smiled. "Remember what the Boulet's say: Drag is art, and art is subjective. Not everyone is going to love you, and that's okay. Stop trying to be perfect, and just be you. A messy, bitchy, emo queen in ripped tights and bad make-up."

"Hey! That make-up is expensive." He was right though. I was overthinking it. I had been all along. Tristan had known it to. He'd even warned me as such when I'd gotten in. But I'd gone from thinking I needed to be someone I wasn't to thinking I had to be the perfect version of myself. Only that didn't exist; there was no perfect Bitch Fit. Bitch was messy, trashy, and funny. Perfect wasn't a word that belonged anywhere near her. I didn't need to sculpt a picture-perfect routine for her because there wasn't ever going to be one. That concept was a myth. All I could do was put together something that made *me* happy, something that encapsulated who Bitch Fit was, something I wanted to perform.

Something *fun*.

"What are you thinking?" Orlando asked, clearly realising I'd drifted away from the conversation.

"I'm thinking I need a pen, a piece of paper, and Spotify." I grinned, an idea beginning to form from the nebulous swirls in my brain. "And I think I want that one." I pointed to one of the wigs in the top row of the page Orlando had open.

"This one?" He tapped the image. I nodded.

"Yep. It's one hundred percent me."

· · ·

The next morning, I felt much more composed. I was completely exhausted from staying up until two in the morning, scrawling all over my notebook and listening to clips on Spotify until I was so tired I could see colours, but I felt a lot better about the whole routine situation.

Tristan found me making coffee. He put his arm around my waist and pressed a kiss to the side of my head. "Good morning," he said. "You look very handsome today."

"Thank you." I smiled at him, hitting the button on the machine and breathing in the heavenly scent of black coffee. "Orlando dressed me today because I overslept. He threw clothes at me and shooed me out the door like I was late for school."

Tristan laughed, flicking the kettle on. "I like his choices."

"So do I," I said, looking down at the shirt, tie, and waistcoat combination. "He has good taste."

I picked up my now full mug and sipped, making a happy humming noise. It was so good I just wanted to sink into it and stay there. Or maybe just inject it straight into my veins.

"Did you stay up late then?" Tristan asked, starting to make his morning cup of tea. If he was down here already, it probably meant he had a string of appointments and meetings lined up. I made a mental note to start prepping things for the meeting room as soon as I was done with my coffee. It would save me a job later.

"Yeah. I had a breakthrough about the routine, so I was up until two making notes."

"That's good. The breakthrough part, not the staying up late part."

"I do fine at the weekends," I said.

"Yes, but then you can sleep until noon," Tristan said. I hummed to myself but had to admit he had a point.

"I'm just nervous, I guess. I really want it to go well."

"It's going to. You're going to be amazing." He smiled at me, radiating that firm, quiet confidence that always made it feel true. "And if you're near the end of the night, the audience will be wankered anyway, so it won't really matter what you do as long as you're vaguely memorable."

I burst out laughing, my body shaking, and I had to put my mug down before I spilt coffee all over the floor.

"You sound happy this morning, Eli," Holly said, appearing in the doorway with a small smile on her face. She and Andrew had a coffee machine of their own, so it was unusual to see her in the break room.

"I am." I choked down the rest of my laughter and attempted to be a professional. "How're you today?"

"I'm good. I was wondering if I could have a word?"

"Of course," I said, picking up my coffee and raising my eyebrow at Tristan as I followed Holly out of the kitchen. Tristan shrugged, looking just as confused as I felt. Usually, if Holly wanted something, she sent me an email. I wondered if I'd made a mistake or if Alistair had ratted me out for my comments on Halloween.

Holly led me into the meeting room, gesturing for me to have a seat.

"Everything okay?" I asked, unable to stop myself from opening my mouth as I pulled out one of the smart, padded chairs around the small meeting table. Holly smiled as she sat down opposite me.

"Yes, don't worry. There's no need to panic," she said. "Tristan tells me that outside of the office you're a drag queen?"

"Yes." I answered slowly, the wheels in my head starting to spin very fast.

"And he tells me you're competing at a local competition in December?"

"Yes… *It's a Drag!*. It's not huge, but it's lots of fun, kicks off the festive season, and raises money for charity."

Holly nodded. "Tristan mentioned that too. It was actually why he brought it up to me in the first place."

I sipped my coffee and frowned. There was a detail missing here that would make this whole conversation make sense, but I didn't have it. I nodded politely, hoping Holly would continue her explanation.

"One thing we've always tried to do here is to raise money for the local community and support local charities," Holly said. "It's why we do our in-house charity fundraising programme." I nodded again. I'd already done some organisational bits for a luxury Christmas raffle we were running. The sort of thing where the prizes were worth hundreds of pounds at a minimum.

"Well, Tristan said this competition is looking for sponsorships and donations, and he told me a little bit about the charities involved," Holly continued. "I'll admit, they're not usually ones we'd donate to, and that's an oversight on my part. I'm going to be looking at how we can diversify the charities we give to so we support our whole community, not just parts of it. And as part of that, I wanted to let you know I've been in touch with the organisers for *It's a Drag!* and have agreed Green & Wodehouse will be one of this year's sponsors. We'll also be making a one-thousand-pound donation to each charity."

I stared at her, momentarily stunned. Of all the things I'd expected Holly to say, this had not been one of them. It hadn't even been anywhere close to the suggestions I'd have made. I'd only been working at Green & Wodehouse for three months, and my contract was only for a year at the most. It wasn't as if she had any obligation to do anything like this at all. It made no sense, but it was still happening.

"Wow," I said finally. "That's amazing. Thank you. That's incredibly generous of you."

"You're welcome. And it's not really me you have to thank. Tristan made some very good points."

Okay, so maybe some of her motivation was guilt related but still. Giving away several thousand pounds was a good way to start making up for it. The fact that Tristan had convinced her was like the cherry on top. He hadn't been ashamed of me or what I did, and he hadn't wanted to pretend a huge part of my life only existed on the weekends when nobody we knew would see. He was proud of me, and he wanted people to know that.

And that fact right there was the reason I loved him.

Tristan wanted me just the way I was. He wasn't going to make me hide parts of myself away; he was going to show them to the world. Having a supportive partner was something I'd dreamt about for so long, and here he was in the form of soft, sweet Tristan Rose. That meant more to me than anything else, and yet somehow I still hadn't told him how I felt because I hadn't been able to find the words. I didn't think there *were* words to convey my feelings, but I'd have to try and find some because Tristan needed to know just how amazing he was. And just how much I loved him.

"He's good at that," I said.

"He really is." Holly smiled at me, letting the moment hang in the air. Then her expression turned business-like, and I knew we were headed back to reality. "So, Eli, while I've got you here, shall we quickly do your three-month performance review?"

CHAPTER TWENTY-SEVEN

DECEMBER

Eli

"Shit, shit, bugger, arse, bollocking fucking shit!" I stared at the shoe in my hand, which was currently in two pieces, the heel snapped clean off. Shoes were not supposed to be in two pieces! This was what I got for buying piece of shit knock-off Pleasers and spray-painting them more times than I could count.

"What's wrong?" Tristan stuck his head around my bedroom door. I held out the pieces of shoe. "Bugger."

"My sentiments exactly." I threw the pieces of shoe onto the bed. I was supposed to be packing for *It's a Drag!* tomorrow night because, even though Nottingham was only an hour or so away, Tristan had insisted on getting us a hotel room for Saturday night. He'd said it was so I'd have somewhere nice to get ready and a space to decompress afterwards, and we wouldn't have to drive home late at night. Plus, it meant we could drink if we wanted to, and I was definitely going to need it. Now, though, I was going to spend the next hour freaking out over shoe choices. Or at least spray painting my other pair and hoping they held.

"Just breathe," Tristan said, coming up behind me and wrapping his arms around my torso. He pressed a kiss to the back of my neck. "It's going to be okay. Will your other pair do?"

"They'll have to."

"Do you need to wear heels?" He kissed my neck again, and I melted against him. That was definitely my weak spot.

"I mean, I don't have to, but I want to." I sighed. I'd been trying out wearing some of my old, battered Converse at The Court, and while it had done wonders for my foot pain at the end of the night, this was an occasion that called for heels. "I know they're uncomfortable as fuck, but they make me feel good. Powerful. Like I'm in full Bitch mode."

"Okay then, heels it is." Tristan was quiet for a second, trailing kisses down my shoulder. My worries suddenly began to feel less significant. This was an excellent distraction technique. "We'll fix the problem in the morning before we leave."

"But—" That definitely wouldn't give me enough time to spray-paint them black and white from the luminous green they currently were.

Tristan turned me in his arms, bringing one hand up to cup my jaw. He smiled softly at me, his stormy eyes full of emotion. "Trust me," he said. "I promise it'll be fine."

I believed him.

"Okay."

He kissed me softly, pressing his tongue into my mouth. My fingers found the front of his shirt, gripping the material tightly. Tristan moaned softly into the kiss. "Let me take care of you," he whispered. "Please."

"Okay."

Tristan sank to his knees.

The next morning, after more sleep than I'd anticipated, I found myself being woken up to soft kisses and a tray of coffee and pastries. I blinked several times, trying to get my head around what I was seeing because I was pretty sure my eyes were lying to me. I didn't think anyone had ever brought me breakfast in bed.

"Good morning," Tristan said, kissing the top of my head. He was already dressed and looked remarkably chipper. "I got you some breakfast, and once you're finished, we just need to nip out before we leave."

"We do?" I looked up at him and then down at the tray Tristan had slid onto the bed next to me. The croissants were warm as were the pain au chocolat. I wondered if he could be any more perfect. "Where?"

"You'll see." He grinned at me, then reached for one of the pain au chocolat.

"Hey! I thought those were mine."

"This one is payment for services rendered."

"I didn't realise I had to pay for breakfast in my own house," I said, raising an eyebrow and shuffling into a better sitting position, propping myself against the pillows like a Victorian lady of leisure. Tristan laughed.

"I can take it away if you want."

"Don't touch my breakfast." I picked up the tray and balanced it on my lap. There was even coffee in a cafetiere. I didn't think I owned one. "I was just expressing my disbelief." I poured myself some of the coffee before picking up one of the pain au chocolat and biting into it. It was warm and rich and buttery and chocolaty and delicious, and I needed a whole plate of them. Which luckily I had. Minus one.

"I'm sorry." He smirked. "Next time you can pay another way."

"Cheeky brat," I said, sipping my coffee.

"You sound like an old man."

I snorted. "I'm definitely becoming one."

"When are you thirty?" Tristan laughed.

"Next year. End of July. I want to have a big party, and the whole theme is going to be 'Funeral for my Youth'. Everyone has to wear black and look fabulous. Like Met Gala fabulous. But, like, budget Met Gala." I reached for a croissant, noting the little scoops of butter and jam Tristan had put on a small plate.

"I can't wait," he said. "I'll make sure I'm suitably dressed for the occasion. Maybe I'll even get a new suit."

"I'm going to insist upon it." I grinned. There was something about the fact Tristan expected us to be together next year and was talking so casually about getting a new suit that made my heart want to burst with joy. It was like it was a given nothing was going to change between now and then.

We chatted while I finished my breakfast and my coffee,

then Tristan took the tray away to wash up, and I got dressed. December had descended upon us and brought unseasonably cold weather, at least for the UK, so I wrapped myself up in several layers before we left, pulling an old My Chemical Romance beanie over my freshly trimmed hair. Tristan looked very smart in his dark peacoat with a red scarf wrapped around his neck and black gloves. We made a delightfully odd pair as we walked hand in hand towards Lincoln High Street.

"So where are we going then?" I asked as we skirted through the crowds of Christmas shoppers.

"You'll see."

"You're really not going to tell me, are you?"

"Nope." Tristan looked down at me and grinned. "We're nearly there anyway."

He steered me towards the Cornhill area, past the doughnut shop that did the most amazing homemade creations which always made me drool whenever I saw them on Instagram. I glanced at the sign, wondering whether we'd have time to stop and get one. Tristan must have seen me looking because he squeezed my fingers. "Let's stop on the way back and get some to take with us."

"Pastries and doughnuts? Do you want me to have a sugar rush?"

"You deserve it. And you can always save it until this evening."

"Fuck no. I'm eating it before then. I want to be able to savour it and not worry about it repeating on me." I hadn't decided if I was nervous or not, and neither had my body. So far, my brain seemed to be thinking it was just another show, and I wanted it to stay that way. I looked at the shops around us, and right before we reached it, I twigged where Tristan was taking me. Robot Monkey, Lincoln's very own alternative store.

Once upon a time, there'd been a huge shop in town called Blue Banana, but it had closed when the company had decided to shrink their operations. I'd loved that shop as a teenager and had been almost bereft when it had closed. A couple of years ago, it had been replaced by something new. The owner couldn't have been much older than me, and I wondered if he'd opened it because he'd also had fond memories of browsing band hoodies and printed tees with cartoon slogans and gazing longingly at the wall of Docs and Vans, wishing they didn't cost so much.

"Here we go," said Tristan, pushing the door open and pulling me into the warmth. Before I could say anything, he dragged me over to the wall of shoes, which included a wide variety of sky-high Mary Janes with cute heart cut outs, stilettos, and those knee-high platform boots with a million buckles I'd secretly lusted after for years. "Pick some new shoes."

"What?" I stared at him and then back at the shoes, my face wrinkling in confusion.

"You said you wanted to wear heels today, but it's too late to order some, and you'll never get the others painted in time. So let's get you some new ones. My treat." He squeezed my hand, his expression a mix of giddy excitement and extreme fondness. "Please," he said, quieter this time. "You do so much for me, and I'm so proud of you. Let me treat you. It's the least I can do."

"A-are you sure?" It sounded unreal, and Tristan did just as much for me. I didn't really think I'd done anything for him except bring him out of his shell a little.

"Positive. Anything you want. I want you to feel like the true bitch you are when you're on stage tonight."

"You are amazing," I said, leaning up to give him a kiss. "Truly, Tristan Rose. I've never met anyone like you." Tristan flushed. I'd forgotten how cute he looked when he was embarrassed. "Okay. Let's pick some shoes!"

I began to peruse the shelves, picking up a couple of pairs of cute Mary Janes and some ankle boots and turning them over in my hands. I'd always considered myself lucky in that, for a man, I had quite small feet. They were only a size nine, and these days most women's shoes went up that far, so as long as they had some in stock, I'd be fine. I dismissed the stilettos because the angle for my foot was too steep, and I wouldn't be able to walk in them. My normal shoes were tall, but they had platforms so my feet were at a smaller incline inside them. They were still seven inches off the floor, but once I'd learnt to walk in platforms and realised I couldn't rely on feeling the ground underneath me, they were pretty easy to wear. At least in my opinion.

"Can I help you?" A pretty person with mermaid hair, blue lipstick, and a variety of piercings appeared from between the racks of dresses. They were wearing a very cute black dress with lace trim that was giving me the most gorgeous gothic Lolita vibes. "Do you want to try anything on?"

"Perfect timing," I said, beaming at them. "Do you have

these in a nine? And those as well? Oooh, and these." I pointed at three different pairs. My eyes lingered on a pair of the taller boots that were patent, knee-high platforms with silver buckles and strapping running across the front. I'd always wanted a pair like them, but they were very expensive, and even though Tristan had offered to pay, I didn't want to take advantage of him.

"Only those three?" Tristan asked. "You don't want to try any of those boots?"

"No, it's fine." I tore my eyes away from them. "They're too…" I tried to think of the right word or at least one that wasn't *expensive*.

"I think you should," Tristan said. He pointed at the pair I'd been gazing at. "Those?"

"Er…"

"He'd like to try those boots too, please, if you have them in a nine," Tristan said to the salesperson. They smiled, looking at us with an almost adoring expression.

"I'll see what we've got! Take a seat. I'll be back in a minute." They disappeared off through the racks of clothing towards the counter.

"Do you need any clothes or anything else while we're here?" Tristan asked, walking over to one of the racks and casually examining some of the dresses. "I don't mind if you want one."

"I'm fine. I'm going to wear one of my old favourites because it's comfortable. It fits, and I know I'm not going to flash the audience while I'm wearing it." Tristan laughed.

"That makes sense."

I'd debated getting something new, but in the end, I

wanted something I felt comfortable in. I didn't want to buy something new and find it didn't fit or rode up when I walked. Spending my whole performance tugging my dress over my ass wasn't the vibe I was going for.

"Thanks for this," I said, reaching my hand out and taking Tristan's. "You really are too sweet."

"Don't thank me yet. We have to make sure they fit first."

I opened my mouth to say something, but the sales-person reappeared, carrying a stack of boxes so high they had to peer around them. "Okay," they said, slowly lowering the boxes onto the nearby padded bench. "I've got the knee-high boots and two of the pairs you wanted. We didn't have the one with the purple hearts, but we do have a really cute pair of ankle boots that we literally just got in, so I brought you those to try instead." They pointed at the bench where they'd left some room for me to perch. "Are you going to be wearing socks under them or tights?"

"Tights," I said, sliding off the old pair of Docs I'd been wearing. "Bugger, I should have brought some with me."

"Don't worry. I brought you some pop socks just in case." They handed me a pair of thin, nylon socks. "I'm River, by the way," they said.

"I'm Eli. And this is Tristan, who has graciously offered to help me buy new shoes since I broke mine."

"Oh no! Broken shoes are the worst! But that is very sweet."

I nodded. "It really is. And in return, I'll buy him a doughnut." River laughed.

"What he's not telling you," Tristan said with a mischievous grin from over River's shoulder, "is that he's performing tonight and currently has no shoes to wear."

"Ooooh, what do you do?" River looked me up and down. "Drag queen?" A look of recognition spread over their face. "Oh my God, you're Bitch Fit, right? My friends and I love you! We all follow you on Instagram. Your Halloween show was amazing!" They flushed. "Shit, I'm sorry. You're here for shoes, not for me to fawn over you like an idiot. Where would you like to start?"

"Thank you," I said, giving them my biggest smile. I didn't meet a ton of fans outside of drag, and whenever I did, I was slightly bowled over by it. "That's very sweet of you. Can I start with the knee-high ones please? They look like the trickiest, so let's do those first." I stared at them. Then another thought popped into my head, and I glanced down at the jeans I was wearing. "Shit. I'm going to be wearing a dress tonight."

"I've got you," River said.

Ten minutes later, in a borrowed skirt and a cheap pair of tights, I slid the knee-high boots onto my feet. They had a zip in the back which made them easier to put on, which was a plus, but they pulled a little around the calf and were heavier than I'd expected. I pursed my lips and stood, walking up and down a few times and examining myself in the mirror. I did look hot. And the boots were amazing. But they weren't quite right. Not for tonight.

"Well?" Tristan asked.

"Not these." I sat down, explaining my thoughts to him. "Next."

The next pair of shoes were a pretty pair of platform

Mary Janes with two bows and a row of little silver studs across the straps. They were cute and definitely a solid choice. After that was a similar pair, only they had a simple T-strap fastening, and the sides had little white stars cut out. I liked them, and the stars were nice, but a niggling voice in my head said they'd stain very quickly, and if I was getting expensive shoes, I wanted ones that would last.

"Okay," River said, opening the last box they'd brought out. "These are the ones we just got in. I'm not sure if you'll like them, but I thought they might fit the vibe you were going for."

River handed me the box, and I gasped. It was a pair of wedge ankle boots with laces up the front and spiked, silver studs decorating the back of the heel. There were two straps running around the boot, each covered in round studs that connected to a large pentagram that sat across the top of the laces, and there were additional chains draped around the side, connected to a loop at the back that were hung with a collection of gothic charms. They were definitely extra as fuck, and I loved them.

"Oh my God," I muttered, lifting them out of the box. "These are amazing!" They had a zip on the inside, which I undid before putting them on the ground and sliding my foot inside. I did them up, took a deep breath, and stood.

"Wow," Tristan said. "They're perfect."

I grinned, walking a few steps to the mirror and examining my reflection. I looked hot as fuck.

The boots were comfy and sturdy, and I didn't suddenly feel like I was going to lurch off to the side or fall over. They were tall but not enormous. I actually felt like I could bounce around in these very comfortably for the whole evening, unlike my normal heels which I usually wanted to remove in ten minutes.

"These," I said, walking over to Tristan. They still made me a little taller than him, which made something hot flare inside me.

"Agreed." He kissed me gently. "Those."

CHAPTER TWENTY-EIGHT

Tristan

THE BALLROOM of the Jewel Hotel and Spa on the edge of Nottingham had been completely decked out for the evening to the point it was almost unrecognisable as the normal beige space these rooms always were.

There were at least twenty round tables spread across the room, covered in crisp white tablecloths with fishbowl centre pieces filled with twinkling fairy lights and eight chairs tucked around each. The walls were hung with dark, gauzy cloths, and there was a large stage set up at the front with a wide runway protruding from the front. At one side of the stage, on a platform, was a judges table that was covered in a glittering black cloth with large golden stars stuck to the front. There'd even been a lighting rig erected, and colourful disco lights rotated slowly around the ballroom, which was rapidly filling with people.

Through two large sets of double doors, I could see into the smaller adjoining room where there was a table set up for people to vote for the winner and a bar where attendees could grab drinks.

The voting was done through the purchase of tickets that people would then be able to pop into the performer's corresponding voting box. All the money was going to charity. There was already someone with a laptop sitting at the table, periodically emptying the boxes and tallying up the votes on what I assumed was a large spreadsheet. You could also vote online through the website in a similar system. Whoever had built it was pretty clever.

From where I stood, I saw a crowd at least three deep around the bar, and the hotel staff were practically throwing drinks across the counter. I didn't think it was going to be as busy as it was, but it made me so happy to see this level of support for the local drag community. Everyone was dressed to the nines, and I noticed a few drag artists mingling with the crowd. I assumed they were either guest performers or previous winners.

"There you are! I thought I might find you lurking here. Are you nervous?" Lewis asked, appearing at my side and snapping me out of my musing. He was clutching several bottles of wine.

"A little," I said. "More so now that Eli's backstage."

We had a room upstairs where I'd spent most of the afternoon trying to relax while Eli was at the dress rehearsal. When he'd come back, I'd forced some room service sandwiches into him before he started getting ready, and about an hour ago, he'd come back down to finish his last few preparations backstage. I'd used the last hour to get ready and then found myself pacing up and down nervously until Lewis and company had accosted me. It seemed like I'd stumbled into this little interconnected network of friends and family, but they'd all welcomed me in with drinks and hugs and open arms.

"He's going to be great." Lewis smiled at me reassuringly. "Do you want a glass of wine? That might help."

"Okay. Sure."

"Jules is getting a couple more bottles for the other tables," he said as I followed him to the far side of the room. When Lewis had spread the news that Eli was in the final, all his friends had decided to make a group outing of it. But when combined with the entirety of Eli's family, Orlando and his men, plus Pamela from the office, it meant there were twenty-four of us. We'd ended up buying tickets for three tables and requested they all be next to each other.

Which in hindsight might not have been a good thing, simply because I could already see things getting very raucous. It was like we'd commandeered an entire corner of the ballroom.

"I found him," Lewis said, putting the extra bottles of wine on one of the tables. "He was pacing again."

"It's going to be fine," Edward, who looked resplendent in blue and silver, said. "If anyone can handle it, it's Eli."

"Exactly," Jules said as she appeared behind us with more wine, this time for the family table. She was wearing a well-tailored suit with an open-collared shirt, her dark-blonde hair slicked back on top and a fresh fade on the sides. "He's gonna be fine." She grinned at me. "And if not, I'm sure you can kiss it better."

"I didn't need to hear that," muttered Richard, taking a bottle of red wine from Jules. Ruby laughed.

"You'll live." Ruby looked around the ballroom, a wild smile on her face. "I'm so excited! I've never been to anything like this before."

"You'll have to come to The Court one day," I said, taking the glass of wine Lewis passed me. "You'll love it."

"I need to come too," said another voice from behind Richard. "I need a holiday." His face was familiar, but I hadn't seen him in a long time. A dark beard dusted his jaw, and he had dark eyes under thick eyebrows. He was the spitting image of a man I'd only seen in an old photo on the family mantelpiece. It was the ever-elusive Oscar.

"Piss off. Your entire life is a fucking holiday," Jules said. "You just spent a fucking month in New Zealand."

Oscar smiled, but it didn't quite reach his eyes. I wondered if any of the others noticed. "I know, which makes coming home a holiday."

"She's just jealous," Lewis said. "She wants to go to Ibiza and look at cute girls in bikinis."

"Santorini. And don't be a little shit." Jules poked him in the ribs.

"Look, if you want cute girls there are definitely some here that are looking at you." Lewis grinned. "Just stop gawking and ask them if you can buy them all a drink."

"Fuck off."

The conversation turned to light family bickering, and I grinned as I watched them. It was clear they all loved each other. Richard seemed to be making more of an effort as well, and although he seemed nervous, like a fish out of water, I was pleased to see him trying.

At the third table, I saw Orlando, looking very dapper in pastel blue, chatting away with Pamela. Beside him were his two boyfriends, Charles and Jude, who were talking to Jason. Orlando had finally introduced Eli and me to them a couple of weeks ago over dinner, which had gone better than I'd expected. Eli hadn't threatened either of them, and we'd all gotten on very well. Afterwards, Eli had been very quiet, and when I'd asked him what was wrong, he'd confessed he'd never seen Orlando so happy, and it was making him rather emotional.

More people flooded into the ballroom, and we took our seats around the tables. There wasn't a meal, and there were no set seats, which meant we could all chop and change throughout the night. I found myself sandwiched between Richard and Jules, and we turned our chairs slightly so we could all face the stage, chatting quietly between ourselves as Jules and I explained to Richard what was going to happen.

The disco lights suddenly flicked towards the stage, and the front of the room lit up like a firework. Dramatic music surged through the speakers. The room around us erupted into cheers and applause as the competition's hosts—a man in a brightly patterned suit and drag queen in a sparking red dress that was slit to the thigh—walked onto the stage.

It didn't take long for everything to get started. The

hosts bantered for a bit, then there was an opening performance from last year's winner, Rick N. Roll—who did an
amazing lip-sync routine to a Queen medley—and they
introduced the four judges and talked a bit about how
everything worked, then it was time for the first
contestant!

There were ten contestants in total, each doing a routine
that could last up to five minutes. The running order had
been randomly assigned the week before with five going
before the interval and five after. Eli was on in the second
half and had seemed pleased with his place in the drawer.

"I wouldn't have wanted to go first," he'd told me when
he'd found out. "But it does mean I'm gonna be waiting for
fucking ever. I won't be able to drink anything, or I'll spend
half my time in the fucking toilet."

The contestants in the first half varied with two stand-
outs in the form of a dancer and a comedian who'd had
everyone in stitches. One very young queen was so nervous
she barely left the back of the stage, and two others were
good but ultimately outshone by the people who came after
them. The audience was lovely though and cheered
everyone on regardless. Even the judges were kind and
constructive.

Jules and I had a bit of a muttered conversation
throughout as we sipped our drinks, and by the time the
lights came up for the interval, I realised I was starting to
feel quite tipsy. I looked down at my glass, which seemed
fuller than it should have been, then around at the table.
Most of the bottles were already empty.

"How many glasses have I had?" I asked Jules. I'd kept

putting my glass down, and clearly someone had kept refilling it. I just hadn't noticed until now.

"Not sure," she said, looking down at her own and then at the array of bottles. "Three?" She laughed. "By the time Eli comes on, the audience is going to be trashed."

As if to confirm this, Finn, Oscar, and a Scottish gentleman appeared out of the crowd with Lewis and Jay, each holding either a couple of drinks or some more bottles of wine.

"I should probably get some water after this," I said, shaking my head with a wry smile. "If I don't remember Eli's performance, I'll never live it down."

"Oh yeah, he'll hold that over you for life." Jules grinned. There was something about her words and the certainty with which she said them that made something inside me burn. Eli and I hadn't made any plans for the future; we'd been too busy to think about it. We hadn't said "I love you" either, but that didn't mean I didn't feel it. I loved Eli more than I'd ever loved anyone.

Whatever happened, I already knew it was always going to be Eli.

I got up, still mulling over the perfect weight of emotion in my chest and headed out towards the bar. It was still packed, but I managed to get a couple of jugs of water for the tables—since I was probably not the only one who'd want some—and wondered whether I should buy some raffle tickets for voting. Would it be terrible of me to drop fifty quid on votes for my boyfriend? The money was going to charity after all.

When I got back, there'd been a shuffle around in the

seating, and I ended up at another table between Lewis and Orlando, who beamed at me and took my hand, squeezing it tightly as the lights dimmed again.

"Are you ready?" Orlando asked, sounding rather breathless. "I'm so nervous I think I might die!"

"I think so," I said. "Ask me again in ten minutes." My stomach bubbled, and I began to feel a kick of anxiety. I looked around the room wondering if, by some miracle, I could spot Eli lurking. But no such luck.

The second half opened with a performance from some of the judges and the previous winners, but I was too nervous to enjoy it. I barely watched the first contestant of the half either... or the second. If I'd been kidnapped and asked, I couldn't have said a single thing about them. My knee bounced nervously, and I sipped a glass of water. I felt like I was going to be sick, and I wasn't even performing.

"Up next," said the male host, a local theatre actor, "please welcome to the stage, Bitch Fit."

The tables around me erupted in cheers and applause, and Orlando squeezed my hand so hard I thought he was going to break my fingers. My chest tightened like I'd forgotten how to breathe as Bitch Fit strutted onto the stage to strike a pose, microphone in hand. She looked incredible, radiating confidence with every step. She was wearing the new boots I'd bought her that morning with ripped fishnet tights, a skintight dress that seemed to have lacing down the side of the skirt, and an incredible new black and white wig with a jagged fringe. Her make-up was the most perfect I'd ever seen with lipstick that faded from purple into black. She looked like a noughties pop-punk emo princess come to life, and I'd never been prouder of anyone.

There was a moment of silence interspersed with a cheer from the far side of the room. Then the opening riff of My Chemical Romance's "I'm Not Okay (I Promise)" crashed through the sound system, and the crowd went wild. Bitch's face split into the biggest grin as she began to move, bouncing around the stage before she began to lip-sync, working the crowd like she was on stage in front of thousands. The song changed, kicking smoothly into Paramore's "Misery Business", then into Avril Lavigne's pop-punk classic, "Sk8er Boi", spinning dizzily into Fall Out Boy's "Dance Dance". With each change, Bitch Fit pivoted her performance, embodying every word she mouthed, drawing the crowd in and encouraging them to clap and cheer along with her. I'd known a little about what Eli had been planning, but he'd been very secretive about exactly what music he was using, saying he wanted me to experience it first-hand. And I could see why. It was incredible.

The energy in the room was electric, building to dizzying heights as we reached the end, and the music made one final change to My Chemical Romance's "Teenagers". Everyone was cheering and singing along at drunken volumes as Bitch Fit conducted from the stage, almost giddy with laughter as she struck a final pose and the song skidded to a close.

The applause was almost deafening, at least to me. Our entire corner was on their feet, screaming themselves hoarse, and I just wanted to laugh. If Eli had ever felt unsupported, I hoped he didn't now.

He and Bitch were so loved, so wanted, and so incredible.

Tears prickled in my eyes as Eli took a bow and walked offstage. I took a breath, my first in what felt like an age. Whatever happened, I knew I'd never forget tonight.

CHAPTER TWENTY-NINE

Eli

As soon as I stepped off the stage, I felt my legs buckle, and I had to sit down. I was breathless and giddy and running on pure adrenaline, which suddenly seemed to have crashed. One of the organisers handed me a bottle of water, and I sat quietly on a chair, watching the next act before I pottered back to our tiny "backstage" area, which was really just a storage cupboard that had been cleared out and converted.

Most of the other kings and queens seemed to be in good spirits since it was nearly over, and they were all chatting quietly, sipping bottles of water and picking at the tray of cupcakes we'd been left. There was a screen in the corner, showing what was happening onstage, and we could hear the music playing as the last act wrapped up.

"You okay?" asked one of the kings, Pump King, sitting down next to me and handing me a chocolate cupcake piled high with icing and sprinkles. He'd performed first in the second half and had been amazing. I'd forced myself to watch instead of pacing up and down.

"Think so," I said, blowing out another deep breath. "Fuck me. I've never been so fucking nervous."

"Tell me about it." He laughed. "You did amazing though."

"Thanks." I grinned. I was very pleased with how it had gone and the way the crowd had responded. A small part of my brain told me it was because most people were quite drunk, but another voice, which sounded oddly like Tristan's, told me it was because my routine had been fucking awesome and nobody could resist a good singalong. It hadn't been my usual mix of comedy, parody, and singing, but I'd wanted to do something fun that would get the audience involved. Plus, comedy was always tricky on people you didn't know. Although, it did seem like half the fucking room was filled with my lot.

If I hadn't known where they were when I'd stepped out, I'd have been able to fucking hear them. There was one corner of the room that made more noise than a fucking rocket launch, and when I'd looked across at them, I'd seen everyone on their feet with Tristan at the front, wearing a smile brighter than the sun. I couldn't put the feeling of seeing them all there together into words. All I knew was that it meant more to me than anything had before.

"How long until we get the results?" I asked, unwrapping my cupcake so I could eat the boring cake bit first. I always saved the icing for last.

"I think there's another quick break where they

encourage voting, and I think people are going around to the tables with buckets to collect any last-minute votes and money. So maybe twenty minutes? Thirty?"

"That's too fucking long. I think I might be dead by then." I shoved more cake into my mouth. The sugar was definitely helping. "Do you think we can go for a wander?" I wanted to head out onto the floor to see everyone. I needed to see Tristan.

"We can ask," Pump King said.

We found an organiser and asked the question, but they requested we stay backstage because it was easier than having to wrangle everyone again.

"Don't worry," she said, giving us a sympathetic smile. "It'll all be over soon. We've been counting votes all evening, and we're nearly there."

Pump King and I lurked backstage, joining in a conversation with a couple of other kings and queens I vaguely knew. My nerves were starting to kick up again, and we heard the music go on again as the hosts returned to the stage. They said a few words, then made way for a final guest performance, which I only half watched. Instead, I touched up my lipstick and tried not to pace.

"Okay," said the returning organiser. "If you all want to follow me."

I took a deep breath. Whatever happened, I was so fucking proud of myself. And there was always next year if I didn't win.

We waited at the side of the stage, and I heard the murmur of the crowd. The hosts were saying something about the amount of money raised through sponsorship, voting, and donations.

"Holy shit," said Lola Lavish, one of the queens who stood in front of me. "Are they having a laugh?"

"What did they say?" I asked. "I missed it."

"Twenty-seven grand," she said. "They raised twenty-seven fucking grand."

"What the fuck?" I probably looked like a damn goldfish with my mouth hanging open. Twenty-seven thousand pounds was an insane amount of money for a charity drag competition to raise. They probably hadn't finished tallying it all either.

A moment later, we were shepherded onto the stage to line up for the award presentation. I took a deep breath, steadying my nerves. I kept telling myself it didn't matter what happened. I was proud of myself, and that was all that really mattered. Even if I really, really wanted to win that fucking crown. I glanced out into the audience, and despite the lights, I could see my lot in their corner. I wanted to laugh because their expressions made it look like I was lining up to be executed, not waiting to find out who the winner was.

"We'll do the first five honourable mentions in no particular order," said one of the hosts. She gave us a brilliant smile. "You should all be so proud of yourselves."

The male host took a golden envelope from an organiser and began to announce the five performers who hadn't placed. The first one wasn't me, and neither was the second... or the third. With every name he announced, the ball of nerves in my chest seemed to grow hotter.

I wasn't any of the honourable mentions, which meant I'd made the top five.

Okay. I could deal with that.

Shit.

We all stepped forward, and all I could do was hope I didn't trip and fall in my lovely new shoes and break my fucking neck.

They announced fifth place.

It wasn't me.

Neither was fourth.

Fucking hell. I'd somehow made the top three. I bit the inside of my lip and glanced across at Tristan and my family. Tristan looked like he might be sick. Honestly, I felt the same. There were just three of us left on the stage now. We all stepped forward. I pictured the ending of *Miss Congeniality*, and I suddenly wanted to laugh. I hoped nobody would try to hand me an exploding crown.

"This year's top three," said the man, gesturing at us. "I think you'll all agree, these performers were spectacular." The crowd whooped and applauded. "In third place, your second runner-up is... Lola Lavish!"

Lola, who'd done a spectacular dance routine, stepped forward to collect her sash and a small bouquet of flowers, graciously waving at the crowd. I applauded. Then the realisation hit me that I was either going to win or come second.

Fuck. Fuck. Fuck. FUCK. I hadn't prepared for this. This was so much further than I'd ever expected to get.

"Are you ready?" said Pump King, who stood next to me. He reached out his hand and took mine, squeezing it.

"Fuck no," I breathed.

"Me either."

We laughed nervously together. I wondered if anyone noticed.

"The next name I announce," said the queen, "will be our winner, and this year's *It's a Drag!* champion. Good luck to both of you."

I swallowed. Thank fuck this wasn't something serious. I'd have fucking passed out by now.

"Your *It's a Drag!* winner is... Bitch Fit!"

The far corner of the room exploded, and it took me a second to figure out why. I couldn't understand why Pump King had let go of my hand and was applauding. I looked around. Everyone was cheering.

OH! HOLY SHIT! It was me. I'd won. I was the winner. Fucking Christ on a cracker.

My legs threatened to wobble as I took a step forward, noise echoing in my ears. Then I remembered my manners and pulled Pump King in for a hug, whispering how amazing he was in his ear. I walked to the front of the stage, and the drag queen placed a sash over me, then placed an enormous, glittering crown on my head. It was heavier than I was expecting. I had something similar that I'd bought last Christmas to crown the champion of the inaugural Christmas Day family NERF tournament—that I'd won— but that one was nothing compared to the one I was currently wearing. I had to remember to get some pictures.

"Congratulations," she said. "You were amazing."

"Thanks," I said. "Gotta be honest, I'm a little bit stunned."

She laughed. "It's always the way. But enjoy it." She stepped back, opening her hand and gesturing for me to walk forward down the runway.

I'd never smiled so wide as I took those steps, music ringing in my ears mixed with the noise of the crowd. As I walked down the runway, confetti canons on either side exploded, showering me in silver paper. I laughed and smiled and drank in every single moment because this was something I'd remember forever.

I reached the end of the runway, and all I could see was Tristan.

He stood at the front of my family and friends' collection of tables, eyes shining as he watched me. He was so fucking perfect. And he was mine.

I really was the luckiest bitch on the planet. I just hadn't told him.

That was going to have to change. Right now.

In fact, why the fuck had I left it this long?

I took my bow, striking a pose or two as we'd all been instructed to do if we won, then strode back up the runway. "Excuse me," I said, hurrying off the stage, one hand reaching for my crown so I didn't lose it. "Can I get out onto the floor please?" The stagehand I'd cornered looked at me with a confused expression. "There is a very important man out there who needs to know that I love him very much because I stupidly haven't told him up to this point, and now I really need him to know."

"Just go through that gap," said the now familiar organiser, appearing from the corridor. "It goes straight out into the ballroom. We don't have the most sophisticated set-up in the world."

"You're a star," I said. "Don't worry. I'll be back in five minutes for pictures."

I dashed towards the ballroom as fast as I could in my platform boots. The room was still full, but the lights had come up slightly and most people were just milling around. Lots of people tried to stop me as I passed, wanting to congratulate me. I brushed them off as politely as I could. Love first, congratulations later.

Tristan was facing away from me, talking to Orlando when I spotted him. Jules tapped him on the shoulder. Tristan turned. His face lit up like the sky at New Year.

My feet carried me towards him at speed as I wove around the chairs, tables, and drunken guests.

"You—" Tristan started to say, but his words were cut off as I threw myself into his arms and kissed him. A couple of people cheered. I made a mental note to kick them later.

"I love you, Tristan Rose," I said, the words tumbling over themselves as they escaped off my tongue. "I should have told you sooner. You are fucking amazing, and I love you so fucking much. More than anything."

"I love you too." He smiled at me, giving me that soft, sweet smile that made my insides melt. The one that made it feel like I was coming home. "More than you'll ever know. I'm so proud of you."

I kissed him again, pouring as much of my love into it as I could. When we broke apart, I chuckled because Tristan was now wearing as much of my lipstick as I was. Tristan put a hand to his mouth and grinned.

"You need better lipstick. I like your crown though."

"Oh? It's not too much?"

"For you? It's perfect." I laughed, and he kissed me again.

CHAPTER THIRTY

Tristan

MUCH LATER, in the early hours of Sunday morning, Eli and I finally made it back to our hotel room.

There'd been a lot of photos and celebrating after the competition had ended, and somehow we'd ended up in a bar in the middle of Nottingham with everyone, watching Lewis and Orlando dancing on the tables. Now Eli stood in the bathroom, naked, peeling off his eyelashes and wiping off his make-up. His crown and sash were laid carefully across the top of the desk that was against the wall opposite the bed, and the enormous crystals shimmered in the soft glow of the bedside lamps.

I stripped off my clothes, glad I'd stopped drinking before Eli was crowned. My whole body ached, and I was tired beyond belief, but I was so deliriously happy that neither of those things seemed to matter.

I climbed into bed, forgoing any kind of sleepwear. The sheets were cool against my bare skin, and I snuggled down under the layers before rolling onto my side so I could watch for Eli. Now that I'd lain down, tiredness was starting to tug at my muscles. My eyelids fluttered, and I yawned, despite my best efforts to fight it. I wanted to stay awake so I could show Eli just how proud I was of him and how much I loved him. I wanted to press my mouth to every inch of his skin, worshipping him until he guided my mouth to his cock.

"I swear," Eli said, stepping out of the bathroom and flicking the light off before walking over to the bed and sliding in beside me. "Those eye make-up pad things say complete and easy removal, but I have to use four of the bloody things just to get rid of my mascara."

He wiggled across to me, finding his place in my arms. His body was warm against mine, and he trailed his fingers across my chest, circling my nipple absent-mindedly. I let out a deep breath, my eyes falling shut. Eli chuckled and pressed a kiss to my skin. "As much as I'd love to be inside you right now, I am far too fucking tired."

"I could give you a blow job," I murmured, still not opening my eyes. Now that I'd closed them I couldn't remember how to open them again.

"You are also far too tired, beautiful boy." Eli kissed my chest again. "In the morning."

"It is morning." I nodded, repeating the words to myself so I could hold them in my mind. When did I get so tired?

"Actual morning. Post-sleep morning. When I'm not sweaty and gross."

"Okay," I said. "I love you. And I'm so proud of you."

I felt Eli's lips against mine. "I love you too. And I like being able to say that."

"Me too. I wish I'd said it sooner, then I could have said it more."

"You're so cute," Eli said. "Especially when you're tired."

"Love you," I said again, pulling him close against me as sleep began to pull me under.

"I love you too."

The following afternoon, Eli and I were stretched out on my sofa, watching *The Lord of the Rings: The Two Towers* while Indy and Solo snored from their respective places on one end of the sofa and the nearby armchair. We'd gone home after breakfast and immediately taken up residence in the living room. Both of us were still exhausted, and I couldn't see myself moving unless it was to fetch food.

"So what's next?" I asked as Treebeard marched slowly through Fangorn Forest with Merry and Pippin. "For Bitch Fit. And you."

"I'm not sure." Eli was lying between my legs with his head on my chest. "I've gotten a couple of messages about some gigs already from Phil and some people who were watching last night. They moved a lot faster than I thought they would to be honest. I probably ought to get some sort of price list of offerings together. Maybe a website."

I kissed the top of his head. "There's no rush. I'm sure someone we know can help you."

"I'm sure they can." He sighed. "Is it weird that I'm kinda… weirded out by it all? I wasn't expecting this, and now that it's happened, I'm not sure how to feel. I mean, it's not like it's going to give me a national platform, but it might help get me something. I don't want to expect too much and then be disappointed if it doesn't happen." He fiddled with the hem of the old *Assassin's Creed* t-shirt he was wearing. "I don't need to be world famous. I just want to be able to do the drag I love and get paid for it."

"I understand that," I said. "I think you just have to take each day as it comes. Be true to yourself, keep promoting yourself like you always do, and see what happens. You're a fabulous performer, Eli, and I hope more people get to see that."

"Thanks." He twisted his head and smiled softly at me, then pouted so I'd lean down and kiss him.

"Did Lewis tell you he got some clips of you from last night?" I asked as we settled back to watch the film. All the *Lord of the Rings* films were comfort watches for me—I'd seen them more times than I could count—and I could virtually quote them line for line. "He managed to get into the centre of the room to get some good footage."

"He never stops working, does he?" Eli chuckled. "He's not even my PA."

"I don't think he can help it. It's just a thing he does."

"Bless him. He's a good bean," Eli said, stretching his legs out and sighing happily. "I haven't seen anything though, but I'd be surprised if he's able to get out of bed today. The last thing I remember was him and Orlando doing fucking tequila shots right before we left."

"Maybe tomorrow then."

"If not, I know where he lives." Eli turned his head to smile up at me. "I can just go and annoy him in person."

We watched the film for a bit longer, chatting here and there about little things and quoting lines of the film at each other. It was my favourite sort of afternoon, and having someone to share it with was something I'd always wanted. I hoped that this would always be the way it was on a Sunday—Eli, me, the dogs, and some films we loved.

"What are you and Alexis doing for Christmas?" Eli asked eventually as the battle for Helm's Deep drew to a close. I thought for a second. Despite the fact that Christmas was only a couple of weeks away, I hadn't given it much consideration.

"I'm not sure. We usually go to my parents, but the last time I spoke to my mum, she mentioned something about her and my dad going away for Christmas. Something about wanting some sunshine. We're not a very close family." I doubted either of my parents had given Alexis or me a second thought when they'd made their plans. As far as they were concerned, they were only our parents when it was convenient for them or made them look good. Spending time with us just because was an alien concept to them. I wasn't sad about it though because that was just the way it had always been. And it wasn't as if we had a lot in common.

Eli patted my knee. "You should come to ours. Bring Alexis and the dogs too. It'll be chaotic as fuck, but it's always fun. Dad and Mimbles do most of the cooking, but everyone usually pitches in to do something. I normally make a trifle. You'll need to bring a NERF gun though."

"You're going to insist on another NERF war, aren't you?"

"Duh. I need to keep my crown."

"You've got a better one now," I said, pressing a kiss to Eli's head.

"Nope. I need two."

"If I beat you, does that mean I get your crown?"

"I suppose," Eli said magnanimously. "But you have to beat me first."

I laughed, deciding not to tell Eli I had a fairly good aim. "I'll do my best."

Ten days later, on the twenty-first, I came down to the ground floor of Green & Wodehouse in search of my afternoon cup of tea to find Eli and Pamela deep in hushed conversation around his desk.

"Everything okay?" I asked, then chuckled as I watched the pair of them jump nearly six feet in the air.

"You know it's not nice to sneak up on people, Mr. Rose," Eli said, looking up at me from his chair. He was wearing a very tasteful Christmas jumper with a red and white fair isle pattern, which he'd stolen out of my chest of drawers over the weekend. It was a little big on him, but he'd folded the sleeves up to give it cuffs. "They could be engaged in secret things."

"Were you?"

"Maybe…" He grinned, practically fizzing with excitement.

"Oh, just tell the poor man and put him out of his misery," Pamela said. "Go make a coffee and show him, or you're going to be useless all afternoon."

"It's the twenty-first of December. I don't exactly have a lot to do," Eli said as he hopped out of his chair, collecting both his and Pamela's mugs off their desks. I had to admit I was intrigued. I followed Eli into the kitchen.

"What's going on?"

"Okay, so… you know how I uploaded some of those clips from *It's a Drag!* to TikTok and YouTube and how I already had a ton of stuff on there from previous shows?"

"Yes." I refilled the kettle and flicked it on.

"Well, this queen I follow called Madam Mercy—she was on the last season of *Drag Stars*, and I think she made the final three—sent me a message today. She and this American queen she knows really well are putting together a kind of UK variety show tour thing for next year… and they wanted to know if I'm interested in being in it." Eli looked at me, waiting for my reaction. "I know I hate *Drag Stars*, but that doesn't mean I hate the people who are on it. And it's so amazing to even be asked. I mean, I've asked for more details because it could turn out to be a shit offer, but—"

Eli's words were cut off as I pulled him into a fierce kiss, wrapping my arms around his waist.

"That's amazing," I said. "I'm so fucking proud of you."

"Thanks." His cheeks flushed, and I grinned because this was probably the first time I'd seen Eli blush. He was usually so calm and collected, but right now, it looked like he wanted to climb to the top of the cathedral and set off a million fireworks while playing "We Are the Champions" over a loudspeaker. "Not bad for some trash goblin from the middle of nowhere."

I chuckled. "Not bad at all."

EPILOGUE

1 YEAR LATER

Eli

"WHY THE FUCK did my brother decide on a winter wedding? Why couldn't he have picked a nicer time of year?" I grumbled, wrapping my coat tighter around me as Tristan and I picked our way across the hotel car park in the rain under the cover of a large umbrella. "It's not even snowing. That's the only reason to have a fucking winter wedding."

"It's romantic, and it's what he and Ruby wanted," Tristan said, unruffled by my grumbling. "And it might snow later."

"I doubt it." I squinted up at the thick clouds and hummed. "I hope they don't want to do pictures outside."

"If they do, you'll only be required to be in a few. And you'll have an umbrella."

"I should probably stop bitching," I said as we reached the door and stepped into the glorious warmth of the hotel lobby. It was festooned with garlands and Christmas trees, which I had to admit would look nice in the photos. I was only grumpy because I'd had a very late Friday night and wasn't expecting my presence to be required so early on Saturday. Who got married before lunchtime? I'd been expecting to sleep until twelve, not be attending a wedding. But when my boyfriend was the best man and my brother was the groom, I had to make some sacrifices. Although I was definitely making them for Tristan, not Richard.

"You? Bitch? Never." Tristan chuckled as he shook out the umbrella and took off his coat. As always, he looked very handsome in his dark grey suit.

"I know. It's such a rarity." I grinned and leant up to kiss him. "But if we ever get married, I want better weather."

"We live in the UK. I can't guarantee anything."

"Fuck it. Let's go to Vegas then. Or Hawai'i. Somewhere warm. I bet there's a list somewhere of places gay couples can get married abroad. Oscar would know." I made a mental note to ask my brother later. I'd corner him during the reception. Tristan smiled at me.

"I thought you wanted to be the centre of attention and have a cake bigger than your head?" he asked, folding his coat over his arm and leading me through the hotel towards the ceremony space. There were already a few people milling around. I interlaced my fingers with his, my chest fluttering because I couldn't believe he'd remembered that conversation we'd had in the kitchen of Green & Wodehouse last year.

"True, but I can be the centre of attention anywhere." I squeezed his hand. "And cake isn't exclusive to the UK." I looked up at him as we walked, drinking in his face for what had to be the millionth time. How I'd ended up with someone like Tristan Rose was a mystery I'd never solve. He was far too wonderful for me, but that made me appreciate him all the more. He made my life a thousand times better just by existing in it. "But if I'm honest, I don't really mind where we get married. If we decide to get married," I said hastily, suddenly realising what territory we were stumbling into. "All I'd really need is you."

Tristan halted, looking down at me with his perfect smile. He kissed me, drawing me to him like a magnet. "I'd still make sure you had cake."

"That's because you are fucking perfect."

He laughed, and we started walking again. Two minutes later, we found ourselves in the ceremony space, and while I got whisked into last-minute preparations, Tristan tried to get Richard to stop pacing and breathe. Truly, I'd never seen a man look so green.

The guests started to arrive, and I greeted relatives I hadn't spoken to in years. Despite the fact that my close family was very big and very gay, some of my relatives still seemed to think I should be holding down a normal job and acting... well, straight. It was fun watching their faces when I got to tell them I'd spent six months of the year doing two different drag shows across the country.

I still wasn't doing drag full-time since I'd come back in between the shows and taken a temporary admin job to boost my bank balance, but it worked itself out. I got the feeling I was always going to hustle for money, but that didn't really bother me. I had enough to pay my bills, pay for my art, and occasionally spoil Tristan, and that was fine. Tristan did very well, and we'd had a serious conversation about money before we'd moved in together in May. He'd tried to insist on paying for everything, but I'd put my foot down and insisted on a proportional split at least.

I think some people were surprised we'd moved in together after only eight months, but it didn't surprise me at all. My contract on the flat had ended, and both Orlando and I were spending more time at our respective partners' houses than there. It just made sense. Besides, I already knew I'd marry Tristan tomorrow if the opportunity presented itself.

I should probably ask him at some point.

The guests settled down, and Richard took his place at the front with the registrar, Tristan beside him. I found a seat with Finn, Gem, and Jules, and we chatted quietly for a second before music began to fill the air.

Ruby looked beautiful in her dress, which was champagne and black with a tulle skirt that made her look like the gothic queen of the fae, especially with her dark hair set in soft curls. The flowers she carried were dark and wild with little pops of cream, red, and gold, and I remembered Lewis saying Leo was doing the floral arrangements after he and Ruby had met and started chatting at *It's a Drag!*. I wondered if I could ask for a finder's fee in the form of a nice piece of cake and a bouquet for Tristan.

The ceremony went off without a hitch, although all my parents cried, and afterwards, we went for a reception with winter Pimms and warm cider and trays of mince pies, warm cheese straws, and tiny cups of soup as appetisers. I tried to eat as many snacks as possible in between being summoned for pictures. Tristan was in his element with a list of photographs and a tiny pencil he'd procured from somewhere so he could tick them off. He wrangled everyone with a quiet but firm charm and only raised his voice a couple of times. I'd have bellowed at everyone like a foghorn. I was definitely going to make sure Tristan got a reward later for being so wonderful. He deserved to be spoilt rotten.

I wondered if our ties would make adequate restraints.

"I tell you what," Lewis muttered to me as we put down our drinks to pose for another family photo. "This big wedding marlarky is a pain in the ass."

I looked at him and grinned. "Thinking of eloping?"

"Maybe." He flushed the same pink as his hair. "Or maybe just not doing this."

"Whatever you and Jason do, at least have some sort of party afterwards," I said. "Just so we can have cake and tell Jason all the embarrassing stories about you from when you were little."

"Haven't you done that already?"

"I'm sure I can find more."

Eventually there was a meal, which thankfully wasn't a Christmas dinner, and then speeches. Ruby's dad made everyone cry, Tristan made everyone cry, and Richard topped it off by making Ruby cry. I wasn't going to admit that Tristan's speech had made my eyes prickle when he'd talked about how thankful he was for Richard's friendship and how perfect he and Ruby were together. Although I did think he could have mentioned some of Richard's previous dating disasters or the fact that he'd punched me, but perhaps that would have been in poor taste. And the wedding was very tasteful.

When I married Tristan, our wedding would be full of drag artists and flamboyant queers. Perhaps we could have some sort of mini cabaret performance as part of it. That would be fun.

Afterwards, there was a short break before the evening festivities began, but any hope I'd had of stealing Tristan away was lost as the pair of us were cornered by relatives and then some of my family insisting on playing card games in the bar. It was fun, but I'd rather have found a very quiet corner for the pair of us to make out. We could probably have even snuck out to the car for some quick fun since we weren't staying the night. But no, that would all have to wait until later.

Finally, the whole thing resumed again with the cake cutting and first dance, and Tristan and I got dragged onto the floor to slow dance alongside the happy couple. I'd hardly ever slow danced before, but being wrapped in Tristan's arms and gazing into his eyes made the familiar fire in my chest spark and grow. I loved him more than I could possibly say. He'd accepted every part of me and rolled with them.

Being out on tour had been hard on both of us, but we'd managed.

The first tour had been in the late spring when I'd still been at Green & Wodehouse. Most of our performances had been over the weekends, but we'd had a couple during the week, and it had meant I'd either had to drive home very late at night or hot foot it up the motorway first thing in the morning. There were some nights where I definitely shouldn't have been driving because I was so exhausted, but I'd made it each time. Thank fuck for Jules who had kept my car running while muttering that I needed a better one than the heap of junk I'd been driving with progressive intensity. Tristan and I had fought about it because he'd wanted to buy me something new, and it was only after a lecture from Jules—and Lewis, who knew what it was like to be in a financially disparate relationship—that I'd given in. I'd spent a long time apologising as thoroughly as I could and then let Tristan help me buy a three-year-old, secondhand Corsa that had barely done ten thousand miles.

The second tour had been this autumn, and I'd been away for up to a week at a time. That had been harder for different reasons, mostly because I missed Tristan so much it hurt. I wasn't sure when I'd gone from being fine on my own, to needing him with such fierce intensity, but it had happened, and it made some of the weeks suck. I loved performing though, and the shows had been amazing, so I wouldn't have changed that. I'd just wished I could magically bring Tristan with me for a couple of nights a week. We'd made it through, and we'd keep making it because that was what we did.

I'd spent a long time talking to Jason about it because out of everyone I knew, he was the one who understood the most since he spent so much of his time in London working on theatre productions. I'd actually ended up going out for drinks with him, his brother—superstar Henry Lu—and Henry's best friend, the incredible Rosamund Jones, after one show. It was a night I'd never forget. They'd even come to see my show the next day, taken backstage selfies with all of the performers, and plastered the pictures all over Instagram.

I didn't want to say that was the reason I was getting more work next year, but it hadn't hurt.

"What are you thinking about?" Tristan asked as we swayed slowly on the spot amongst all the other couples. "You look very pensive."

"Just thinking about you and me and what a weird year it's been."

"It's been a good year though."

"It has. Not really one I'd have predicted." I smiled at him. "How long do you think we have to stay tonight?"

Tristan smirked. "Why? Got plans?"

"For you? Of course." I kissed him slowly, pressing my tongue against his lips. When we broke apart, Tristan looked at me with desperate eyes and sighed.

"I don't know... Maybe another couple of hours? I'm best man, so I'll need to help clean up and sort everything out."

"You're too good." I pressed my hand to his chest and leant in close. "That's going to earn you more rewards."

"This is where I need time to go faster," he muttered. I chuckled.

"Don't worry. We have the whole of tomorrow to do nothing," I said, kissing him again. I was already planning to make the most of it. "There's no rush at all. I can wait a few more hours to spoil you."

We circled slowly on the floor as the song drew to a

close. I took Tristan's hand and interlaced our fingers together, leading him off the floor. Whatever happened, wherever we went, I knew Tristan would be there for me and I'd be there for him.

It was going to be the two of us, forever and all time.

Always.

The End

ACKNOWLEDGMENTS

From the moment I first created Lewis's big, queer family in *Proficiency Bonus*, I knew that Eli was going to get a story. He was far too fun to resist. And the fact that this ended up being novel number ten somehow made it more special— I'm very glad Eli and Tristan are the ones to take me to double digits, a place I never imagined I'd be.

As always, I must extend my eternal gratitude to a selection of wonderful people, without whom I would be nothing.

To Susie, who knew I needed to write Eli to clear my head. Thank you.

To Toby, Carly, Ali and Jayne for letting me ramble, for cheering me on and for never letting me give up on myself.

To Charity: friend, PA and all-around superhero. I'd be lost without you.

To Natasha, for the beautiful covers that make up this series. Seriously, wait until you see the rest of them.

To Lori, for catching my mistakes.

To my husband for being there every single day, even the ones when I am a grumpy trash-goblin. I love you. And to the dachshund asleep on my leg while I write this, I love you too but my foot has gone numb.

To Rosie, who introduced me to *Drag Race* and *Dragula*, and all my Queen Bee crew. You are incredible.

To all the Queens, Kings, and Non-Binary Drag Superstars—you inspire me.

And last, but never least, to you, my fabulous readers. Whether I'm new to you or you've been here since the start, I am grateful for you love and support.

If you enjoyed *Always Eli*, please consider leaving a review. Reviews are invaluable for indie authors, and may help other readers find this book.

Until next time.

Love,
Charlie x

ALSO BY CHARLIE NOVAK

FOREVER LOVE

Always Eli

Finding Finn

Oh So Oscar

HEATHER BAY

Like I Pictured

Like I Promised (July 2022)

ROLL FOR LOVE

Natural Twenty

Charisma Check

Proficiency Bonus

KISS ME

Strawberry Kisses

Summer Kisses

Spiced Kisses

OFF THE PITCH

Breakaway

Extra Time

Final Score

The Off the Pitch Short Collection

Off the Pitch: The Complete Collection (Boxset)

STANDALONES

Screens Apart

SHORT STORIES

One More Night

Twenty-Two Years (Newsletter Exclusive)

Snow Way In Hell

AUDIOBOOKS

Always Eli

Finding Finn

Natural Twenty

Charisma Check

Proficiency Bonus

Strawberry Kisses

Summer Kisses

For a regularly updated list, please visit:

charlienovak.com/books

charlienovak.com/audiobooks

CHARLIE NOVAK

Charlie lives in England with her husband and two cheeky dogs. She spends most of her days wrangling other people's words in her day job and then trying to force her own onto the page in the evening.

She loves cute stories with a healthy dollop of fluff, plenty of delicious sex, and happily ever afters — because the world needs more of them.

Charlie has very little spare time, but what she does have she fills with baking, Dungeons and Dragons, reading and many other nerdy pursuits. She also thinks that everyone should have at least one favourite dinosaur...

Website: charlienovak.com
Facebook Group: Charlie's Angels
For day-to-day-musings, giveaways and teasers.

Plus sign up for her newsletter for bonus scenes, new releases and extras.

facebook.com/charlienovakauthor

twitter.com/charlienwrites

instagram.com/charlienwrites

bookbub.com/profile/charlie-novak

amazon.com/author/charlienovak

Printed in Great Britain
by Amazon

79983061R00185